Lloy

THE MINISTER

THE MINISTER

MAURICE EDELMAN

redcliffe

First published by Hamish Hamilton 1961

This edition first published in 1994 by
Redcliffe Press Ltd
49 Park Street, Bristol

© 1961
© Introduction 1994

ISBN 1 872971 53 9

British Library Cataloguing-in-Publication Data.
A catalogue record for this book is available
from the British Library.

Typeset by Mayhew Typesetting, Rhayader, Powys
and printed by The Longdunn Press Ltd, Bristol

Introduction

Maurice Edelman, who was a Labour MP for Coventry from 1945 until his premature death at 64 in 1975, was the most successful political novelist since Disraeli, a figure who, appropriately enough, fascinated him. This may sound a bold claim, but it is in my view an incontestable one, although it should not be interpreted to mean that Edelman equalled Disraeli, which he did not, manifestly not as a politician, and not as a writer either. His work lacked the length and breadth and depth of the Young England trilogy or the late serenity of *Endymion*, and Edelman, who was a measured craftsman rather than a megalomaniac messiah, would not have put himself up against his hero.

Nevertheless there was no one between the two, or post-1975, who could challenge Edelman for the second plinth. There have been greater writers in the House of Commons. There were Morley and Churchill amongst major politicians, but they were not novelists, except for Churchill's one-off *Savrola*, published when he was 31, and to which he never attempted a follow-up. There were Hilaire Belloc, and A.E.W. Mason, and Harold Nicolson (although I would regard Mason's claim to be a better writer than Edelman as distinctly shaky) but they were none of them other than short-term politicians – Nicolson, although politics was the least of his talents, would like to have been longer-term – and Belloc and Nicolson wrote little fiction. More recently Wilfred Fienburgh wrote one good film-script (in the form of a novel) before his early death in a car crash. Julian Critchley showed that his excellent political jokes could be as well-clothed in fiction as in fact, and Douglas Hurd, with quite a little *oeuvre* to his credit, is the first Foreign Secretary to write in office since Lord Rosebery in 1892–4.

None of these, however, can show anything comparable with the solid list of twelve novels which Edelman produced between 1951 and 1975. They were supplemented by four works of non-fiction and by numerous television and radio plays and adaptations. But the core of his literary output lies essentially in the novels which very professionally came out, give or take a few months, at almost regular two-yearly intervals. The neatly chosen titles mostly indicate the extent to which he was a 'political' novelist, not in the sense that his life or his stories were bounded by politics, but in the sense that were a sizeable proportion of Trollope's novels. He began with *A Trial of Love* in 1951, which as I recollect after a gap of more than forty years since reading it, was a bit goggle-eyed about the glamour of dalliance by mock Greek temples in a country house park. But it is a tribute to its vividness that over such a span it should have left in my mind a firmly surviving physical image.

After this the style became more restrained, more worldly perhaps, as we progressed through *Who Goes Home?* (1953), *A Dream of Treason* (1955), *The Happy Ones*, (1957), *A Call on Kuprin* (1959), *The Minister* (1961), *The Fratricides* (1963), *The Prime Minister's Daughter* (1964), *Shark Island* (1967), *All on a Summer's Night* (1969), *Disraeli in Love* (1972), and *Disraeli Rising* (1975). There was a hint of Ian Fleming as well as Trollope and even of Anthony Powell in one or two of the titles, but the treatment was much less two-dimensional than the formula of Cold War violence embellished with high life accessories which gave the Bond stories such a 'sixties success.

Of all these Edelman books, the two Disraeli ones at the end had a special quality which stemmed from the author's absorption of every detail of his subject's life, including making his own home in part of Hughenden Manor, the gothicized Buckinghamshire house which became a very vivid symbol of the Disraeli legend. These apart, however, *The Minister* is one of the most characteristic and perhaps the best of the lot. It is therefore a very good choice for re-issue thirty-three years after it first saw the light of publishers' day.

In 1960, which was presumably when *The Minister* was being composed, Edelman was just under fifty years old, had been in the House of Commons for fifteen of them, and had probably abandoned much thought of a straight line ministerial political career. He was a victim in this respect partly of the Labour Party having just lost its third general election running, but also of his own tendency to become something of a detached observer of politics. For this rôle he had a very good and by then experienced eye.

The context of the time was that Harold Macmillan, at the

6

height of his success, with the great electoral victory of 1959 just behind him and the disasters of 'the day of the long knives', the de Gaulle veto and the Profumo scandal still well ahead, was putting on an increasingly stylized performance as Prime Minister; that African affairs in the era of 'the wind of change' were still a major influence on British politics, and made personally tense by the clash between Iain Macleod, an adventurous Colonial Secretary and the champion of the Tory left on the one hand, and Duncan Sandys, a monumentally stubborn and more right-wing Commonwealth Secretary on the other; that Hugh Gaitskell as leader of the opposition was a high profile and much discussed figure, both politically and socially, and that Lady Pamela Berry and Mrs Fleming were the two dominant hostesses in the frontier zone where the worlds of fashion and achievement mingled, the former the more political, the latter the more literary.

The influence of all these circumstances and personalities can be seen in Edelman's novel, just as, for instance, the influence of the Conservative Party's boxing of the compass over franchise reform in 1866–68 can be seen in Trollope's *Phineas Redux*. This does not mean that Edelman's imagination is confined to writing up contemporary politics. His characters are never copies, and as soon as there is a feeling that one can be securely identified he or she turns into someone else. But the background is nonetheless firmly contemporary, and the strength of the book, apart from its technical skill in narrative, is its portrait of political society at the height of the Macmillan era.

In the book, there is as good a debate sequence as anything I know in fiction. Authenticity, suspense and shafts of insight into character are well-mingled. Yet, despite all the impressive displays of parliamentary and Whitehall knowledge, the book is in reality an anti-political novel. It is about political triumph built round a hollow shell of a sense of personal failure. It is in a way the opposite of Trollope. Trollope would have loved to have been in the House of Commons, but on his one attempt to be elected met with an ignominious set-back. Edelman had a safe seat for thirty years, but I suspect spent most of them searching for some greater satisfaction, and partly finding it through his writing of fiction, of which this is a conspicuous example.

Roy Jenkins March 1994

I

The coffee stain spread into a map of Africa. Where the tablecloth rippled, a white ridge cut across the ooze like a line of latitude, and the waiter muttered, 'I'm sorry, sir.' The Minister edged his chair away from the table and said, 'Don't worry. That's Capricorn,' and smiled.

'You're electioneering,' said Mrs Drayford.

'Not a bit, Julia,' said the Minister. 'I've got the fourth biggest majority in the country.'

'That's all very well,' she replied. 'But the trouble with you politicians is that you have to be loved all the time. You're always soliciting.'

'Oh, come!'

'But you are. Take that poor waiter. First of all you fuddle him with Capricorn. Then you give him the Constituency Smile. It's hardly fair.'

'You've only known me twelve years,' said the Minister, moving his saucer over the stain. 'You must avoid premature judgements.'

Mrs Drayford puckered her forehead as if to give the matter thought; and then she turned her face towards him and laughed.

'I judged you the first evening we met in the Harcourt Room. I said to Edward, "Who's that pretentious looking young man who's talking so much?"'

'What did he say?'

'He said, "That's Melville. He'll be Prime Minister one day."'

'That's the most dangerous of prophecies. The back benches are littered with ageing, putative Prime Ministers.'

'Oh, I didn't agree with him. I took a look at you, and said, "Parliamentary Secretary, Minister of Pensions more like it."'

'I haven't any ambitions. My progress is all accidental.'

The Minister turned to Mrs M'landa. 'Have you found the trip very tiring?' he asked.

'Not really, Mr Melville,' she said, and in the drifting light of the candelabra her large dark eyes had red flecks. 'You must remember that my mother was Indian and my father African. So you see I am accustomed to the heats.'

9

Melville smiled and moved the saucer again.

'Africa – India – it's the new axis of the world.'

'Perhaps one of them,' said Mrs M'landa in her cadenced voice. 'That is what Aloysius says.'

Melville followed her look along the table to his wife, Elizabeth, who was listening attentively to M'landa, as he inclined towards her, two thin rivulets of sweat advancing down his temples. For ten days during the constitutional talks, the Minister had faced M'landa's jaws, angrily opening and closing, or the back of his closely cropped lambswool head turning to his advisers, but this was a new aspect of him. M'landa *galant*. Mrs Melville and M'landa were preparing for the climax of the joke. The white teeth, the pink tongue moved faster. His wife was looking at him with her eyes narrowing, the grin set hard. At any moment, the guffaw! And then, in duet, the African laughter mingled with what he called Elizabeth's Putney Chortle, overriding the conversation and making the heads rise. The Minister looked rapidly down the table, observed the amiable expressions, and his uneasiness disappeared.

'Elizabeth,' said Mrs Drayford, 'has a hearty laugh.'

'Yes,' said the Minister. 'I like it.'

Mrs Drayford leaned across the Minister and her bare shoulder, its freckled skin rather loose over the muscle, rested against his sleeve.

'It's a very great asset, Mrs M'landa, to have a devoted wife when you're a politician. Do you write all your husband's speeches too?'

Mrs M'landa stopped playing with the green fern which entangled the roses of the centrepiece, and said in bewilderment,

'My husband would never agree to such a thing. He never writes his speeches. He always speaks straight out.'

'Oh, it's different here. Elizabeth, for example – she always adds a few epigrams to the Minister's speeches – you know, a few little things like "Too many cooks spoil the broth", and so on.'

The Minister frowned, and then seeing that his wife was smiling to him from the other side of M'landa, smiled back to her, half-tender though half-irritated that a strand of her hair was drooping untidily over her face, as he compared it with Mrs Drayford's *coiffure*, a pale pattern of carefully assembled light. He said to Mrs M'landa,

10

'You mustn't believe everything Mrs Drayford says. She doesn't herself.'

Mrs M'landa said, 'Banter is the secret of your success.'

'That's an interesting thought,' said Melville. 'Why?'

'Well,' said Mrs M'landa, turning her dark face to Mrs Drayford, who half looked away, 'you can say one thing and then pretend you're joking, and that we haven't any sense of humour.'

'The peonies this year are magnificent,' said Mrs Drayford. 'I forget – do you have peonies in your part of Africa?'

'My husband is very fond of bougainvillaea,' said Mrs M'landa, as if that disposed of the subject.

The toastmaster whispered in the Chancellor of the Exchequer's ear, and tapped the microphone to see if it was 'live'. The Chancellor pushed his chair away from the table, and in the seconds before the toastmaster's gavel fell surveyed the chandeliers and the gilt mouldings of the ceiling with his melancholy, hang-dog eyes.

'The Right Honourable Gerald Ormston . . .' called the toast-master, 'a member of Her Majesty's Privy Council.'

Ormston rose, and began to speak in his light, hurried, but precise voice.

'My Lords, Ladies and Gentlemen,' he said. 'In the last two months I've got used to saying, "I have been asked to reply. . . ."' The audience composed itself in preparation for a witticism. 'Unhappily, the Prime Minister's illness made this necessary.' The audience readjusted its expression. 'But tonight I am glad to tell you that his convalescence is following its normal course. We are all delighted.' (A murmur of 'Hear, hears'.) 'And I will convey to him, on your behalf, good wishes for his speedy and total recovery.' (Loud 'Hear, hears' and a mild thumping of tables.)

'Tonight I am not replying. I am proposing. And what I propose is the good health and the long life of the newest independent African state whose Prime Minister we are so delighted to have with us tonight. Aloysius M'landa is a name which we have for some time associated with the upsurge of what I might call the New Africa – an Africa young, eager and – if I may say so – responsible. Aloysius M'landa has at one and the same time achieved a constitutional settlement and reaffirmed the intimate nature of his people's links with our family of nations – the nations of the New Commonwealth and the nations of the

West. That is, indeed, the path of advancement.'

His gaze, turning to right and left, rested on Melville before he went on,

'Yet there is one whom it would be ungenerous not to mention tonight – one who played a major part in the decision to set up a constituent assembly – one to whom our own country's thanks are unreservedly due and without whom the Conference could never have succeeded.'

Melville stared down at the débris of the dinner and fingered his unlit cigar. It was good of Ormston to refer to him, although in a sense it was inevitable since he had, in fact, personally drafted the main statutes of the constitution. But Ormston, he knew, didn't like him; and listening to the rapid words, he felt for him a reciprocal distaste which not even an accumulation of compliments could temper.

They had both been elected in the same General Election sixteen years before. When he had been appointed Under-Secretary to the Ministry of Supply, Ormston had been made Financial Secretary to the Treasury, and their careers had since then advanced in step until, at last, Ormston had become Chancellor, and he himself, with the amalgamation of the Ministries, Secretary of State for Commonwealth Relations and Colonial Affairs. They had constantly met each other in committee meetings and official cocktail parties, and on ceremonial occasions with their wives, but neither he nor Elizabeth could suffer what he had once called the *froideur à deux* of the Ormstons.

He watched Ormston speaking, and realized that he knew him little better now than when they had first met. With his pallid face and somnolent eye, Ormston had the air of a man who spoke dutifully but had other preoccupations.

Chief among them was the premiership. When Vincent Telfer, the previous Prime Minister, collapsed at the Royal Academy banquet, Ormston was attending the San Francisco Monetary Conference. After an interval of one day which the Press felt it seemly to occupy in eulogy of the dead Prime Minister and descriptions of the arrangements for the State funeral before speculating about his successor, they began to publish a short list of heirs, together with the constitutional procedure for the appointment by the Queen of the new Prime Minister.

At the same time as Ormston, the Chancellor of the Exchequer,

12

was named as the natural incumbent, the anti-Ormston movement formed.

After Prayers on the Thursday, the Speaker made the announcement in the simple and traditional terms of regret on a Member's death. Almost immediately, there was a drift from the Chamber into the Members' Lobby, where groups of M.P.s stood about, discussing the Old Man and his last and characteristic words.

'The best of celebrations is the celebration of one's own work – but I must add of this year's Academy – that if you're looking for a monument, don't look around!' It was thought fitting that he should die with an insult on his lips. It made it easier to talk of his successor.

'Not Ormston – not if we can help it,' said Lockhart, the Chairman of the Fuel Committee, on his way to the Smoking-Room. 'Why not?' asked the correspondent who had accosted him. Lockhart paused and said, 'It's indefinable. When you meet Ormston – even if you've known him all your life – it's as if he's never set eyes on you before. It's that cold, hang-dog look. I'd rather have Collard – Melville – Dawson-Pratt – the Chief Whip – anyone.'

'Are you serious?'

'Why not? But – hello, Geoffrey.'

Melville had taken Lockhart's arm and they had walked together to the Smoking-Room, talking about the succession. As they approached it, they saw an unusually large group gathered around the clacking tape machine, reading the message with an incredulous absorption.

'Chancellor of Exchequer returning to England. *San Francisco*: The Rt Hon. Gerald Ormston told reporters before leaving for England that in view of the P.M.'s tragic death he was returning to England at once in order to put himself at the disposal of his colleagues. Asked if he expected a summons from the Queen, Mr Ormston said he couldn't anticipate events.'

That same evening, while Ormston was flying home, Melville told four Cabinet Ministers that he had been asked to talk to them on behalf of a hundred and eighty-three back-benchers led by Lockhart as Chairman of the Private Members' Committee. The Cabinet, they felt, should request the Queen to send for the Lord Privy Seal, the Rt Hon. Andrew Collard who, although sixty-eight, commanded 'the united respect of the Party which for various reasons could not rally without reservations behind the leadership of any alternative candidate'. Melville presented each of the Ministers with a copy of the memorandum signed by the Chairmen of the Party's six most influential Committees.

When Ormston arrived at London Airport he was met by his Parliamentary Private Secretary who told him that the Cabinet had met earlier in the evening and that it had humbly offered Her Majesty the advice that Collard should be asked to form a new Government. He added that Melville had spent the whole day canvassing support for the proposal, and had announced in an emphatic voice while walking in the Library Corridor that 'the country couldn't have a fellow like Ormston at Number 10. His dismal face would cause a flight from sterling.'

Ormston hadn't replied, and drove in silence to London, throwing only a casual glance at the headline in the newspaper which his P.P.S. had brought him. *Melville the Kingmaker.* 'The absent,' he said wearily, 'are never right.'

'It's an argument against foreign travel,' said his P.P.S. Ormston smiled his melancholy smile, and said, 'Melville will no doubt be rewarded.'

'He wants the F.O.,' said his P.P.S.

'As long as he doesn't interfere with my Bank Rate –!' said Ormston, and shrugged his shoulders. The night air of the suburbs had the mingled scent of lilac and decaying laburnum, and he thought irrelevantly of his twelve-year-old daughter who had died many years before, and of Telfer's condolences. Caesar's child stuffing a hole in the wall.

'The Prime Minister's illness, so soon after his assumption of office,' Ormston continued his speech still facing Melville, 'was, of course, a blow to us all. We all know of his great interest in Africa. And while he has temporarily laid down his burden, he has asked me on his behalf to convey his special thanks to –'

The faces turned towards Melville, who folded his arms and looked down at the table-cloth.

'– to Mr Edward Drayford who, I can disclose, was directly responsible for the drafting of the Instrument of Agreement. We are delighted to see among us Mrs Drayford – even though her husband is still with the Commission in Africa.'

14

Ormston bowed and smiled to her, and Melville forced himself to smile too. But feeling one hand trembling with resentment, he steadied it by putting it on his knee beneath the table.

Drayford had been put on the Commission primarily because they needed a leading industrialist with business connexions in Africa and to a lesser extent because his television company could promote the Commission's work. In Africa, he had, in fact, constantly to be left behind by his colleagues, 'to study the situation'. The Government had reported to him privately that immediately after his arrival, Drayford had succumbed to what he euphemistically called 'inertia', but what was really a total boredom with abstract thought, and that in order to hasten the Commission's work he had been appointed host to the native chiefs — a function which he was still discharging. His part in framing the new constitution had been nil. That had been essentially the work of Melville, who, with his official advisers, had drafted a working agreement in London. The idea of a Constituent Assembly with a transitional year before full independence had been Melville's personal invention which, as Ormston knew, he had himself presented to the Cabinet. Melville looked at Ormston, who was contentedly bringing his speech to an end, and from him to Mrs Drayford, who whispered, 'Poor devil! You'll have to explain it to him!'

Melville waited till the applause for the Chancellor had exhausted itself before adding a few desultory claps himself.

'He is such a brilliant speaker,' said Mrs M'landa, ecstatic. 'He is a very handsome man.'

'A little theatrical,' said Mrs Drayford, and Melville's smile returned.

'In what way — theatrical?' Mrs M'landa asked.

'In the theatre,' said Mrs Drayford, 'you have to exaggerate. Everything must be a bit more so — gestures, make-up — everything.'

'But Mr Ormston is so quiet,' said Mrs M'landa.

'That's just it,' said Mrs Drayford. 'Exaggerated understatement!'

Mrs M'landa was already absorbed in her husband's opening words as he stood, his black face glistening over his white shirt front, behind the drifting smoke of the candles. His voice was thick and soft and slow, and Mrs Drayford put her elbows on the table, cupping her chin, to listen to him.

'A few minutes ago,' he said, the 'o's' flattened out, 'when I was looking at those very beautiful chandeliers, I noticed a lady observing me. "I wonder," she seemed to be saying, "if Mr M'landa is going to swing from the chandeliers at any moment."'

Melville led the laughter.

'No, madam,' said Mr M'landa, 'my ancestors stopped swinging at about the same time as yours. But all the same, I think it right for me to tell you tonight about my translation – if that is the word – Mrs Melville assures me that it is –' M'landa bowed to Elizabeth – 'from the banks of my African river to the banks of the Thames.

'I went to a Mission School, ladies and gentlemen, where I was presented with the name which for so long made my English friends – if I may call them that –'

'Hear, hear!' said the Chancellor.

'– the name Aloysius, which used to make my English friends smile. And then at last, thanks to the British Council, to which so many of my colleagues owe so much, I came to study at the London School of Economics and then at Jesus College, Oxford, and became eventually the President of the Oxford Union Debating Society.

'But this did not conclude my education. Oh, no! I also went to one of the finishing schools which H.M.G. used to prescribe for future Commonwealth Prime Ministers. My four years in Ombala Gaol were the most educational of my life.'

The Minister caught a quick glance from Mrs Drayford, and composed his face in a neutral expression. M'landa's voice had become reflective, as if he were thinking aloud and guiding his audience to a conclusion which might or might not be agreeable.

'I read a lot – Laski, Shaw and Shakespeare. I learned the difficult art of patience. I learned that the reign of empires is brief and that peoples as well as tyrants can be rubbed out from the pages of history, and go to hell.'

M'landa paused, and for three or four seconds there was an uneasy hiatus as his audience wondered whether his silence was deliberate. M'landa looked up and smiled.

'Let me not digress, ladies and gentlemen. I have come here to praise Caesar and to bury old hatchets.' He laughed at his joke, and Elizabeth joined in until the laughter rippled around the table, and someone began to clap.

'It is not, I fear, a very good joke,' said M'landa. 'I merely wanted to change the subject. Let me, therefore, thank you, Sir, for your very gracious toast, but, above all, the Secretary of State for his conspicuous success in bringing our labours to a happy end. My friend Mr Drayford entertained us in Africa with his convivial presence. Mr Melville sustained us here.'

He waved a pink palm towards the Minister who bowed an acknowledgement.

'To introduce a personal note, I have known the Minister for a number of years. I heckled him in Conway Hall when I was a student. I have clashed with him over the Draft Constitution. But I have always held him in great esteem – as one who is destined to take a steadily more important place in the Government of Britain, as one who may well one day lead his country as now I lead mine – and one who has at his side a lady who I am sure is not the least of his assets.'

'He really is a charmer,' said Mrs Drayford when M'landa sat down.

'I dislike the term, Julia,' said Melville. 'It's old-fashioned and coy.'

Mrs Drayford's cheek-bones became touched with a slight flush.

'Well, if you don't believe me,' she said goadingly, 'you'd better ask Elizabeth.'

Ten years earlier when he was still a back-bencher, Melville had received a letter from Mrs Drayford which ended:

'And since we both admired your speech so much – we specially liked the bit about Bardsley always "accusing people of wagging their faces in his fist" – we hope you will come to luncheon on Thursday the 20th.'

Flattered, he had accepted the invitation. Drayford was abroad, and the other guests at the party were Gareth Tyler, the former Ambassador to Spain, a newspaper proprietor and his wife, a New York publicist, Lady Fierling and Alfred Yates, an Opposition back-bencher who had been a Cambridge don.

Mrs Drayford had preened herself as the conversation bounced between Tyler and Yates.

At three o'clock when the guests were leaving, she said to Melville, 'Do stay a little. You've hardly spoken to me at all.' And Melville, who had been feeling neglected, stayed and drank

17

Armagnac with her, lounging on the sofa and watching the gauzy curtains billowing in the summer afternoon breeze. They spoke about South America where he had been seconded to the Ministry of Economic Warfare in 1944, after he had been wounded at Calais in 1940, and she explained to him that Drayford was twenty years older than herself. Then there was silence, the ticking of the ormolu clock, her eager wet mouth tasting of alcohol, his hands groping at the buttons of her spotted blue dress, and curving like a scoop around her breast, and, in the discomfort of their entanglement, their knees striking together, the slow dying of desire. Over her shoulder beyond the lime-coloured brocade, he could see a Poussin landscape with figures; a brown faun was carrying off two naked nymphs. Their pink bodies and the light blue sky combined with the stale fumes and his sweating forehead in an anaphrodisiac harmony.

After a few minutes, Mrs Drayford said, 'It really is too hot. Perhaps we might play canasta.' He disengaged himself with humiliation and relief, and walked to the window while she rebuttoned her dress.

'You must tell me something about your constituency,' she said, returning and offering him a cigarette. She was cool as if there had been no interlude, but when he left and thanked her, she didn't reply. Afterwards, they met often on social occasions, but neither ever referred to the episode.

Now that he was speaking and commanding his audience, he felt virile and dominant. Occasionally, he would select a face and address himself to it, pausing, emphasizing, qualifying, jesting, exhorting, reassuring, intimidating. This was the part he loved best, even when there was dissent. Tonight there was only applause, and watching Julia's face turned upwards towards him with its mocking expression temporarily subdued, and seeing Elizabeth gazing at him with the steady fervour which she always showed, though she had heard him many hundreds of times, he felt exultant. The Conference had undoubtedly proved a triumph. His two television appearances when he had explained the details of the settlement had won enthusiastic approval both in the Government and the Opposition Press. And there was M'landa himself, wagging his head, murmuring 'Yah, yah, yah,' and applauding every passage in which he mentioned cooperation.

'. . . I will end, then,' said the Minister, 'with a statement of faith. I see Mr M'landa unfurling the banner of a new era in Africa. It is a challenge to those who, because of certain recent events, have lost their faith in Africa's capacity for progress and self-government. To the faint-hearted I say that they should watch carefully the evolution of the new State whose provisional constitution we celebrate tonight. Men like Mr M'landa are not only the leaders of a new Africa. They are, I believe, the leaders of a New World which will one day stand in the same relationship to the Old as America once stood to Europe.'

Melville stopped, then speaking more slowly, said,

'Those who now fail to recognize the ineluctable movement of history will be overwhelmed by it; they can't stop it. Modern science has made the world shrink. We have perforce been made neighbours with the other races of the world. This is the age of the multi-racial society. And tonight, in proposing the toast of the new State, I want to make this declaration. The African is my friend; I want him to be my brother.'

As he sat down, applause swept the room, and continued long after it might have politely stopped. M'landa, clearing his throat, walked over to the Minister, shook his hand, said, 'Thank you very much,' and returned to his seat.

'You were terribly good,' said Mrs Drayford. 'I liked the bit about the multi-racial society, although I never quite know what it means.'

Melville dabbed his face with his handkerchief and said,

'It means what I said, Julia. I want the African to be my brother.'

Mrs Drayford frowned. 'But does that mean —?'

'Oh, no,' said Melville in a whisper. 'I want the African to be my brother – not my brother-in-law.'

They looked at each other, and burst into loud laughter.

'What are you laughing at?' asked Mrs M'landa, rejoining the conversation.

'Oh, something silly,' said Mrs Drayford. 'Mr Melville was telling me about a friend who's getting married for the fourth time. She always marries colonels in the Horse Guards.'

'Yes,' said Melville. 'She's had three shot from under her.'

He laughed again, and Mrs M'landa joined in the laughter till it moved along the table and through the room, lasting in a subdued

19

form throughout the final speech and emerging again in a burst of general friendliness when the dinner ended and the guests began to rise.

2

As Melville entered the vestibule outside the Prime Minister's bedroom, the secretaries rose to greet him. The chairs seemed stacked with hydrangeas, and the air was heavy with the scent of roses and, sickly-sweet, of lilies overflowing from an elaborate basket on the table. Before he could inquire about the Prime Minister's health, the bedroom door opened and his physician, Sir Gregory Broome, backed out reassuringly, 'You'll be there before I will.' He closed the door behind him and greeted Melville with a grave movement of his hand.

'Let's go into the garden, Geoffrey,' he said, and they walked together down the staircase and the broad stone steps on to the lawn.

'How is he?' Melville asked.

Broome trod on a weed thoughtfully, and said,

'He's very tired. He can't return before at least six weeks.'

They walked without speaking for a few moments till Melville said,

'I am asking you this for the most responsible reasons – it isn't an idle curiosity. They've asked me to find out –'

'Don't ask me for details,' Broome said quickly.

'I want to know,' Melville said deliberately, 'whether he'll *ever* come back.'

Broome stopped, and looked him straight in the face with his normally cheerful blue eyes become solemn.

'I will answer you frankly,' he said.

'Well?'

'He might –'

'You damned doctors are impossible,' said Melville with a shrug.

'– but it's unlikely.'

Melville paused, and looked away over the lawns descending in terraces towards the Greystoke Gardens with their alleyways of Italianate statuary.

'I'm terribly sorry.'

'That's how it is,' said Broome. 'I don't want anyone –'

'Of course not,' said Melville. 'It's very sad. He was always very kind to me.'

They turned and walked back to the house, which now was ambered by the afternoon sunlight.

'Don't stay long,' said Broome.

'No,' Melville answered. 'I don't want to exhaust him.'

'It isn't that,' said Broome. 'We don't want you to be late for your party.'

'My party –?' said Melville. And then he remembered and walked smiling into the house.

Inside the room, the chintz curtains were half-drawn, and the light fell only at the foot of the bed. The Prime Minister sat propped up against two pillows, his head lolling, with his mouth open so that an ooze of spittle trickled from its corner. His blue pyjamas were open, his white hair lay uncombed over his moist forehead.

Melville closed the door quickly behind him, and sat in a chair waiting for Collard to awaken, half guilty as he watched him sleeping that he had taken him, vulnerable and indecorous, at a disadvantage. After a few seconds, the Prime Minister stirred and mumbled.

'Can I get you anything?' Melville said, approaching.

The Prime Minister said, 'What's that – what's that?' and dozed again. Then he opened his eyes and said, 'Bartlett?'

'No, it's Melville – Geoffrey Melville.'

The Prime Minister grunted and opened his eyes.

'They never draw the curtains in the morning. What time is it?'

'Twenty to five – it's the afternoon. Would you like me to draw the curtains?'

Without waiting for a reply, Melville drew the curtains and the sunshine came pouring in, illuminating the Rowlandson prints on the walls, and turning the bed, where Collard now sat, alert, into a throne.

'How good of you to come, Geoffrey,' he said. 'I'm beginning to find my secretaries and nurses and doctors – tedious.'

'I'd have come much more often, Prime Minister, but –'

'I know. M'landa! Never mind. You're here. . . . How is Elizabeth?'

'Very well – she asked me to give you her love.'

'I like Elizabeth. The very first time we met – you were a young Member – she mistook me for the Serjeant-at-Arms. A touch of baldness, I suppose. . . .'

'You are looking very well,' said Melville, who had heard the anecdote many times before. The Prime Minister's face was pallid, and he had become thinner, but his voice was strong and at ease.

'Oh, that's all behind me,' said Collard cheerfully. 'I'll probably go to Aix-en-Provence or somewhere like that for a few weeks – I always think that sea-cures are overrated. . . . Never mind about that. I want to know all the gossip.'

He rang the bell for tea, and motioned Melville into the armchair by the bedside.

'It's all very much the same,' said Melville, smiling. 'M'landa went off grinning – which I suppose is satisfactory.'

'You saw him off?'

'Yes,' said Melville. 'I always make a point of seeing my Africans to the airport. It makes certain that they don't come under unsuitable influences on the way.'

The Prime Minister propped himself on his elbow.

'That's very good, Geoffrey – very good. And Yates – how did he take it?'

'Well, Prime Minister, Hansard didn't quite give the picture. If you can visualize the deputy leader of the Opposition standing at the box choking with every word of congratulation, you'll be able to image Mr Yates – taking it.'

'He really is insufferable.'

'Quite insufferable!'

The nurse came in with a tea-tray, and Melville said, 'Thank you – I'll deal with it.'

'Brilliant, of course,' the Prime Minister continued, musing. 'It's fatal, though, to be a triton among minnows in your youth. So frustrating later when you find the other tritons in the sea. He's lucky to have Newman as his leader – virtuous and null.'

'The trouble with Yates,' said Melville, 'is that he's a natural Tory who strayed into the Socialist Party because he didn't like his family. He's perfectly happy with the working classes as long as he's lecturing them.'

22

'He's perfectly happy as long as he's lecturing us,' said Collard. 'But I do wish he'd keep that finger to himself.'

They laughed, and the room was transmuted from a sickroom into an annexe to all the places in Parliament where Collard had taken Melville by the elbow for a rapid burst of confidence or advice.

'Is he still friendly with Julia Drayford?' the Prime Minister asked.

'Not as friendly as he was,' said Melville. 'I think he's last year's friend.'

'That's very satisfactory. I wouldn't like to think of Drayford talking to Yates via Julia.'

'I don't think there's any danger of that, Prime Minister. I doubt if she ever speaks to her husband except to say, "More gin."'

'Yes,' said the Prime Minister. 'If we can get Drayford safely back in the next week, I think that all will be well with Mr M'landa. You mustn't underestimate Drayford, you know. The Africans like him.'

He relapsed against the pillows and with a brooding expression, his finger moving back and forth on the counterpane.

'Geoffrey,' he said at last.

'Yes, Prime Minister?'

'I'm glad you handled the thing so very well.'

Melville said, 'Thank you.'

The Prime Minister continued to speak without looking at Melville.

'You now have a great national reputation. You were excellent in the Party political broadcasts. You're well thought of in the Party and the Government. And you're a good-looking man. How old are you?'

'Forty-five.'

'And your health?'

'Excellent.'

'Does Elizabeth like public life?'

'She likes it very much.'

'And your children?'

'There's only Sylvia — she's at Oxford.'

'Yes,' said the Prime Minister, 'yes. She's a nice little girl. I remember her. . . .'

He fell into a doze, and after waiting for a few minutes Melville stood up carefully in order not to disturb him, and took a pace to the door.

'No, don't go,' said Collard, opening his eyes. 'I wanted to tell you this, Geoffrey. If the M'landa business goes well, I want to reconstruct the Government – you know, give some of the younger men a lift.'

'What did you have in mind, sir?'

'I'm thinking –' the Prime Minister hesitated, '– I'm thinking of sending Ormston to the Lords.'

'Ormston – Gerald?'

'Yes,' Collard said calmly. 'I feel uneasy with him at my elbow. For the last ten years, he's done nothing but wait for the current Prime Minister to die. He was like that with Telfer. It makes me uneasy. It sterilizes his own office. It unsettles the Cabinet. Elevation, Geoffrey – that's the new cry.'

Melville smiled.

'He won't like it, you know. I doubt if he'll accept.'

'We'll see,' the Prime Minister said flatly. 'If he doesn't like the Lords, he can have the corner seat in the third bench below the gangway. We'll give it a month. By the way, do you know the portrait of my ancestor, Sir John Copeland, in the Salon?'

Melville nodded.

'Well,' said the Prime Minister, 'after he was Speaker of the House of Commons in the eighteenth century, he didn't get a pension. He got all the silver in the official residence . . . It's come down to me – 240 pieces. When I'm better, I want to give a great dinner party.'

'I hope to be invited,' said Melville.

The Prime Minister sank his chin into his chest till his jowls wrinkled in a thin corrugation.

'Mind you,' he said, in a self-critical afterthought, 'you have an important handicap as a politician.'

Melville waited, and the Prime Minister continued,

'I've sometimes watched you with your friends. They talk to you, and you stand there with a distant look as if the one you can talk to hasn't arrived. They think you're arrogant.'

Melville shrugged his shoulder, helplessly.

'I'm sorry,' he said. 'It isn't my intention.'

'In politics,' said the Prime Minister, 'it's not enough to have a private language – one that does for a few high priests and the family. You must communicate –'

Stiffening himself to resist an impulse of anger, Melville said, 'I'm not sure that I agree with you, sir. The hell of politics is that we reduce everything to the average truth that can be squeezed into a slogan. It's then the ready-made, pre-packaged truth that we can market at elections. I get paralysed with boredom when Forbes and Lockhart and Ardrossan start trotting out Party resolutions as if they were quoting divine revelations.'

'That may be,' said the Prime Minister. 'It may well be. But you've got to be careful. Average truth, as you call it, is for average people. And if you appear to think you've got a private line to God, they won't like it. Be careful, Geoffrey?'

Melville laughed.

'I'll be careful,' he said.

The Prime Minister turned the pages of a book at his bedside, and said,

'You mustn't patronize them. Nobody likes to be patronized. They'll want you to fall flat on your face.'

'I'm sorry if I seem –'

'It doesn't matter. . . . I was saying –'

He brooded for a few moments, then fell asleep. Waking suddenly, he asked,

'How are Surrey doing?'

Before Melville could answer, he dozed again. When he awoke, he said, 'I think you'd better go now. I'm tired.' Melville waited for him to speak, but now the Prime Minister was pretending to sleep.

At the gate, a group of photographers was waiting, and Melville, with the friendly smile which gave amiability even to his caricatures, ordered the driver to stop.

'Any news of the P.M., sir?' asked one of the journalists.

'Yes,' said Melville, leaning out of the window, 'he's in splendid form – bursting to get back.'

'Any idea when?'

'Well,' said Melville reflectively. 'I can't really say – but if you want a guess, within the next few weeks.'

Another journalist joined in.

'That's very good news, Minister. Could you tell us if your visit had any special significance?'

'Yes, Peter,' said the Minister. 'I wanted to see the P.M., to ask after his health.'

'And the new Constitution?'

'Everyone seems to be delighted. I hope you'll forgive me. It's my wedding anniversary, and I'm meeting my wife.'

The photographers, as he expected, made him pose for another group of pictures, and within a few minutes the ministerial car was heading, with its pennant flying in the evening breeze, towards London. Melville triumphant, a conqueror about to enter a city, felt power stirring inside him. Ormston! Ormston in London waiting for bulletins. Since the Prime Minister's operation, the provisional had become the permanent, but the permanent only enjoyed the prestige of the provisional. Ormston! 'I have been asked to reply . . .' There were only two jobs that Ormston had wanted – the P.M.'s or Saunders' at the F.O. And now Ormston was to be bundled into the Lords. Melville smiled to himself as his car moved into the third lane of traffic, and passed an aggressive sports car with a surging acceleration. Ormston wouldn't like it one bit.

The prospect gave Melville a special satisfaction.

Wearing a mauve silk dress, Elizabeth stood greeting her guests who walked straight through the open door of the small Adam house in St Martin's Street. Around her, the party was beginning to coalesce, the interstices gradually filling with faces inclined towards each other, lip reading and straining or retreating from each other's spray. Half a dozen diplomats and their wives, a handsome Ghanaian, the son of the High Commissioner, Bagnari the sculptor, the Lord Chamberlain, Gregory Broome, three young M.P.s, two of them with model girl wives, Sir Brian Upjohn, Marcus Prebble-Keir, Sir Gareth Meade, the curator of the National Gallery, Lord Claddishe, Lord Ardrossan, Sir Julian Greenhill Waters, John Ingleborough, Sir James Twist, Janet McIver with one of her petalled hats – Elizabeth surveyed her guests and felt satisfied.

'Hello, Elizabeth,' said Broome, bending slightly to her cheek.

'Hello, Gregory,' she said. 'You're looking terribly like a fashionable doctor tonight.' He patted her arm affectionately.

26

'I wonder why,' said Melville, who had come up behind him. 'I think it must be those striped pants.'

'Not a bit,' said Broome. 'Today's fashionable doctor wears an unpressed suit, and tries to look like a scientist. Striped pants are strictly for the Ministry of Health.'

Elizabeth had taken Melville's arm, and was guiding him to the table where the drinks were laid out. 'My poor darling,' she said, 'you must be so tired.' She took the bottle from the barman's hand, and herself poured out a double whisky and guided the syphon for her husband.

'What happened?' she asked.

'I'll tell you later,' he said hurriedly as a group of guests began to move in his direction.

'What an idyllic picture!' said the Chief Whip, Rupert Scott-Bower, who reached Melville first. 'Hebe pouring nectar for Jove.'

'It sounds very improper,' said Elizabeth. 'I thought a Hebe was something you didn't mention.'

'Hetaira,' said Melville.

'And they were most respectable,' said Scott-Bower. 'They provided relaxation for philosophers and politicians.'

'I know a lot of those,' said Elizabeth.

'Yes, darling,' said Melville, laughing with Scott-Bower, 'but we only talk of that *in camera*.'

'I'm told,' said Scott-Bower, 'that today's a very important anniversary. What number?'

'Number twenty-two,' said Elizabeth, linking her arm in her husband's. 'And I won't pretend it's less.'

'Well,' said Scott-Bower, 'you both look indecently young.'

Helen Langdale, a film actress, approached, and Elizabeth remarked to the two men, 'Here she comes – all claws and plunge-line.'

'You must let me defend myself,' said Melville. 'Go and circulate.'

'Only for five minutes,' said Elizabeth, and she began to edge through the crush, smiling, offering drinks, asking questions and ignoring answers until she reached her post at the entrance again.

'It must be a change for you, finding yourself among whites again,' said Helen Langdale.

'I'm not anti-white,' said Melville. He looked into her *décolleté*, and said, 'You're *en grande beauté* tonight.'

'That's nice,' she replied. 'I was hoping to attract your attention.'
'You've been busy,' he answered. 'How's "The Enchanted Grove"?'

'Coming off,' she said, 'any day now. Our fairy prince couldn't get on with the anti-fairies. Tell me about yourself.'

She was looking him straight in the face, her grey-green eyes steady, her neck with its short dark hair poised in the characteristic way which had made her famous, and he remembered how for one week fifteen years before he had yearned and hungered for that face and how after a short episode at Cap Estel – Elizabeth had said that he needed a holiday – he had returned to a new Session; and the panic joy and the exultation had subsided, dying into an occasional meeting during Helen's abortive marriage. She seemed no older. Perhaps a line or two at the corner of her mouth. The slightest sag at her jaw-bone. Otherwise she was the same – at ease, articulate, beautiful. He looked from her to Elizabeth – Helen, tall, slender-shouldered, gentle-voiced: Elizabeth – not short nor tall, physically strong, loud-voiced.

'There's nothing much to say,' Melville answered. 'I've been absorbed in a steamy jungle of African affairs.'

'I always forget,' she said. 'Were you in Africa during the war?'

'No,' he replied, 'France to begin with – fighting to get home, and then South America – fighting for drinks at countless parties. I was in the Ministry of Economic Warfare.'

And, irrelevantly, he remembered the Ambassador, towering and off-handed above the head of his new father-in-law, leaving the reception after little more than half an hour, the Ambassadress, calm and elegant, saying good-bye to Elizabeth who stood clumsily at his elbow, and he frowned at the twenty-one-year-old memory. He had seen Sir Thomas Runcorn at the Palace only a few weeks earlier, and each had made a swerve to avoid the other as if they were conscious of an old indelicacy which they didn't want to recollect. Perhaps it was because Grundie, Elizabeth's father, the clerk turned vice-consul, called Runcorn 'Sir' too often.

Elizabeth passed, and, brushing against him, said,

'One more minute.'

'What did she say?' Helen asked.

'She said, "One more minute." She holds the view that anything more than that would be risky.'

'That's very tolerant of her . . . But, seriously, Geoffrey – she's amazing. How could she have put up with you all these years?'

Melville took glasses from the butler and handed one to her.

'Elizabeth,' he said, 'has a natural wisdom. She has always made life easy for me.'

'You mean – by being a Madame to your affairs?'

She asked the question sharply, and Melville thought that her small nose looked smudged.

'No,' he said calmly. 'By understanding her own importance in my life – and perhaps, mine in hers.'

'All right,' said Helen, smiling again. 'Don't get miffed. When are you going to have a drink with me?'

Melville looked at her fingers as she held the glass in her right hand, the other carefully feeling around its base. He hesitated, and said, 'I'll telephone you.'

'Soon?'

'Very soon.'

They moved apart as Elizabeth approached with Scott-Bower.

'I've got to go, Geoffrey,' said Scott-Bower, 'but I just wanted to wish you both the very greatest happiness. Speaking as a bachelor –'

'You've no right to say anything,' said Elizabeth. 'You *must* get married!'

Melville put an arm around Elizabeth's shoulders, and said,

'I've always thought Disraeli rather a bore, but he wrote it all in a dedication to his wife – "the most severe of critics but a perfect wife".'

'What a ghastly idea!' said Elizabeth. 'How awful to have to live up to that!'

Melville patted her lightly on her cheek and said,

'You've got no say in the matter.'

'Well, I'm going to be very imperfect,' she said. 'Gregory's had an urgent telephone call – some little girl's ill – and I'm going to take him to Ebury Street. I'll only be gone ten minutes though. Will you keep everyone happy?'

Melville looked across the room at Helen Langdale and said, 'I'll try. But don't be long, darling. . . . Anyhow, why doesn't he take a taxi?'

'There aren't any – and besides, the little car is right outside.'

She kissed Melville, and hurried away with the two men

29

looking reflectively after her.

'You're very fortunate,' said Scott-Bower, and the years of Melville's marriage became focused in the second when his wife had kissed his cheek, and all the love and resentment and hostility and reconciliation and sacrifice and fear and relief and joy and bickering and serenity came together in a single tenderness. He walked thoughtfully in the direction of Helen.

By a quarter past eight, the evening air had become chilly, and the waitresses were already putting the empty bottles away, and ranging the unopened ones in their hampers, although half a dozen stragglers still lingered, reluctant to give up their carefully acquired euphoria. Melville, who had been impatiently looking towards the door for Elizabeth, had suddenly become anxious. He had asked Waters, his Parliamentary Private Secretary, to telephone Broome's house to find out if there had been any message from him, but the reply came that he wasn't expected back till eleven o'clock.

Ten minutes later, Elizabeth arrived, panting as if she'd been running.

'Really, Elizabeth —' Melville said in a combination of irritation and relief.

'I'm so sorry,' she said. 'Do forgive me, darling. It was an operation, and I had to take him to Great Ormond Street. I left him there.'

'I did the "good-byes" on your behalf.'

'I bet they didn't even notice I wasn't there. You know that everyone comes to see you, not me.' She kissed him in full view of the staff. 'Get me a gin and tonic, Geoffrey. I'm so hot. I'm going to sit down.'

She sat on a gilt chair while he got her a drink, and when he joined her she said, 'You're looking singularly handsome tonight. Did they fall for you while I was away?'

He raised his chin slightly, pleased and reassured by her compliment.

'Not everyone,' he said. 'Just a few.'

'That Helen Langdale,' she said lightly. 'I must be mad leaving you alone with her.' And then, changing the subject, she said, 'Did you see the bit in tonight's paper about Sylvia?'

'What bit?' he answered sharply.

'It's here,' she said, turning over the pages of the evening paper which she had brought with her. 'Look – here it is in "Behind the Talk".'

Melville took the paper from her hands with distaste.

'We really oughtn't to touch this filthy stuff,' he said. And then he read.

'*Brothers Under the Skin*. Miss Sylvia Melville, the twenty-year-old daughter of the Secretary of State, is having a busy time at St Anne's College, Oxford, as secretary of the New Commonwealth Society. Her most constant companion is the joint secretary, Mr William Akebo, twenty-year-old son of Justice Jonah Akebo. But in Oxford romance is discounted. For why? Because at Lancaster House the Commonwealth Minister was heard to add to his splendid peroration, "I want the African to be my brother" – "But not my son-in-law."'

Melville flung the newspaper in disgust on to the arm of a chair where it tipped over an ash-tray full of cigarette butts, before sprawling in a litter of ash and used matches on the floor.

'They're unspeakable,' he said.

'Yes,' said Elizabeth, bending to pick the paper up. 'They'll invent anything. I do hope Sylvia won't get upset.'

3

'Thirty-four – thirty-five – thirty-six . . .' Melville listened to the cadence of the teller's voice as he waited to pass through the 'Aye' lobby where, he felt, everyone he wanted to avoid invariably accosted him. Howard Forbes, the Minister of Works, had edged forward along the green carpet, and now, with his lips quivering, would attend him back to the Front Bench.

'Melville!' He gave his name to the clerk at the desk who marked it in the register.

'Forbes!'

They bowed in turn between the tellers.

'Fifty-three – fifty-four . . .'

Instead of turning left into the Chamber, he decided that he would release himself from Forbes by going through the

Members' Lobby to the Smoking-Room. But Forbes was already at his heel, talking about some plan to link the Palace of Westminster by a subterranean tunnel with an annexe on the Embankment. 'It's so damned difficult to get a decision, you know. It isn't even the Treasury. Ormston likes the idea.'

'Well, what's the problem?' Melville asked wearily. The stifling march through the Voting Lobbies at the end of the day was the Parliamentary activity which he had always liked least. They walked to the Dispense and he ordered two whiskies and soda which they took to his favourite place near the Chess Room.

'I'll be frank with you,' said Forbes. 'It's the absence of leadership. We really can't go on like this, you know. I'm pretty sure we're going to lose Merchison North.'

'Why?' Melville asked quickly. His interest was aroused because three days earlier he himself had spoken at the by-election rally.

'Brinton's a very good candidate,' he said. 'A bit dim about policy. But that's what you want in a candidate. Nothing too specific.'

'That's not quite it, Geoffrey,' said Forbes, stretching out his legs from the leather armchair. 'In my view –'

He was interrupted by the annunciator rattling on its ribbon the result of the vote. 'Ayes 243, Noes 221.'

From his corner of the room came an 'Ah' like a jeer from Yates and his friends who had begun to take up their posts in twos and threes, so that the Smoking-Room seemed divided by the sofa, now empty, where the Prime Minister usually sat, in the same opposition as the Chamber.

'That's what I mean,' said Forbes. Melville noticed that Forbes, who had recently married for the first time at the age of forty-seven, had developed a winsome manner which went badly with his protuberant jaw muscles. He visualized the new wife whom he had met at the Speaker's Tea Party – a thin, middle-aged widow with a tight belt – and had a distasteful recollection of her coquetries with Forbes.

'I think I'd better push off,' said Melville. 'Elizabeth's waiting for me in the Central Lobby.'

'Oh, Rosemary's there too,' said Forbes reassuringly. 'She's a great admirer of Elizabeth. But to get back to what I was saying . . . look at tonight's vote. We've got a nominal majority of thirty-six. Tonight it was down to twenty-two.'

'What's your conclusion from that?' asked Melville.

'Leadership.'

'In what way −'

'Every way. We're just not getting it.'

Melville frowned. Forbes was talking loudly, and Melville had no doubt that he would soon draw the subject to the question of the Ministry of Health which he felt that he should have had in place of Mabel Walpole.

'What do you think we ought to do about it?' he asked, looking at the bottom of his empty glass.

'You tell me,' said Forbes.

Melville turned his face to his, and said amiably,

'I'm not complaining about the leadership.'

'Well,' said Forbes, smearing the wet marks on the table with his glass, 'I don't think we can go on like this.'

'You think,' said Melville, 'we ought to do something −' he was about to say '− do something about the P.M.' but looking at Forbes' expectant face he knew that if he asked the question, the other would translate it as an affirmation. He stopped, and Forbes finished his drink.

'We must do something,' said Forbes. 'He'll be a sick man when he gets back.'

'I don't think so,' said Melville. 'I saw him today. He looked fine.'

Forbes dropped his voice, and said,

'I'm told it's cancer.'

'Nonsense,' said Melville. 'He looks as fit as − as you do.'

Forbes shrugged his shoulders. 'I'm sorry for poor old Collard, but it can't go on, you know. We're losing support in the country. There's no leadership.'

Melville stood up and said, 'I don't think it's like that. We've two years to go.'

'Just a minute, Geoffrey,' said Forbes. 'I want to put something to you.'

'I can only stay a moment,' said Melville with a quick glance at the clock that said 10.20.

'I want to put it to you, Geoffrey, that the P.M. should be asked to stand down for Ormston, and you yourself −'

'No,' said Melville. 'No. I don't want to hear it, old chap. It's not on.'

33

He hesitated as he decided which route he would take through the tangle of noisy tables; then, turning, he said,

'What does Ormston say about it?'

'I haven't asked him,' said Forbes, and Melville knew he was lying. 'A few of us −'

'It's the wrong time,' said Melville, and he strode past the legs, waving and nodding as he went.

At the door, he was met by Francis Waters, his Parliamentary Private Secretary, wearing the apologetic but contented smile of one who brings disturbing news.

'There's an urgent telegram you ought to see,' he said. 'Lincorne brought it himself.'

Melville stiffened his features and took the telegram from Waters. It was from the Governor, Sir Rupert Benning, and said,

'Mr M'landa asked me to see him today in a request for an explanation of remarks attributed to Secretary of State at Lancaster House following dinner. He has taken deep offence.'

Melville held the telegram in his hand for a few seconds, and then he said,

'Tell the Office to send this message to the Governor.'

He wrote on the back of the telegram, 'Statement attributed to Secretary of State is a journalistic fabrication which he deplores.'

'Is that all right?' he asked Waters.

'Oh, it's fine,' said Waters idly, his face, already pink, flushing deeper at the illusion that his Minister was asking his opinion.

'See that it goes at once,' said Melville. He patted Waters on the shoulder, and walked rapidly to the Central Lobby.

Beneath the statue of Earl Granville, Elizabeth stood in a group of Members and their wives, their voices echoing under the vaulted roof. The policeman at the barrier to the Chamber was gathering up his papers under the green lamp, and the door leading to St Stephen's Hall was open for the Members now hurrying down the stairs towards Parliament Square. Elizabeth left her friends as soon as she saw Melville, and ran towards him.

'Don't run, darling,' he said with a smile. 'One day you're going to slip on the floor, and cause a lot of embarrassment.'

'I know,' she said, taking his arms, 'they'll lay me out on one of those leather benches − groaning slightly but bravely. The policeman ringing for an ambulance. You bending over me with a white face – an emergency operation at Westminster Hospital – reporters in the corridor –'

'Don't,' said Melville, 'you're exhausting me. Just don't run on slippery stone floors.'

'You're a dear,' Elizabeth said. 'I'm going to cling to you.'

'I've got to make a telephone call,' said Melville, 'and then I've got to go to the office.'

'What – at this hour?' she said.

'I'm afraid so,' said Melville. '*Semper aliquid novi ex Africa.*'

'You mustn't tease me,' Elizabeth replied. 'You know I'm uneducated. What does it mean?'

'It's a corny quotation,' said Melville. 'It means that anyone doing my job can always expect something new when he wants to go to bed. But I'll be back soon. Before midnight.'

He kissed her cheek and said sternly,

'I expect you to be awake when I get back.'

'Aren't I always?' she replied meekly.

The policeman in New Palace Yard opened the door of a taxi, and Melville waved to his wife as she blew him a kiss before she sat down.

'Shall I ring for your car, sir?' asked the policeman.

Melville thought for a moment, and said, 'I don't think so, Bob. Tell them I won't need it again. But I will want another taxi in about five minutes.'

He pushed the heavy oak doors of Westminster Hall, and walked rapidly through its deserted cavernous expanse, his footsteps resounding from the stone walls. Two small lights burned in the vast arcaded ceiling, giving a russet glow to the oak beams. Otherwise, it was in darkness or shadow, except where the buttresses gave off a faint reflection. He didn't like Westminster Hall, he decided. The ghosts were unfriendly. William Rufus – Charles I – Warren Hastings – the Seven Bishops. The plaques glimmered in the darkness. Cold in summer, colder still in winter. Windowless except for its modern stained glass, it was noble, dark and damp. He associated it like a school hall with boring ceremonial processions. Morning coats. Gentlemen-at-arms. Coronation luncheon and catafalques of kings. Summer chill, parties of school-children. The dark grey flagstones. Westminster Hall. Treading on history. He left the Hall for the warm and well-lit telephone booths with relief.

35

He dialled a number, and when a woman's voice answered, he said cheerfully, 'Julia?'

'Who is it?'

'It's Geoffrey.'

'Oh, Geoffrey. How very nice of you! I see you were at Collard's today.'

'Yes.'

'I hope you're going to tell me all about it.'

'Of course,' said Melville. 'Everything.'

'Well, that's wonderful.' She became silent, waiting for him to tell her why he had telephoned.

'Can I come and see you, Julia?'

'I'd love you to. Why not lunch next Wednesday – if you can bear the Adrian Stewarts.'

'I can't. But Wednesday's too far away.'

'Geoffrey – how flattering! What about – let me look at my book – what about a drink tomorrow – half past six?'

'I want to see you tonight, Julia. There's something that's worrying me – and it affects you.'

'Me!'

Her voice had hardened.

'Yes – it affects you. There's something I have to clear up. May I call on you – for a few minutes?'

He heard her laugh.

'Of course you can,' she said. 'Will you bring your detective? It'll be very cosy.'

'No,' said Melville, laughing too. 'I've sent him back to Scotland Yard or wherever they come from. Since Mr M'landa's become more friendly, I'm on my own.'

'Don't be long,' said Mrs Drayford, and put down the receiver. Melville sat with his head resting against the panel in the tele-phone booth. The whole thing was tiresome. But it was important to get the record straight. Julia was, after all, an old friend. He stood, took a deep breath outside the booth, and returned to New Palace Yard where the taxi's meter was already ticking.

Mrs Drayford herself opened the door, and preceded him upstairs to the drawing-room.

'I've lit the pictures for you specially,' she said. 'And I've sent the maids to bed. But don't be alarmed. It's their usual bedtime.'

'Thank you,' said Melville, taking a seat on the brocaded sofa. 'Is that a Degas?'

'No,' she said. 'It's a Forain. Their ballet dancers are often confused. You can tell the Forains, though, by all that burnt umber he uses on the left.'

Melville looked politely at the picture and then he said, 'Julia —'

'You're just in time,' she said, 'for the topping-up. What will you drink? It's an unfashionable hour but I'm drinking dry Martinis. It's the *modern* form of secret drinking, as Edward's TV ads. would say.'

'I'd like a small whisky and soda,' he said.

'Well, do it yourself,' Mrs Drayford said sulkily, seating herself in an armchair.

'A *mauvaise ivre*,' Melville reflected, and poured out his drink.

'I'm tired,' Mrs Drayford said, 'and I'm feeling inhospitable. Why does one go on living?'

'It's a habit,' said Melville.

'A disgusting habit,' said Mrs Drayford, and burst into tears.

Melville waited for her weeping to subside. Her eyes had become inflamed, and the tip of her nose had a bead of mucous.

'Oh, God,' she said, reaching for her wet handkerchief, 'it's been like this the whole evening. God, how I hate you bloody politicians!'

'Is he being unkind to you?' Melville asked sympathetically.

'Very,' she said in a more restrained voice, sniffing. 'He's so cruel. I sometimes think there are only two real Parties in Britain — the Sadists and the Masochists. He shouldn't be Deputy Leader of the Opposition. He ought to be Minister of Sadism.'

Melville laughed, and she laughed too.

'All the same,' she went on. 'It's very hard when everything in your life is public, including your private life.'

'Yates never could keep a secret.'

Mrs Drayford stood up, and said coldly,

'What on earth do you mean?'

'Nothing,' said Melville. 'Nothing — except that your friendship is much discussed.'

She walked over to the cabinet, and poured the rest of the dry Martini into her glass.

'There's nothing to discuss any more,' she said. 'Nothing at all. I wish there were.'

Melville watched her carefully as she returned to the armchair, her fingers glistening from the overspill of the glass. An aggression in search of an object, he said to himself, and he waited for her to speak.

'It's gone on too long,' she said at last, 'and it's stopped growing.' Her face became bright. 'You know, Geoffrey, I've suddenly had an idea about love. It's got to grow and grow all the time if it's to go on living. Once it stops growing, it starts to decay.'

She drank her Martini, and went on,

'The day before yesterday was wonderful.'

'Why?'

'I met him at Gradwell's, and we went for a long walk together.'

'And you enjoyed it?'

'No – I was bored. Bored – bored – bored. For the first time, I faced the fact. I was bored. And I was delighted. It's gone on too long.'

Melville wondered when he could ask her the question which he had phrased and re-phrased during his journey, and he looked over her shoulder at the wall-clock. It was late, and he didn't want to prolong her confidences which, in any case, were neither novel nor confidential.

'Listen, Julia,' he said, 'why don't you chuck the whole thing?'

She took a cigarette from a shagreen box on the table, and Melville reached across to give her a light. She took one puff, and then put the cigarette out.

'I don't know,' she answered. 'It doesn't work like that. You can decide that you don't want somebody for this reason or that; and that if they do this or that, you'll drop them. But then they do all those things – and you still want them. You can even be ashamed to want them. But you do – and then, there's – oh, Christ, there's something wrong with my lachrymal ducts!' She wiped her eyes and then she smiled at Melville.

'I'm so sorry, Geoffrey. Here you are, calling to see me in the middle of the night –'

'Ten past eleven.'

'– and anyone coming in would think you're doing me a violence. Have another whisky!'

'No, thank you,' said Melville. She had begun to make up her face, and gradually its blotches disappeared beneath the powder.

'Do you really think that – how can I put it – do you really think that the way people behave to us has nothing to do with whether we love them?' he said.

'I didn't say that,' she answered. 'Good behaviour has a lot to do with the beginning of love, but misbehaviour – once it's begun, it makes no difference.'

'Well, I don't know,' said Melville, standing. 'I wouldn't like to be tested.'

She scrutinized him for a moment and opened her mouth to speak.

'Yes?' said Melville.

'Oh, nothing – nothing at all. You're lucky, Geoffrey – you have no need to be tested.' Cheerfully, 'What a lovely party you gave tonight! Elizabeth looked very nice too. She's got exactly the right face and figure to set off her handsome husband.'

It was curious, Melville thought, that he could be sitting alone with Julia at this house without the least embarrassment at the possibility that Drayford might walk in. If he did so, he would regard it as normal that Julia should be entertaining. And yet, if he himself had returned from the House late at night and found Elizabeth receiving some solitary man, he would have felt a sense of outrage. He dismissed the prospect from his mind, and took refuge from Julia's compliment in a banality.

'Elizabeth believes,' he said, 'that M.P.s' wives should be seen and not heard.'

'Oh, no,' said Julia, her smile falling away as if she had a private memory that angered her, 'Elizabeth believes they should be both seen and heard – and overheard. Why doesn't she pipe down a bit?'

'What on earth do you mean?' Melville asked, frowning. He had himself heard Elizabeth tell Monroe that he would be opening the Colonial Affairs debate the following week although the week's business had not yet been officially announced, and her indiscretion had irritated him.

'I mean,' said Julia, 'that Elizabeth is a compulsive talker. She was very objectionable to Scott-Bower about my husband. You ought to know, Geoffrey, that the only person I allow to be objectionable about my husband is myself.'

She laughed privately, and Melville said in apology, 'I'm sure she couldn't have said anything deliberately offensive. You know

Elizabeth. I've never heard her say anything unkind –'

'You must listen harder,' said Julia. 'She said to M'landa only the other night, on the steps of Lancaster House, "Geoffrey likes Drayford. He calls him 'that ambulant hangover'."'

'I certainly have never called him that,' Melville protested. 'In any case, I can't imagine that M'landa would know what it meant.'

'Don't be absurd, Geoffrey,' said Julia, twisting her necklace in her fingers, her expression of malice changing into one of distraction as if the subject now interested her. 'M'landa said, "That's rich! That's jolly rich! . . ." It's strange how these blacks pick up worn-out public school slang. But I can tell you he didn't like her insolence about Edward. Never mind. It's all unimportant.' Her voice trailed away. 'What did you want to ask me, Geoffrey?'

Melville walked over to the fireplace, and looked at a photograph of Julia and the Prime Minister, taken at the opening of the new runway at Gatwick. She was laughing in it, not with the embarrassed air of those who pose for photographers, but easily, like a woman who is sheltered and without anxieties. Melville turned back to her as she sat on the sofa sullen and lacerating a matchstick.

'Well, what is it?' she asked.

'Julia,' Melville said, sitting down again. 'It's a small matter – but it's important in its way. Did you see the evening papers?'

'Yes,' she said. 'I've read them from cover to cover. I'm like Elizabeth – compulsive – but a compulsive reader. Why?'

She was speaking fast and defiantly, and Melville lowered his voice as he was accustomed to do when provoked in the Chamber.

'You saw the piece about Sylvia – and myself – in "Behind the Talk"?'

'Yes – I thought it rather apt – very funny – all that stuff about you not wanting an African son-in-law. Is Sylvia thinking of getting married?'

Melville looked at his nails, and said,

'Please be serious, Julia – What appeared in the paper tonight is a garbled report of something that I might have let fall – I've forgotten exactly what it was – in a flippant aside. I don't know how they got hold of it . . . Perhaps you do. At any rate, I want you to know that it can lead to a lot of trouble, and I'm going to deny it.'

Mrs Drayford looked away from him, and said, 'It's got nothing to do with me. I don't know why you're bothering me with it.'

'I just wanted you to know the position.'

She smiled at him, a generous, unforced smile that twisted at the end of her mouth into enjoyment that Melville's self-assurance was about to be disturbed.

'The position?' she repeated in a query. 'I know the position. You want me to forget that you said, "I want the African to be my brother – not my brother-in-law." Is that it?'

Melville returned her look carefully, and decided he would be cautious.

'It would be easier, Julia,' he said, 'if we were all to forget.'

'I'll forget it,' she said obligingly.

'Thank you, Julia,' Melville said with a sense of relief. He strode across to her, laid his face against hers for a fraction of a second in which its warmth, her scent and a staleness of dry Martinis exuded into his consciousness as the emanation of her personality, and turned to go.

'And no more tattle to Yates,' he said lightly.

She pushed him away from her, and her smiling air of a second before changed into one of fury.

'What do you mean?' she said. 'How dare you talk to me like that?'

'Oh, come, Julia,' he said wearily. 'I was only being flippant.'

'Flippant,' she said, her voice rising. 'Flippant! Why do you bloody well think you can come here to my house and insult me?'

Melville looked towards the door, overwhelmed by the sudden feeling that he wanted to leave quickly before the interview became catastrophic. He put his hand on her arm to calm her, and she flung it away.

'How dare you speak like that,' she said in a scream.

'I'm sorry, Julia,' said Melville, retreating in anger and uneasiness. 'I sometimes think you ought to take control –'

'Control,' she said, sitting on the nearest chair. 'Don't you start lecturing me. Look after your own affairs. Look after your own innocent little wife.'

'What has Elizabeth to do with it?'

'Nothing,' said Mrs Drayford. 'Nothing at all.'

41

Under the lampshade as she started to rearrange the bowl of roses, the veins on her quivering thin hands seemed mauve, and her maculae orange.

'Elizabeth —' Melville began. Then he shrugged his shoulders and left.

He walked rapidly through the Park towards his house past the black silhouette of trees, the flash of water, and the deserted buildings with their occasional abandoned lights. 'The rotten bitch,' he said to himself, and a night bird squawked an accompaniment to his rage. He breathed deeply the air that was puffed with the smell of privet, and gradually, as his footsteps became slower, his anger began to ebb as well.

He let himself into his house with his key, paused for a moment to see if there were any messages for him in the hall, and then went straight upstairs. By the bedside, Elizabeth had as usual during the Session left a tray of sandwiches and a thermos flask of coffee. She had fallen asleep with the light still on. Her book, a novel by Georgette Miller, which she had borrowed from Boots' library, lay tumbled on the bed. Melville looked at her, sleeping with her mouth slightly open, and thought that she was plain and dear to him and his wife; and that Julia was a bitch.

'Elizabeth,' he said quietly.

She stirred and put her arms around his neck, and said, 'What time is it, darling? . . . You work much too hard.'

4

During the last four overs, the Lords and Commons had only scored two runs, and their supporters in the deck-chairs on the boundary of the cricket field were beginning to get restless. The Law Society's slow bowler, a specialist in entails, started a crab-like waddle to the wicket. Dallow, a solicitor who had regularly played in this annual event but who this season had injured a thumb, turned to Yates who was tying on his pads, and said,

'He doesn't bowl them out. They just die of boredom.'

The batsman carefully played the ball back, and Yates replied, 'That's how it should be. Dying in the illusion of permanent summer – nothing happening suddenly – everything blending into an afternoon snooze.'

He closed his eyes to assure Dallow that he didn't want conversation, but Dallow who a few days earlier had successfully acted in a libel action on behalf of a Government back-bencher against a newspaper, was in a mood to talk about politics.

'I don't quite know how you work these things,' he said to Guest, an Opposition Junior Whip who was lying on the grass at Yates' feet. 'If you're a Whip, how do you get the day off?'

'We have influence,' said Yates, opening his eyes and looking gravely at Dallow. 'We arrange for the day of our match against the Law Society to be Welsh Day in the Commons. Our absence isn't noticed.'

'That's it,' said Guest.

'We leave the Chamber,' said Yates, 'in a Celtic twilight. Nothing is heard except a rising *hwyl*.'

'That's right,' said Guest.

'No votes?' asked Dallow.

'Not till the match is over – nothing but incantation and exorcism if an English Member intrudes . . . Oh . . . first class!'

The entail bowler had repeated his slow spinner once too often, and Reynolds had driven the ball hard towards the shadows of the beech trees. It came bouncing and hopping over the rough grass of the outfield, struck a root, leapt in the air and ran a few yards up a tree trunk before falling near their feet. Guest tossed it to a fielder, and Dallow rose, saying, 'I'll see you later.'

'Not if I can help it,' said Yates after he had gone. He glanced behind him at the Palladian club-house which formed a background to the cricket held and croquet lawns, and decided that he liked it there. It was as if he were in a stockade excluding the outer world with waiters serving iced drinks. The sky was a hazy blue, and he remembered how during his African tour he used to wake up longing to see a white cloud appear in the unchanging copper colour in the sky. Once it had been darkened by a flight of locusts. In England he sweated more. His sleeves were rolled up. A land-crab waddling from the sand. The dark hairs of his forearms bleached golden. He had never been far south in the desert. The Kalahari. The morning air – the morning

43

light. He dozed, and was wakened by a shout from the pitch. Reynolds had been caught.

'Hit the shoulder of the bat,' said Guest. 'Swiped too late.'

Yates joined in the clapping as Reynolds made his way to the deck-chairs with his bat under his arm. He had made seven runs in an hour.

'Well done,' Yates said. 'I don't think Hobbs could have done much with that one.'

'Think so?' said Reynolds, seeking comfort as he took off his pads. 'There's a tuft out there – you've got to watch for it. He keeps dropping them on each side, and it's a matter of luck where they twist.'

'Cunning lot, these solicitors,' said Yates, looking to right and left. Reynolds, a director of a public relations firm, had evolved what he called the Reynolds Syndrome Theory. It meant that every action was related to a pattern, the action being to the pattern what a symptom is to a disease. The drawback to Reynolds' discovery was that he had become almost incapable of making a statement without a commentary on its origin.

'In my view –' Reynolds began. Yates heaved himself from his chair, and said,

'I think I'll lumber about a bit. I'm after Mackay.'

He glanced at the scoreboard. The Law Society had been all out for 123 before lunch and Lords and Commons were 81 for 5.

'I'll come too,' said Guest.

They walked away in the direction of the nets, and Guest, who had been a school-teacher before he became a Member of Parliament, said,

'Chaps like Reynolds give me the willies. They're every bit as dogmatic as our lot. And they call themselves the empirical party!'

Yates laughed loudly, and some of the spectators turned their heads as they heard the familiar sound which had become as much part of this TV *persona* as his boxer's shoulders were part of his caricatures in the Press.

'Well,' he said, 'there are two kinds of dogmatic thinking. There's the dogma of conformity, and the dogma of non-conformity. Reynolds isn't dogmatic because he sells soap or whatever it is. He's dogmatic because he's an earl's nephew – went to Eton and Magdalen – and because one of his ancestors chopped off Charles I's head before becoming a royalist.'

Their boots crunched on the gravel.

'It's a great mistake,' Yates went on, 'to assume that the British are inherently more equable in temper than anyone else. We're just cleverer. We had our revolution three hundred years ago, and got it over. We learnt then that it was better for the Opposition to want to change the Government than the constitution. Makes life so much easier.'

'It's true, of course,' said Guest, walking in step with his Deputy Leader. 'Didn't someone say that Parliament's the substitute for civil war?'

'I said it,' Yates answered. 'Everyone's said it.'

He stopped, and took a deep breath.

'God,' he said, 'it's a wonderful day! I can't remember a summer like this.'

The figures on the cricket field were a brilliant white against the grass, the deck-chairs made a confusion of colour and the club's standard every now and again fluttered from its limp posture as a breeze lifted it up, dangled it and dropped it. A group of women in light-coloured, short-sleeved dresses approached the deck-chairs, and the men hoisted themselves from their chairs.

'The wives are here,' said Yates. 'Perhaps we ought to go back.'

The commotion of greeting, the female voices introducing a new and gayer sound into the somnolent afternoon, the changed demeanour of the men who after lolling on the grass now stood attentively behind the chairs – all this displeased him. He thought of his wife, Elsa, with their three children at home near his Northumberland constituency. She was happy to be a housewife and help in his local affairs, and wasn't for ever fussing to be with him at their flat in London. He couldn't stand political wives who were always treading on their husband's heels.

'M.P.s' wives really are a special kind,' he said.

'They're a bit like Service wives,' said Guest.

'Camp-followers,' Yates went on. 'Where do you live?'

'As a matter of fact,' said Guest, 'we did live in High Wycombe but we moved to London three months after the Election. Mary didn't like being left. You know how it is. They get pretty lonely when we're away all the time.'

'Yes,' said Yates reflectively.

He felt that he had spent long enough with Guest, and he was already making up his mind about whom he should talk to next.

45

Burton, Thornby, McLennan – they were grouped around Reynolds who was still explaining away the ball that had got him. Farleigh and Jasperson were absorbed with their wives. Lord Horley – he would talk endlessly in his thin, distilled voice about the days when his father should have captained Sussex. No, he couldn't face Horley or any of them. He walked over to Stour-Benson, the team's opening batsman, and said,

'Hello, Raymond. How's it going?'

Stour-Benson looked up, wrinkling his eyes against the sun, and said,

'I think it's all right. As long as we're not interrupted by a cloudburst or something. Edwards is doing us very nicely.'

He stopped to applaud an easy glide which brought two runs off the fast bowler.

Yates sat on the grass, and examined Stour-Benson – Sir Raymond Stour-Benson. The name tripped off the tongue like the beginning of a poem. With his baronetcy, his patrician cheekbones and his passion for cricket, he should have spent all his days on his estate reviving squirearchal customs instead of legislating at Westminster. Except for this cricket match, Yates hardly ever saw him during the session. From time to time they would nod to each other briefly as they passed each other in the Members' Lobby; and occasionally, Stour-Benson would ask him for a 'pair'.

They sat watching the cricket for a few moments till Yates said,

'Are you speaking in the African debate next week?'

Stour-Benson pondered as if he needed to invoke guidance before answering so direct a question from the Deputy Leader of the Opposition.

'I may be,' he said at last.

'You ought to, you know,' said Yates. 'After all, there aren't many who know Africa as well as you do.'

Stour-Benson picked up a bat and patted the turf.

'To be quite frank,' he said, 'it's one reason why I don't like talking about Africa in the House. I'm afraid, Alfred, you wouldn't like my views any more than most of my own Party.'

'Oh, no, not a bit,' said Yates, propping himself on his elbow. 'There's no single view on Africa that's right – I'm sure of that. The thing to do is to see it as a spectrum. Don't you think the Constitutional Settlement is a step forward?'

Stour-Benson put his arms behind his head, and said,

46

'Frankly – no. I don't like appeasement in any form. It's what we objected to in 1939. I spent five years fighting the result. Why should we appease a man just because he's black?'

'But don't you think,' Yates said, 'that it's better to offer what you'll have to yield anyhow?'

'I don't agree – I think we have a place in Africa that no one should ask us to yield – and if necessary we ought to fight to keep it.'

'But say,' Yates persisted, 'say this policy – I mean the policy of the Constitutional Settlement – say it satisfied the settlers as well as M'landa?'

'I can tell you for certain,' said Stour-Benson, 'that the white settlers don't like it. I have a brother and several cousins out there. They don't regard themselves as settlers. It's their home – and their children's home.'

He had begun to speak angrily, and Yates looked around quickly to see if they were attracting attention. He tugged at a blade of grass, and began to suck it.

'What I don't understand,' he said, 'and I'm really not being political – really not – what I don't understand about your Party is why the back-benchers take these views so supinely. Obviously, we don't share your views, but if there were a real difference of opinion, we'd have one hell of a row – the papers would be full of it.'

Stour-Benson had become suspicious of Yates' *bonhomie*, and he said,

'We believe in keeping our differences in the family.'

'Of course,' said Yates, 'the Gentlemanly not the Brotherly Party. Mind you, it's a bit bovine.'

'Bovine? What d'you mean?'

'It's bovine,' said Yates, rising to his feet. 'I never can understand why you chaps can never show the public that you're something more than a bunch of castrated cattle being pushed into a pen. You say yourself that you consider the settlement a bad one –'

He tightened the buckle of his pad, and added,

'– but what happened? Not a squeak – not a question – not a Motion on the Order Book – not even a letter to *The Times*. Nothing but a dismal lowing.'

'I think you'd better wait and see,' said Stour-Benson, resisting

47

Yates' provoking tone. 'There's something unnatural about the new coalition.'

'Which one?'

'Collard – Newman.'

'Yes,' Yates said, 'that's an interesting combination – like harnessing the ox and the ass – or is that *lèse-majesté*?' Then he added hastily, 'It wouldn't do at all – not even for Africa. . . .'

'I quite liked Newman's crack the other day,' said Stour-Benson good-humouredly, 'about Melville catching up with *The Times*.'

'Poor old Newman,' said Yates. 'I sometimes wonder what he'd do without the Oxford Book of Quotations and *The Times* first leader.'

'There's always "I remember when I was a boy. . . ." He's quite indestructible, isn't he?' Stour-Benson said. 'I think politics must be a healthy exercise – seen as a game.'

'It isn't a game,' said Yates coldly. He had gone far enough in familiarity with Stour-Benson, and wanted to leave his dissent on record. A member of the Club's staff came up, and said, 'You're wanted on the phone, sir. The House of Commons.'

Yates hesitated, then made his way to the telephone booth inside the cool, well-polished entrance.

'That you, Alf?' said Newman's voice, snapping like a biscuit. 'Been hitting them for six?'

'No,' said Yates. 'I've spent the afternoon inhaling the grass. I haven't been in yet.'

'Well, I'm sorry to interrupt, but it's quite important. I think we ought to have a meeting tonight.'

'What about?' said Yates, restraining his irritation. The Parliamentary Committee normally met in the early evening, and it meant that he might have to leave the game before it ended.

'Africa,' said Newman crisply.

'That seems to be doing all right without us,' said Yates. He never could understand why Newman was constantly fussing about vast and unmanageable subjects. Africa, the world, outer space – truth, beauty, God. If only he gave as much attention to Parliamentary Bills as he gave to universal sentiment –! Yates shrugged his shoulders. It was perhaps better like that. It was a convenience that Newman as Leader of the Party dealt in generalizations while he himself coped with the day-to-day business of the Party and the House. He recalled in a parenthesis

48

that he had arranged to meet a group of leading trade unionists the following day, and decided that he wouldn't emphasize the fact to Newman, who as an old trade unionist himself had always tried to keep the handling of industrial relations as his prerogative. The line was bad, and he had difficulty in hearing what Newman was saying.

'. . . I was saying,' Newman repeated, 'that I've just had a telegram from the Ahuru Party signed among others by Ngura.'

'What does he want?' said Yates, alert now with his mind focused on the practical consequences of the information. Ngura was M'landa's chief opponent at the Lancaster House Conference, the most suspicious and intransigent of the African delegation and the one least willing to accept the final compromise. On two occasions, in front of television audiences, he had said that the only future for Africa lay in the extermination of the colonialists, and at the end of the Conference, although he had acquiesced in the settlement, had refused to appear at the side of the Minister in the official photograph.

'I've got the telegram here,' said Newman. 'No – wait a minute – just one minute – I've put it aside somewhere . . . Anyhow, the point is that for some reason or other – oh, here it is.'

Yates heard the voice of Newman's secretary as she handed him the telegram.

'"Respectfully request you and your colleagues ensure Constitution introduced in the spirit of Lancaster House without chicanery –"'

'That's a splendid word!' said Yates.

'"– or evasion stop have reason to believe that Government in concert with local settlers will seek whittle away essential provisions following Minister's green-light racialist sentiments M'landa dinner." What do you think of it?' Newman concluded.

'I don't quite know what it's all about,' said Yates.

'I imagine,' said Newman, 'it's that piece in "Behind the Talk" about Melville not wanting his daughter to marry a coloured student.'

'I think,' said Yates, 'we've got to be pretty careful. First of all, we don't want to look as if we're encouraging opposition to the agreement.'

'No,' said Newman.

'Then again, there's not much substance in what Ngura says.

He's a bit of a paranoiac, you know. I met him when he was over here. I can't quite understand why Africans who study law in Britain, seem to go mad.'

'I think,' Newman said mildly, 'that they become conscious of rights.'

'I don't think so,' said Yates. 'I think it's the wig and the little white bib. It's like the witch-doctor's top hat. . . . Anyhow, Ngura's definitely not our man.'

'A polite acknowledgement, I think.'

'Yes – assure him that the Opposition has the best interests of Africa at heart.'

'Yes.'

'And that we will carefully follow the unfolding of events – something of that kind . . . I don't really think we should have a special meeting – it all seems pretty innocuous.'

'I don't know, I am a bit worried. I think they may be brewing something up. I think there's more behind it, Alf.'

'Oh, but there always is,' said Yates calmly, glad that Newman was only half-hearted about the meeting. 'I think we ought to see what line Melville takes next week. He's very cock-a-hoop.'

He could hear Newman sucking his pipe at the other end of the line, and he said,

'I think I'd better get back.'

For a few minutes, he stood watching Lockhart at the wicket. He was fidgeting with his cap, tugging at his shirt, patting the crease and taking centre. He was one of the best organizers on the Government side, a man who rarely spoke in the House but whom all the Government back-benchers regarded as their spokesman to the cabinet. He had been playing himself in for about three-quarters of an hour, stolidly returning the ball to the bowler or occasionally scoring a run to leg where a semicircle of fielders surrounded him. The slow bowler tripped and sent down a short ball. Lockhart examined it with a frown. It was unprecedented, out of rhythm with his defensive play. He hesitated, played forward to it, and the ball rose in a slow parabola to fall securely into the hands of mid-on.

'We need twenty,' Stour-Benson said to Yates who had begun his walk towards the wicket. Yates grinned over his shoulder, and said,

'It's only a one-day match.'

His pads flopped against his knees, his boots, which he hadn't worn since last year, hurt, and he had forgotten whether he needed his reading glasses for cricket. But there was something very agreeable about going in to bat. Your opponents were in a cheerful mood; they had, after all, just got rid of one of your team. There they stood, heaving the ball to each other, expecting to do to you what they had done to him.

I, on the other hand, thought Yates, have a different idea. He felt the muscles of his forearm harden at the prospect. He was in the mood to hit three sixes in the first over. Dazzling innings by Yates – fifty runs in first hour. It was a reverie from the prep. school which walked with him to the wicket. From the boundary, the pitch had seemed an even green. But approaching it, he saw that the grass had been rubbed away by the cricketers' boots, exposing the dry, brown earth. The stumps and bails seemed larger than they used to be, and all in all, the man at the crease was alone in a hostile world. It was no good thinking of Newman and Africa and the Party Committee. What he had to think of now was the thin man at the other end who was rather contemptuously tossing the ball in the air and catching it. Yates hadn't played for a year. Perhaps he should have had an hour at the nets. He took centre, and prepared to receive the first ball.

It came very fast, hit a small rut and rose sharply at Yates's head. He ducked, and heard a sound of laughter from the spectators. He waited for the next ball with an angry determination, but it swung wide and he watched it go. The third ball was a full toss which came hurtling at his groin. With a feeling of outrage, he swung his bat, and hit out with the whole strength of his powerful shoulders so that the ball soared in the air and seconds later crashed through the upper branches of one of the beech trees on the boundary. The spectators clapped, and the other batsman who had begun to run waved him back. Yates rested on his bat while the ball was retrieved. He felt exhilarated. He liked argument and disciplined vigour. He looked at the thin bowler, who wore a chastened expression, and decided that before the over ended, he would hit another six.

The bowler took a somewhat shorter run, and this time the ball came sweeping in from leg with a sudden break. Yates, who had been preparing to hook it, played it back respectfully. The last ball came perfectly straight and pitched in a classical length. With an air of total contempt, Yates advanced to meet it, couldn't quite reach it, lunged, and then when the ball was past him heard a gentle snicker. It was the sound of the bails falling to the ground. For a second, he couldn't believe that it had happened to him. The missed ball, the broken wicket, the smiling faces – they happened to other people. He put the bat under his arm, and taking off his gloves began to walk back to the spectators, who applauded him as he approached. He had been in for exactly three and a half minutes.

'Bad luck, old chap,' said Stour-Benson. 'It was a dicey one.'

Yates grunted, and knelt to take off his pads.

When he stood again, he saw that Forsyth who had followed him had hit a clean four with his first drive, and that close by there was a flutter of activity which had suddenly taken precedence over the cricket. Julia Drayford, wearing a slim sheath dress, had arrived with an Afghan hound which disposed itself at her feet as if to harmonize with her afternoon elegance. Forbes, Ardrossan, Da Silva and Penderton were standing around her like squires while their wives, made uncomfortable by Mrs Drayford's easy invasion, concentrated on the cricket. Yates caught her eye for a fraction of a second; then he looked away, and stretched himself flat on the hot grass, watching the progress of insects through a jungle, hearing the summer sounds of birds and tea-conversation from the verandah by the croquet lawns, and thinking that she would demonstrate to the others her brilliance and influence and independence, and that then, she would come to him as if by accident, talking of cricket and politics and Lord knows what while her eyes groped for his beseechingly.

Behind him, the dog had begun to pant.

The sun had gone behind a wisp of cloud, and the air suddenly became cooler. The voices seemed to fall in sympathy, and the sounds from the field became precise and remote against the background of silence. Grass and acacia trees, hills of bare rock, the glistening women making huts of fronds, red earth, dust, ritual and fetich, the pure air of the deserts, the roar of water heard against the great hush of Africa. Yates recalled his journey through the continent four years ago, and he raised himself on his elbow.

The hush of Africa, the abrupt sunsets, the stillness and the stir

52

of magic within the silence. The old divinities had been overthrown and in their place M'landa with the aid of the Government and Opposition was offering a property franchise, a University at Kadowa and a Bill of Rights. It wasn't going to be as easy as Melville thought; there was bound to be trouble from the Europeans. They had no experience of being a minority protected by the law of the majority. A Bill of Rights was only of value when it had lasted so long that its performance was habit and its provisions forgotten. It would be all right in a few years. The Chiefs would die off. The whites would acquiesce.

Yates reached for his sweater which was lying on a deckchair, and pulled it over his head.

'Mr Yates,' Mrs Drayford said, coming up behind him with her dog panting at the end of the lead, 'it's not very seemly – dressing in public.'

Her voice had a faint tremor, as if she were afraid that Yates might disapprove of her approach. He rose grudgingly to his feet, and said,

'You've arrived too late. I was hitting them for six.'

'No, you weren't,' she said more boldly, so that those around could hear her. 'You hit one six, and then I started willing you to get out. It worked, didn't it?'

Yates pulled up the left sleeve of his sweater, and her gaze followed his hand over the hair of his forearm.

'Yes,' he said, 'I never thought you were on our side.'

'Oh, but I am,' she said, lowering her voice, 'I didn't want you to spend the rest of the afternoon hitting a harmless ball. I wanted you to have one lovely slog, and then I wanted you to come back to me.'

She sat on the deck-chair, and he stood next to her.

'Did you see my six?' he asked with a touch of vanity.

'Yes,' she said. 'You had your savage look. I adored it.'

Stour-Benson joined them with Lady Ardrossan and Mrs Forbes, and Yates said, as if summing up their conversation,

'And so I couldn't telephone Edward, but if he'd like to get in touch with me –'

'I think he'd love to,' said Mrs Drayford. 'He's been wanting to talk to you about Africa ever since he got back this morning. You've no idea, Gillian, how tired he gets when he flies.'

'It's the meals,' said Lady Ardrossan. 'I once flew from Beirut to London and had three dinners all in one night. They changed crews at Athens and Geneva.'

'Did you think of refusing one or two of the meals?' Yates asked.

'Certainly not,' said Lady Ardrossan. 'The Government was paying, and it would have been terribly wasteful to refuse.'

She drew her companions away with an air of offence, and left them.

It was the last over before tea, and the spectators were rising.

'I have to talk to you,' said Mrs Drayford. 'It's very important. . . . He came to see me last night.'

'Who came to see you?'

'Geoffrey Melville.'

'What happened?'

'Nothing.'

'What did he want?'

'He asked me to forget what he said at Lancaster House.'

'Did you?'

'No – he annoyed me.'

'What did he do?'

'He didn't *do* anything – he mentioned you.'

'And what did you say?'

'I told him – I told him that he was insulting.'

'And then?'

'He left.'

Yates stroked the dog's long ears, and it nestled its face against his thigh. The teams were approaching, chatting and joking, and Yates began to walk towards them. Mrs Drayford took a step behind him and said,

'Are you angry with me?'

He stopped and looked in silence at her imploring face before he said,

'I'm not sure.'

'Darling –' she began, but Yates was already surrounded by the lawyers.

'You nearly brained a High Court judge,' said one of them. 'He was resting under the beech tree.'

'It was self-defence,' said Yates.

They laughed, and moved cheerfully into the clubhouse.

5

The gorilla sat brooding, immobile, with its back against a tree. After a time, it stroked its black belly, and slowly turned its apathetic eyes towards the spectators, who were observing its monstrous size amid the litter of banana skins on the floor of the cage. Then, it looked away, frowning, as if the circle of children and their parents had deepened its melancholia.

'He looks sad, doesn't he?' said Melville, coming up behind his daughter and kissing her cheek.

'You're twenty minutes late,' she said reproachfully, 'and I've been feeling so sorry for poor old Paul. What do you think he's thinking about all the time?'

'That he'd like a stroll around the Zoo,' said Melville.

'What a wonderful-looking beast!' said Sylvia. 'It seems uncivilized to keep him behind bars.'

'On the contrary, it's highly civilized. Tame the beast!'

'He looks so dignified,' Sylvia said, 'I'd simply adore to let him out and see what happens.'

'Come on,' said Melville, taking her arm and drawing her away. 'I've got enough trouble already. Let's go and look at the panthers.'

Sylvia, nearly as tall as her father, looked happily up at him, and said,

'It's terribly exciting. I always wanted you to take me to the Zoo – and I had to wait over twenty years.'

'Are you twenty? I always forget.'

'Nearly twenty-one – and you shouldn't.'

She disengaged herself from Melville, and took his arm instead. A few passers-by threw curious glances at them, and she went on,

'I like you being anonymous. I adore it when people give you a sort of half-look, and then turn back and can't make up their minds. I suppose they can't believe that the Secretary of State for Colonial and Commonwealth Affairs would go to the Zoo with his popsie.'

'Conceit!' said Melville. 'Anyone can see you're my daughter – besides, you're not wearing stockings.'

'What does that show?'

'It shows you're my daughter. Ministers' popsies wear stockings.'

She looked down at her light-brown legs and sandalled feet, and said,

'I've got nice legs, haven't I?'

'Yes,' said Melville. 'Let's go and look at the snakes.'

'Let's not,' she answered, turning her face to the hot sun. 'I like it in the fresh air. I loathe slimy things and creepy things.'

They paused, and watched two panthers rolling over and over in their cage.

'They don't look unhappy. They're well fed,' said Melville.

'Pampered panthers from the pampas,' Sylvia replied. 'I'm talking nonsense because I'm happy.'

'Do you still like Oxford?'

'Oh, it's quite lovely. All the lilac's out,' she answered. 'I'm going to hate going down. . . . By the way, I wanted to ask you, Daddy, whether you'd mind very much if I stayed on another year and did a diploma in sociology.'

'What on earth for?' Melville asked quickly. 'Don't you think you'd better – if you want to go on – why not go to the Sorbonne for a year?'

'I don't want to do that,' she answered. 'I'd really like to have more qualifications for a job where I could do social work of some kind.'

'Where?' Melville asked.

'I think I'd like to go abroad – perhaps Africa.'

'Listen, Sylvia darling,' said Melville, taking her hand in his, 'why don't you leave Oxford – and do sociology at London? It's absurd to make plans so early. We'd like it so much if you'd spend more time at home. The last four vacations you've been away. It would be very nice if you'd use your room a bit more. It looks at me like a reproach every time I go past it.'

She turned her face to his in an unfamiliar proximity, and then she released his hand.

'I'm sorry,' she said, 'I can't really explain – I simply feel stifled at home.'

'But why, Sylvia?'

He drew her aside to avoid a children's cart pulled by a llama.

'It's not because of you –'

'Who, then? Your mother is terribly unhappy in your absence.'
'Is she?'
Sylvia asked the question in surprise.
'Of course she is,' said Melville, 'she's most anxious for you to
come home for your birthday next week – you'd do her a great –'
he was about to say 'kindness' but he corrected himself '– you'll
make her very happy if you do.'
Sylvia looked down at the dusty pathway as they walked
towards the lions, and said,
'I don't really like my birthday. I hate remembering it.'
'Oh, stuff –' said Melville. 'That's when you're my age, not
when you're twenty.'
Sylvia tied her silk scarf around her loose, fair hair, and said,
'It's not that. It reminds me – ever since I was fourteen – of
mummy giving me a birthday present – that musical box with the
three tunes – and – don't make me say it –'
'Say what, darling?'
'Well, you coming in with the telegram about the car crash and
Robert.'
'He's dead,' said Melville. 'And it's a long time ago.'
'But the musical box went tinkling away, and then you and
mummy went out of the room – you were so white – and then
her screaming – that horrible screaming – I still dream about it.'
Melville put his arms around his daughter's shoulders.
'That wasn't an ideal present for a little girl. I'm sorry. You
must forget about it.'
'Tell me, Daddy,' she said, turning to him, 'were you very
attached to your brother?'
'Yes – very. It's a long time ago. Why do you want to talk
about it on this lovely day?'
'I'm not upset – really not. You know how it is when you're a
child. There's so much that's strange and bewildering that passes
over your head.'
'What didn't you understand?'
'Well, Robert seemed to live with us as long as I can remember
– on and off at any rate. Why was that?'
'He came out of the army,' said Melville, 'and couldn't make a
go of things. So we helped him.'
'He was always gay – and very sweet to me.' She put her head
against her father's arm as he stood holding the railings outside

the lions' cage, and she repeated pensively, 'He was always very sweet to me.'

'Poor Robert!' said Melville, and thought for a moment. 'Enough of that, Sylvia. Is this what you talk about when you take your father out for a treat? What are your views on Nyasaland?'

She opened her mouth to answer, and he said, 'Don't tell me. I know them.' She kissed his cheek, and he went on, 'Seriously – how is the New Africa Group going?'

'Awfully well,' she replied. 'Not that we've been helped by that idiotic paragraph in "Behind the Talk".'

She studied his expression carefully, and said, 'You couldn't possibly have said anything as moronic as that. Could you, Daddy?'

'I could have,' said Melville. 'But I didn't.'

'Well,' she said affectionately, 'I never can tell with you. Anything for a laugh. All politicians are like that when they're showing off.'

'We won't talk about politics,' said Melville. 'Not this afternoon. I've got to be back at six o'clock. Let me enjoy you.'

'All right,' said Sylvia, her face turned to the sun with her eyes closed. 'I do love being alone with you. I always did, you know. I remember when I was very small – you took me out to lunch when I was away at school, and you towered above me . . . I was so proud of you. Miss Fountain, the science mistress, said to me, "Your father's extremely attractive," but I didn't tell you in case you got conceited.'

'Most thoughtful of you to care for my moral welfare,' said Melville. He hesitated, and Sylvia looked at him inquiringly.

'I don't like mentioning it again, Sylvia,' he said, 'but have there been any repercussions from the "Behind the Talk" paragraph – journalists telephoning you and that sort of thing?'

'Yes,' she replied. 'I had two calls.'

'What did you say?'

'I said what you told me to say if ever I'm bothered. I said "I have no comment." "No comment" sounds too American. And when they asked about you, I said, "If you're inquiring about my father, you will find him at the Colonial and Commonwealth Office."'

'That was very good,' said Melville approvingly. 'First-class. But what exactly did they want to know about you?'

Sylvia laughed.

'They wanted to know if I was going to marry Akebo.'

'I see,' said Melville. His face became sombre. 'And you said, "I have no comment."'

'Yes.'

Melville reflected, and said,

'Quite right. They've got a damned impertinence. Let's go and have tea.'

'I wish we didn't have to return so soon,' said Sylvia. 'When I think back – as long as I can remember – you were always going away somewhere, or saying good-bye when I was being packed off.'

'I'm very contrite,' said Melville. 'It's the job of being a politician. Why don't you see more of us now?'

'Now,' said Sylvia, studying the signposts that pointed to the tea-lawn. 'Now, I don't need you in the same way. Don't be offended. I no longer feel the same pang when I'm away.'

'But we'd like to see more of you – your mother as well as myself.'

'Would she?' Sylvia asked. Her tone was sceptical, and she added ruminatively, 'She was always so busy – always preoccupied with some terribly important outside work – always busy with being your wife and scattering good deeds – I used to think it was normal.'

She changed her step to fit his.

'Well, for your mother it is,' said Melville. 'I don't think you ever realized how she always – yes, always – had to plan things when you were growing up. She had to look after the house and help in the constituency, and committees –'

'I know all that,' said Sylvia. 'She was a most excellent M.P.'s wife – rushing and running from one thing to another. A peck on my forehead – an order to a maid – and then I'd arrive at school with half my things forgotten. Do you realize, Daddy – it all sounds so childish now – but I was a sort of joke at school because she never planned my clothes properly for the right term. It was all so frustrating and humiliating.'

'You mustn't misjudge her,' said Melville, 'she really loved – loves – you very much. She had such a lot to do in those days –'

Sylvia undid the bow of her headscarf, and tightened it fiercely. 'Yes,' she said, 'mother had a lot to do. She was very busy – too busy. I remember once – I came home early – oh, never mind. I'm quite sure she's a splendid woman.'

'You'd better finish your anecdote, Sylvia,' said Melville.

'It's finished,' said Sylvia.

'It's rather a lame anecdote that begins and ends "I remember once – I came home early – oh, never mind."'

'I'm sorry, Daddy,' she said, putting her arm in his again. 'I was only going to tell you some boring little story about coming home early years ago – and having had to wait for her.' Her voice trailed away.

'What a pity!' said Melville. 'I really expected something rather scabrous.'

'Oh, no,' said Sylvia, 'I never quite know what scabrous means. But you'll never hear that about her. . . . Isn't that a charming restaurant? I do like the red umbrellas.'

Melville didn't answer. The day's joy had strangely disappeared, and walking next to Sylvia towards a vacant table he felt resentful that at a time when he wished to concentrate on a political problem she had introduced a vague and personal uneasiness into his thoughts.

The policeman saluted as Melville hurried through St Stephen's Entrance.

'They've been looking for you, sir,' he said.

'Who?' Melville asked curtly.

'They rang through from the Colonial and Commonwealth Relations Office,' said the policeman, offended by Melville's unexpected irritation.

'Why did they ring you?' Melville asked.

'That's all I know, sir,' said the policeman. 'They've been looking for you all the afternoon.'

When Melville reached the Members' Lobby, one of the Government Whips who was sitting on guard at the door, reading an evening paper, stood up and said,

'Did you get a message?'

'What message?' asked Melville.

'Ormston asked me to tell you – he'd be grateful if you'd have a word with him in his room.'

Melville forced himself to smile; he liked to be on good terms with the Junior Whips.

'All right, Roger – thank you so much.'

He turned to the Parliamentary Messenger, in the tail-coat and chain of office, who was standing with a pink sheaf of telephone messages in front of him.

'All for me?' he asked.

'Yes, sir,' said the messenger. 'I believe Mr Ormston's looking for you. And Mr Waters too – he's been inquiring after you.'

'No peace,' said Melville. 'A man can't take his daughter to the Zoo nowadays without a general alarm.'

The Junior Whip composed his face sternly. He disliked this practice of fraternization with staff which the Opposition had introduced and some members of his own Party had adopted.

'The Chancellor said it was urgent,' he said primly, ignoring the messenger, and returned to his evening paper.

The messages which Melville opened were from Ormston, his Private Secretary, and Scott-Bower, the Chief Whip, asking him to get in touch with them as soon as possible, and he wondered what matters could need such pressing attention.

'Hello,' he heard a voice say, and looked up into the shining bespectacled face of a trade union Member of Parliament whose practice it was in the long summer afternoons to stop other Members on their way from the Library to the Chamber and address them with his reminiscences and analyses.

'Hello, Bill,' said Melville, and made to pass him. But Parsons, with his legs apart and one finger in his waistcoat pocket, was already barring the way. Melville paused.

'You know,' said Parsons, 'I often think that you fellows who built an Empire in a fit of absent-mindedness are going to lose it the same way.'

'How d'you make that out?' Melville asked, accommodating his own voice and manner to Parsons' crackling *bonhomie*.

'Well, look at what's happening in Africa –'

'Sorry, Bill,' said Melville, welcoming an excuse to break off the conversation, 'that's for next week.' He gave Parsons a friendly nod and strode on.

'Here – wait a minute,' said Parsons. 'It's coming up tomorrow. When I was in Washington –'

'We'll fight it out then,' said the Minister, and walked on

wondering about the arrogance of bores which makes them so fascinating to themselves.

He walked through the group of Civil Servants outside Ormston's door, and entered the Secretary's room. A girl wearing a cardigan despite the afternoon heat rose to her feet and said,

'I'll let him know at once.'

Within a few seconds, Ormston came out and said,

'Thank you so much, Geoffrey. I'm sorry to bother you.'

His manner was agreeable and unruffled, and Melville felt relief that an ill-informed anxiety which had begun to grow in him during his progress from New Palace Yard to the Chancellor's Room seemed to have no basis. Ormston took his seat and said,

'We've been trying to get you the whole afternoon. Do you think your people could arrange to be in closer touch?'

Melville frowned.

'My Departmental arrangements are perfectly adequate,' he said stiffly.

'Oh, my dear fellow!' said Ormston. 'I don't wish to interfere. It's just that – have you seen this afternoon's telegrams?'

With a sense of guilt as if he had been caught in an untruth, Melville said,

'No. I don't usually see them till the evening.'

'But a matter of urgency –'

'Naturally, I see the urgent telegrams at once.'

'Well,' said Ormston, lighting his pipe and waving the smoke away, 'let's not dwell on it now. There's been trouble at Kadowa. It's on the tape already.'

'There's always trouble at Kadowa.'

'This has been rather more serious, I'm told by Ledbury.'

Melville stood.

'Do you mean that my Permanent Secretary has been in touch with you before seeing me?'

Ormston changed the position of the glass paper-weight on the table before replying.

'I'm sorry, Geoffrey. They couldn't find you. You really should let your Department know about your movements. Never mind –' he said, as Melville began to protest. 'There's been what sounds like a ghastly mess just outside Kadowa. The Governor's car was attacked after a protest meeting of the Freedom Party. Thirty-six Africans were killed by the guard.'

Melville sat down again and looked out through the Gothic windows at the hazy blue sky now tinged towards the north with a white mist. Thirty-six Africans killed. It was a statistic. In the Minister's absence, thirty-six Africans were killed. It was a departmental entry.

'I'd better see the telegrams,' he said.

'Yes,' said Ormston. 'But there's rather more to it than that. In another riot, Lady Benning, who's been opening the Cunningham Child Welfare Centre ten miles away, was made to get out of her car – the ADC was surrounded – and they made her kiss the feet of a number of the rioters.'

'That's the usual sort of story,' said Melville. 'It's probably apocryphal.'

'Well,' said Ormston, 'we'll see. The main point is that Yates has put down a Private Notice question for tomorrow which you'll answer.'

'Of course . . . How did all this begin?'

'No one quite knows – except that you've been widely quoted – well, I don't know if quoted can be the right word – at any rate, you've been quoted as saying something about not wanting a black man in the family – and it all began with the Freedom Party organizing a protest march.'

Melville stood and said, 'It's quite outrageous, Gerald. Those damned gossip writers are murderers.'

'You can't help it,' said Ormston, shrugging his shoulders philosophically. 'All you can do tomorrow is say how sorry you are, repudiate the *obiter dictum* which they've fastened on you, and look forward to a growing association with M'landa.'

'I suppose it's all one can do,' said Melville. 'At any rate – thank you.'

'I will, of course, back you up,' said Ormston as Melville rose to go.

'I take that for granted,' said Melville.

'How did you find the P.M.?' Ormston asked as he paused with his fingers on the door handle.

'I think,' said Melville, feeling with the question that once again the balance of their relationship had been restored in his favour, 'I think – he'll be all right.'

63

'Do you really?' asked Ormston. 'It's very difficult – these long absences. We miss, I think, the prestige that accumulates around a leader.'

'It takes a long time to create prestige.'

'I doubt it,' said Ormston, and the pouches under his eyes seemed to become heavier. 'It's the job that elevates the man.'

'What would you say,' said Melville, 'if we had our Prime Minister in the Lords?'

'Never do,' said Ormston quickly. 'It would never do. Neither the Party nor the country would have it. It's difficult enough, as you ought to know, having your own Parliamentary Secretary there.'

Melville looked straight at Ormston and said,

'Luckily, we don't have to face that possibility. I think Collard's still got a long way to go. Besides, I like him.'

At the entrance to the Chamber Melville was stopped by Waters, who came hurrying up behind him with a red-tabbed message from the Colonial and Commonwealth Office. He opened it rapidly and read,

'M'landa has repudiated the London Agreement in view of this afternoon's events. May I see you at once? Arthur Ledbury.'

'I'm going to the office,' said Melville. 'Will you tell my wife I won't dine at home tonight?'

He walked in silence with Waters across Whitehall through the columns of men and women released from their work who in queues and motor-cars and on foot were hurrying towards another room in their lives. Despite the presence of his secretary, he had a sense of being alone, and, like an explorer, of entering a jungle inhabited by invisible mysteries and dangers from which he couldn't turn back. A newspaper placard had the title, '36 Africans slain. Governor's wife assaulted.'

'Extraordinary how soon they get it. They treat it like a cricket score,' Melville said.

He bought a final edition of the paper which showed a radioed photograph of Lady Benning on her knees apparently embracing the naked foot of an African in the middle of a jeering crowd.

'That means more trouble,' said Waters.

Melville said nothing.

He left Ledbury and his staff at half past nine to telephone Elizabeth.

The maid answered and said, 'Madam has gone out to dinner.'

'Tell her . . .' said Melville. 'Oh, never mind. What time did she say she'd be back?'

'She never says.'

Melville put the telephone down and returned thoughtfully to the discussion on whether the killings should be described in the Parliamentary reply as 'tragic' or 'unfortunate' events.

6

As the laughter drowned Granger's voice, the Speaker rose to his feet till his head seemed nearly to touch the green canopy and said, first in a throwaway voice and then, like a headmaster, 'Order! Order!' and the instruction, echoed from both sides of the House, gradually stilled the uproar.

'Caponized chickens . . .' Granger began again in the brief silence that followed, but the words were extinguished by cries of 'Question!' and 'Reading!'

Squaring his shoulders and putting his notes behind his back, Granger, well known for the power of his voice – he had been a sergeant-major in the Regular Army before becoming a gentleman farmer – shouted,

'Is the Minister aware of the alarming biological effects on the population produced by the artificial caponization of chickens?'

The Minister of Health, Miss Mabel Walpole, put her hands on the Despatch Box, and looked over her shoulders at Granger's indignant expression.

'There is no evidence,' she answered, 'to justify my Hon. and gallant Friend's anxiety. At any rate, *he* doesn't seem to have any immediate cause for alarm.'

She gave a quick smile to Yates sitting opposite her and, clutching her papers, sat down, gratified by the renewed burst of laughter. She was often quoted in 'Sayings of the Week' by the Sunday newspapers, and felt that she had sustained her reputation for retort.

'But, Mr Speaker . . .' said Granger, rising again.

'Mr Granger!' said the Speaker faintly, as if already exhausted by the questioner's persistence.

'Is it not the case,' Granger went on, 'that in certain areas of Scotland, there has been a distinct falling off of the birth-rate *pari passu*' – it was his standby tag – 'with the development of caponization?'

Miss Walpole rose again and said,

'That is a different question, of which I'd like notice. But if my Hon. Friend would like to see me in my room later on, I'll endeavour to give him every satisfaction.'

There was a moment of silence, and then a rumble of 'Hear! Hears!' and guffaws that ran along the benches. 'Every satisfaction.' 'She'll give him every satisfaction.' Members liked the phrase and repeated it, and the cheers rose loudly as Miss Walpole, half-pretending that she had intended its ambiguity, subsided in the crush of the Ministerial Front Bench.

'We must get on,' said the Speaker. 'Question Number 38 – Mr Porson.'

'No. 38,' said Porson, rising, and the Parliamentary Secretary to the Minister of Health climbed over the outstretched legs to make his way to the Despatch Box. The questioner asked whether the Minister would invite the Prime Minister to set up a Royal Commission to inquire into the pharmaceutical industry.

'No, sir!' the Parliamentary Secretary said firmly.

Yates, slumped on the green leather bench, studied the Government Front Bench from between his feet which he had stretched on the Table. Then he said to Basil Jones, the Opposition Chief Whip, 'They look just like the cast of a Restoration Comedy. Moody – a misanthrope . . .'

'Starkie – an exhibitionist.'

'That's very good,' Yates murmured.

'Loveitt – a man of strange habits.'

'Twist – an attorney.'

'Miss Goodbody –'

'Yes,' said Yates. 'The possibilities are enormous.'

He looked at the crowded benches opposite which were falling into an afternoon gloom as the electric blinds slowly rose above the clerestory windows. In the Press Gallery, the journalists had begun to crowd forward in expectation of the statement on Africa which had been forecast earlier in the day, and the Ambassadors' Gallery above the clock facing the Speaker was already full with the familiar faces of important occasions – Von Henel, Alexandrov, Marecchi and Gillet – Yates' eyes travelled like the lens of a film camera over the scene, past the occasional light suits that varied the traditionally dark clothes of the Government supporters to the Gallery where Mrs Speaker sat in her customary place wearing a brilliant red hat. There was a blur of flowery dresses. And then, the pale yellow hair. The pale yellow hair. Yates was pleased. His eyes rested deliberately on a neighbouring figure and returned to greet in a second of time the eyes of Mrs Drayford.

'Mr Yates,' said the Speaker. 'Private Notice Question.'

The mutter of conversation died away, and Members leaned forward in curiosity and expectation.

'I wish to ask the Secretary of State for Colonial and Commonwealth Affairs a question of which I've given him private notice – to ask whether he has any statement to make on the situation in Kadowa.' Yates asked the question and then resumed his place, holding the copy of the Minister's statement which had already been issued to him.

Melville read his reply in a rapid, authoritative voice. He described the events, deplored the loss of life, expressed sympathy with the relatives and dependents of the British troops involved as well as with the Africans, and ended with the assurance that the Government were gravely exercised by the riots, and were watching the situation closely. When he sat down, there was a sympathetic murmur from the benches behind him.

Yates heaved himself from the relaxed posture in which he had listened to the Minister, and with one elbow on the Despatch Box, slightly inclined towards the Treasury bench, said,

'We are obliged to the Right Hon. Gentleman and will watch with interest – and some anxiety – the developing situation.'

Melville gave him a faint bow of acknowledgement, the nod of a rich patron to a client. He felt relieved that the question had been asked and answered, that yesterday's fears were dissolved and that Members, no longer interested, were beginning to leave the Chamber.

As Yates fumbled behind him for his place between the Chief

Whip and the Leader of the Opposition, he seemed to have an afterthought, and turning his heavy body towards Melville again, he added, folding his arms over the Despatch Box,

'But there is one small matter which ought to be cleared up . . . It has been stated by Mr M'landa that a somewhat indelicate observation by the Minister' – the Government back-benchers groaned and Yates raised his voice – 'a somewhat – if I may use the term – racialist observation was a precipitating cause of the outbreak. Would the Right Hon. Gentleman confirm that the remarks attributed to him have no substance?'

Melville raised his legs to the Table, and crossed his ankles. Immediately, there was an angry clamour of 'Answer!' 'Answer!' from the Opposition back-benchers. Melville looked up at the roof, his features set, and Yates rose again.

'Perhaps,' he said, 'the Right Hon. Gentleman would like me to put it differently.' The uproar behind him subsided and he went on. 'Is he aware that his offensive reference to Africans at the conclusion of a dinner given by Her Majesty's Government in honour of an especially distinguished African resulted in an outbreak of violence at Kadowa for which the Right Hon. Gentleman must accept personal responsibility?'

Melville uncoiled his legs, and paused at the Despatch Box. Yates, he noticed, had a half-smile on his face like a schoolboy bully provoking his victim. He knew the formula for dealing with Yates – a swift, contemptuous answer that flushed a hidden guilt.

'The Gentleman,' he said, 'has been listening to the grubbier rumours of Fleet Street. The one which he has reported to the House has no basis in fact.'

Amid the cheers that followed, half a dozen back-benchers rose to ask supplementary questions.

'Mr Barry,' said the Speaker, and a Government supporter, well known for his docile endorsement of Ministerial statements, said,

'Is the Minister aware that his handling of the Constitutional Conference has won the admiration of both Africans and Britons?'

Melville bowed and gave him a grateful half-smile which he at once regretted, since it was like a compact with a sycophant. He stiffened his features as Parsons, standing with his feet apart and playing with the watch-chain medallion which he had been given for long and meritorious service to his trade union, rose from the Opposition benches below the gangway.

'But, Mr Speaker, sir,' he demanded in his ponderous button-holing voice, 'is it not in fact the case that the Right Hon. Gentleman did state at Lancaster House that while he was ready to accept the African as his brother, he didn't want him as his –'

'– mother-in-law!' a Government Member called out, an interruption followed by a din of laughter in which even the Clerks at the Table joined. The public in the galleries, the Members standing at the Bar, the attendants, the American and French Ambassadors, Lord Gradwell bending over the Peers' Gallery and the Speaker himself were all swept by the breeze of gaiety which the anonymous shout had blown into the argument. Melville smiled. The whole thing was too absurd for words. But all the same, thank God for Parsons! You could trust him to turn melodrama into farce.

'I think we'd better get on,' said the Speaker, looking at the clock which now stood at ten to four.

'On a point of order, sir,' said Yates, rising. 'The Minister, abdicating somewhat from his usual courtesy, has refused to answer a question to which we really do want a reply.'

'He's answered already,' a voice called out.

'Indeed not,' said Yates. 'He obliges me to put into words a question I would have preferred him to deny unasked. Would he tell the House whether or no he said at Lancaster House "I want the African to be my brother" – and then added in an audible aside- "but not my brother-in-law"? I put that question to him. Will he answer it?'

Melville hesitated, but before the cries of 'Answer!' became too insistent he replied,

'It is not my practice to deny imputations made by Hon. Gentlemen opposite. They would keep me far too busy. . . . In this case, however, since the Right Hon. Gentleman himself has assumed – with some enthusiasm, I observe – the role of a scavenger of rumours, I think it not unfitting to tell him that, even in that humble role, he has met with no success. My reply to his question is – "No, sir."'

A number of Members rose on both sides of the House as the Government back-benchers roared their cheers in the face of the silent Opposition. But the Speaker got to his feet quickly and announced, 'The Clerk will now proceed to read the Orders of the Day.' The episode was over. Hands in pockets, Sir John

Overbank, a Member who had obtained a baronetcy for twenty-five years of loyal and pertinacious silence, whispered to Edgar Haslett, the 'Baby of the House', as they passed the Speaker's Chair in the general movement of Members from the Chamber,

'You will notice in time' – and Haslett's ears went red as the older man gave him his confidences – 'that you can sing "The Clerk will now proceed to read the Orders of the Day" to the tune of John Brown's Body.'

'That,' said Haslett, frowning, 'is very interesting.'

On his way to his room, Yates detached himself from the small court which had formed around him – his P.P.S., the Party's Press Liaison Officer, two secretaries and three Members, and turned in the direction of the Tea-Room. When he had first come into the House, the Right Hon. Paul Homerton, an elderly Etonian who had been in a pre-war Cabinet, rumbled in his ear, 'Never forget the Tea-Room! If you look after the Tea-Room, the Tea-Room will look after you.' At the time, he hadn't realized that the House was divided into sodalities of the more prosperous Members who used the Smoking-Room and the more modest who used the Tea-Room. In the long afternoons when the debate in the Chamber went stale, the arguments in the Tea-Room, usually led by trade union M.P.s, were always lively. Often the most articulate were those who in the House itself were silent. As Parsons said, 'They didn't leave their unions like sages just to make fools of themselves in the Chamber.' The Tea-Room was also a passageway, heavy with the smell of 'bangers' and toast, between the exit from the Division Lobby to the Smoking-Room, where transients could glance at the headlines of the newspapers which strewed the armchairs and tables. In the course of six Parliaments, Yates had learnt that many a political reputation which had begun well in the Minister's corridor had ended badly by the time it passed the scrutiny of the recumbent Tea-Room observers. 'Cultivate the trade unionists,' old Homerton had advised, and Yates had diligently distributed his benevolence in these regular promenades through the Tea-Room. The rise of his vote in the elections to the Parliamentary Committee from twenty-seven to a hundred and twelve in four years, after which he had come top of the poll, could be attributed, he often felt, to his

70

martyrdom to tea and the easy way with which he who had always been called Alfred because of a remote collateral link with Tennyson (his other names were Hallam Godwin, nor had any of them ever been shortened by family or nannies) was now generally greeted in the Party as Alf.

His progress down the long aisle between the tables was a cheerful one. A wave and the name of the liegeman was his usual salute. 'Bill!' 'Walter!' 'Tom!' Sometimes he varied it with 'All well?' or 'Very fine speech the other day' or a friendly pat on the arm. That was when he forgot the name. On this day, he saw, sitting alone near the piled trays of the cafeteria, Owen Armstrong, who ten months earlier had won a by-election for the Party with the slogan, 'The man from the mines will speak for the miners!'

'Well, Owen,' he said, pausing, 'how d'you like it here?'

'I don't,' said Armstrong calmly.

'Why not?' said Yates, sitting at the table.

Armstrong smiled to himself, and put his hand to the scar on his forehead.

'It's like this, boy,' he said. 'I miss Cwmbrau – see?'

'You'll get used to it,' said Yates. 'There's nothing so bad that you can't get used to it.'

'It's not bad, Alf,' said Armstrong in his quiet voice. 'It's just not real.'

Yates glanced from Armstrong to the queue of Members at the cafeteria and said, raising his voice above the conversation, 'They look real all right.'

'Yes,' said Armstrong, 'but are they? Do you trust anyone here, boy?'

Yates laughed and said, 'Trust might be going a bit far.'

'Well, watch yourself,' said Armstrong, and he returned to his paper.

Later, meeting Jones, the Opposition Chief Whip, in the Members' Lobby, Yates said, 'Tell me, Chief, have you ever spoken to Armstrong – Owen Armstrong?'

'Yes,' said the Chief Whip. 'He came to see me the other day. He said everyone in the House seemed unreal, and he doesn't like it. It wasn't like the pit.'

'He's quite right, of course,' said Yates.

71

It was a long time since he himself had been down a coal mine. To be exact, not for fourteen years, when he had been Parliamentary Secretary to the Minister of Fuel and Power in Madingley's short-lived Government. There had been a national drive for more coal, and various junior Ministers had visited the coalfields in a campaign of exhortation. When he had arrived at the Northumberland pit, the manager had dressed him in pit overalls and a miner's helmet and given him a stick, and the party went down the shaft into a broad, dimly-lit gallery, silent except for the sudden clanking of trucks, a shout of warning or a mutter from the blackness beyond the rays of the helmet-lights. They had trudged through the thick coal dust, steadily reducing their height beneath the timbering till Yates felt his thighs aching with the strain.

'You'll have to bend a bit, sir,' said the manager. 'The face is only two foot six where we're going.'

Near the coal-face, they had to crawl on their hands and knees. At first Yates could see no one. Then he glimpsed three men stripped to the waist, with sweat making a pattern of lace over their begrimed bodies, their eyes white circles in the penumbra of the lights.

'This is Mr Yates,' said the manager. 'Ministry of Fuel and Power.'

'Aa – ah!' said the men together. They shook hands.

'Everything all right?' asked Yates.

The men were silent till one of them said, 'Aa – ah!'

Yates felt his own clothes soaked with sweat beneath his overalls, and he decided that he'd had enough of the pit. At that moment there was a tearing, creaking sound, and instinctively Yates put his hands over his head. The miners laughed.

'It's the timber,' said the manager. 'They say it's the pit talking.'

'Talks too bloody much,' said one of the miners.

'Where are we now?' Yates had asked.

'A mile and a half under the sea,' said the manager.

'Well – we're all very grateful to you,' said Yates, turning on his knees to go.

'We thought you'd come to give us a hand,' said the oldest miner of the three, a man of over sixty. His voice was unsmiling, but his manner was good-natured.

'I need a hand myself,' said Yates, and they all laughed and

72

helped him to scramble over the conveyor belt which was being repaired.

When he breathed again in the open air at the pit-head, he had made a short speech to a group of journalists and assembled officials which began, 'We who are winning the coal for the nation . . .'

If every politician remembered the speeches he was ashamed of, Yates thought, the House would have nothing but penitents.

'No,' he repeated to the Chief Whip, 'it's not like the pit.'

'Any chance of a "pair" Thursday?' Yates heard a voice behind him say. 'I've got a dinner party.'

'Let me look at my book,' another Member said. 'Yes – fine. I'm going to the *première* of "The Logician".'

The Members made their arrangements to be absent like lovers making agreements to meet. A P.P.S. approached a third Member, and began with a coy smile, 'My Minister would like a "pair" . . .'

'I'm done already,' McAlpine answered sourly. The P.P.S.'s smile was turned off as if by a time switch.

'No,' said Yates again, 'it's not like the pit. I sometimes think it's Gehenna itself. I'm going out.'

'Don't forget, Alf,' said the Chief Whip. 'You're on the Bench at 8.30.'

The summer rain had stopped, and the Millbank pavements steamed with the heat of the sun on the evaporating puddles. A procession flowed alongside the river – typists in print dresses leaving their offices and tourists dawdling down the Embankment and lingering by the parapets as if they were backwaters of the main stream. Yates joined it happily. After the mausoleum lights of the Chamber, he was glad to be in the open air with the white façades of ferro-concrete across the river, turning the cobalt of the sky by contrast into a Prussian blue. The sun dazzled his eyes as he strode, and when he looked at the coal barges, they were black silhouettes against the white water. He felt released and fit, and he wanted everyone to feel free. Britons – Africans – Russians – Chinese. Everyone. He felt sorry for anyone who didn't feel as fit and free as he did at that moment. He felt sorry for people shut in offices. Sorry for coal-miners. Sorry for bus drivers. Sorry for the eight Riflemen who'd been killed; for their mothers; for the thirty-three – or was it six? – Africans whose photographs in death, looking like bundles of rags with sleeping feet, had been published in the afternoon papers.

Melville's dismissive manner had exasperated him. They'd never learn. It was *hubris*. And, as always happened, it would end badly. Melville had made the jibe and that was that. He had to take responsibility if his words led to violence, and Yates hadn't hesitated to discuss them with Henry Lovell of 'Behind the Talk'. Lovell was the natural recipient of every calculated indiscretion. He was accurate. And since his business depended on never betraying a confidence, he never betrayed a confidence. He wore a permanent half-smile as if to say, 'Don't hit me. I'm wearing my glasses.' His trade-name was Scanner. 'Any background?' he had asked Yates after the Lancaster House Conference. Yates had told him Mrs Drayford's anecdote.

Yates shrugged his shoulders as he walked. Why not? Melville had asked for it. From the pavements he looked up the long flight of stairs leading to the pillars of the Tate Gallery, and the pale hair was already there. Yellow hair against grey stone. He made a gesture with his hand and she rose from her seat and walked through the swing doors. In an old habit which had grown on him in the last few years, he glanced quickly round to see if any of his colleagues or familiar journalists were in sight. Then, he hurried up the stairs, pausing only long enough at the top to take breath before following Mrs Drayford to the far room where she sat on the leather bench in front of 'The Parting of Hero and Leander.'

They sat silently for a few minutes looking at the fervent yellows and reds of the vast picture. An elderly custodian who had seen them many times together before approached, circled the bench and then returned without speaking to his own chair at the entrance.

'One of these days,' said Yates, 'Turner is going to become popular. And then where will we be?'

'We'll be in the Gainsborough Room,' she answered. 'In any case, there's no law against politicians looking at pictures.'

'Too many coincidences –'

'It's unimportant,' said Mrs Drayford. They rose and walked slowly past the pictures with Mrs Drayford touching his elbow.

'I thought it went very well this afternoon. But he was very offensive to you.'

Yates stiffened; he felt that his own doubts about his part at question time were being confirmed.

'But you slapped him down beautifully,' she went on.

'You really thought so?' Yates asked, his brow wrinkling.

'Of course,' she said in her emphatic voice. 'You made him look oafish. He didn't like it a bit.'

They paused near a picture by Stubbs, and Yates moved his hand along her forearm to the crook near the elbow.

'I like that very much,' said Mrs Drayford.

'I like it very much too,' said Yates.

'Why can't we go to bed?' said Mrs Drayford.

'Here?' Yates asked.

'Yes,' said Mrs Drayford. 'Here – but we're being followed by that old *voyeur* . . . Seriously, darling –'

'It's impossible,' said Yates hurriedly. 'Elsa's in London . . .'

'Elsa!' said Mrs Drayford in disgust.

They had returned to the Turner Room and were standing again in front of 'Hero and Leander'.

'You fuss too much,' said Mrs Drayford. 'Just look at Leander about to swim the Hellespont. I don't think you'd cross Parliament Square for me – not if it rained.'

'There was a time, Julia, when I would have walked across Parliament Square in my bare feet for you.'

'And now?'

'It's too late,' he answered. 'Five years too late.'

'You were afraid,' said Mrs Drayford. Yates shrugged his shoulders. They were about to start, he thought, an old, unrewarding recrimination, and he tried to distract her.

'Are you going to the McCartneys' tomorrow?'

'You were afraid,' Mrs Drayford persisted. 'We should have –'

'Not now, Julia,' said Yates uneasily. 'I don't want to go through all that again.'

'But that's what you always say,' Mrs Drayford went on, her voice rising. 'Why won't you face things as they are? How do you expect me to go on like this – all these furtive meetings – like schoolboys and schoolgirls –'

Yates stood up.

'I'm not going to talk about that now – not here.'

'Well, where then? You used to manage to find time –'

She was looking up at him and her eyes had become red with tears.

'We will,' said Yates appeasingly, and thought of how it had been six years before, when they had first met and, for a year after they became lovers, had seen each other almost every day except for what they called the 'high days of family and the holy days of politics' and how he had longed to give up his seat and return to the University; but he was constantly being elected to something or other and the children were growing up and the habits of marriage made for inertia. The sharp joy became duller. And Julia stayed with Drayford because he was comfortable for her and she had no wish to be the backroom mistress of an ex-politician. Yet, there had been a time five years before in Scotland, waking in the silence of an autumn night and seeing the hills through the violet window, when they had loved each other with a poignant intensity, and had vowed never to leave each other. But that was in another country.

'We will,' said Yates, stroking her hair, and thinking, all that was dead and why go on pretending.

'When?' she asked.

And Yates said, 'Do you know an M.P. called Armstrong?'

'No,' Mrs Drayford said sulkily. 'Should I know him?'

'He's an interesting man,' said Yates. 'A miner – he told me he wants to go back to the pit.'

'It's probably all he's fit for,' said Mrs Drayford.

'That's not a bad thing to be,' said Yates, withdrawing his arm from hers. 'I've often wished myself that I had the guts to give up politics.'

'You will never give up politics,' said Mrs Drayford. 'You like power. I've often noticed – you don't like or dislike people according to whether they're good or bad. You like them if they're powerful – whether they're Tories or Socialists or Trade Unionists or Flat-Earthers.'

She paused, drew her head away like a long-sighted person making a critical examination, and said,

'That's why you'll never be Prime Minister – not even if you win the next nine Elections in a row. You're always looking for someone to be No. 2 to.'

'Go on, Julia,' said Yates. 'I love it when you're being specially unpleasant.'

'How tall are you – six foot one?'

'Six foot and half an inch.'

'And all those shoulders,' she said, thoughtfully, and prodded his arm. 'I suppose you were a great rugger hero at school.'

'No,' said Yates, flexing his muscles and imprisoning her hand between the bicep and forearm. 'I boxed.'

'Iron glove and velvet fist,' said Julia. 'I don't know what I saw in you. Liking, I suppose, is a habit.'

'Why do I like you, Julia?'

'You like me – liked me at any rate – for just that reason. Because we were as we were, and because Edward's wealthy – owns a television network – entertains the Cabinet – you felt flattered by your connexions.'

Yates flushed, and said, 'Rubbish! I liked you – because I liked walking upstairs behind you at the Hallidays.'

They passed through the swing doors and stood at the top of the steps, looking down at the Thames glittering in the sunlight. Yates drew her to the balustrade, where they watched the coming and going of the visitors to the Gallery.

'Darling,' she said.

'Yes?'

'You know that what I told you about Melville is the absolute truth?'

'Why do you say that?'

'Because every woman who lies to one man about another must seem a potential liar to the one she lies about.'

'Of course.'

'I've never lied to you.'

'You will when it's necessary.'

'I never will.'

A wave of affection, an old longing, moved into Yates' mind. 'Would you like to have a drink at Marjorie Galt's?'

Yates hesitated. 'I ought to get back, you know.'

'A quick one,' she said, and he could see the tip of her tongue between her lips.

'Marjorie's such a bore,' Yates said.

'But she won't be there,' Mrs Drayford went on. 'She's in Italy. She gave me her key and asked me to look in occasionally –'

'Hello, Mr Yates,' said a brisk voice. Yates looked up and nodded to Philip Anderson, a political correspondent.

'Christ!' he said under his breath. 'The Town Crier.'

'Oh, Philip,' Mrs Drayford called out. 'Do come here a moment.'

Anderson, his intelligent face wary, approached the plinth near which Mrs Drayford and Yates were waiting.

'We were talking about you at lunch,' she said.

'Really?' said Anderson, surprised.

'Yes,' said Mrs Drayford. 'My husband was saying – and Mr Yates agreed – that you were so good on "Press Call" at the beginning of the year – you ought to do it more often.'

'Well,' said Anderson, 'if only they'd ask me –' and he explained that Gayforth, the producer, had his own coterie of interviewers to which he personally would never belong because of his professional integrity.

'But that's just it,' said Mrs Drayford. 'It's what we all admire. Where are we now? July. Yes – July. Will you come and lunch with us after the Recess? Don't say "No".'

'I'd be delighted,' said Anderson eagerly.

'Well, propose yourself,' said Mrs Drayford, saying goodbye to him. 'Propose yourself.'

'After the Recess,' said Yates ruminatively, when Anderson had gone. 'That'll be October!'

'Yes,' said Mrs Drayford. 'There's nothing like a lively sense of future favours to keep journalists and politicians happy. I've been thinking, you know, about corruption. Take Anderson – there isn't enough money in the whole world to make him write a line or a word that he didn't believe. And yet, the prospect of a television appearance – an invitation –'

'You underrate us all,' said Yates. 'You have to fix prices on everybody. But you and your friends suddenly find that there are some people who don't fit – who can't be bought – so you thrash around for some price-tag to fit the ones you can't buy with money or snobbery.'

'Money,' said Julia, 'is only the most obviously corrupting element in our lives just as language is the most obvious means of communication. But there are other ways of communicating and other ways of bribing. Don't be so hypocritical, sweetie. You know it all – patronage, hospitality, publicity, decorations, titles –

heavens, there's no end to it. Some men get sent to gaol for taking five pounds to show favour. And others travel like princes as the guests of foreign governments who hope to win their favours. I really think there are as many abuses in public life today as there were in the eighteenth century.'

'What are you going to do about it?' Yates asked ironically.

'I've acquiesced,' said Mrs Drayford, 'long ago.'

'Well, what's your price, Julia?' Yates continued in the same tone.

'A kind word from you, my darling – and if that doesn't come off –'

'What then?'

She reflected, and said,

'I have a thought or two. What about that drink?'

'Yes,' said Yates, making a decision. He didn't have to be on the Bench till 8.30. 'You take your car, and I'll go by taxi – it's No. 28, isn't it?'

'Tell him to gee-up,' said Mrs Drayford.

Yates ran down the steps to the taxi on the rank, and lay back in it with a sense of triumph. 'Well, propose yourself.' He liked that very much. 'Propose yourself.' He laughed to himself. 'We were just talking about you.' After the Recess. Next winter. In the after-life. And she had proposed herself to him.

But as the taxi turned into the Square, he wondered whether he really wanted to be there at all.

7

Because of the demonstration, Melville and his wife had been obliged to drive three times around Covent Garden before turning in to the Floral Street entrance. Here, their car had become wedged in a mass of shouting men and women who had begun to rock it with their pressure. Someone threw a firework, and within seconds a kicking youth was being held down by two policemen while a woman who had come to his help was dragged away on the wet pavement. Her skirt had ridden up exposing her thigh and torn stocking, and her plastic handbag, with a few pennies, a two-shilling piece and a looking-glass falling out of it, lay abandoned on the pavement.

'It's horrible,' said Elizabeth. 'I hate seeing policemen without their helmets. It makes them look so ordinary.' And Melville replied sharply, 'Well, don't look.'

In the roadway, among the torn home-made posters, was one which said, 'Thirty-six Murders – How Many More?'

And another, simply, 'Melville – Murderer.'

'Who on earth are they?' Elizabeth asked. 'They're absolutely terrifying.'

'They're the Campaign for a Free Africa – the Yates fellow-travellers,' said Melville contemptuously as the car with its escort of police nudged slowly forward towards the striped canopy. 'Just hold my arm and smile.'

'I'll hold your arm all right,' said Elizabeth. Behind the double row of police who were keeping the crowd back, she could see that the demonstrators had hoisted new banners.

As soon as Melville put his foot on the carpet and gave his hand to his wife, the shouts rose into a furious tri-syllabic chant.

'Mur – de – rer! Mur – de – rer!'

Melville smiled to the photographers, and turned and waved to the crowd which instantly swayed forward, breaking through the cordon. One demonstrator lunged at Melville with a pole. A sergeant grappled with him, and Melville with his arm around Elizabeth advanced a few paces. A bearded student raised a stick at Melville.

'No,' Elizabeth exclaimed, putting up her arm.

For a few seconds, there was a mêlée in which they were surrounded by the panting, struggling police and the white-faced, angry demonstrators, and then they were in the foyer with the doors being locked behind them.

All around stood the earlier arrivals at the Gala, the women slightly subdued by the peacock air of the men in white ties and decorations, yet excited by the clamour outside.

'I must comb my hair,' said Elizabeth, rummaging in her handbag.

'Not here,' said Melville, turning to smile to Lord Gradwell who had limped up to him.

'They didn't get you?' Gradwell asked in his hoarse voice.

'Not yet,' said Melville.

'What a show to put on for the Italian Prime Minister! No good
– that fellow Yates,' said Gradwell. 'We'll have to deal with him.'
Melville didn't answer.

'Well, my boy, *we're* starting a campaign in your favour,' said
Gradwell, and limped away to his secretary, who was standing
sulkily apart, scowling at her protector with an adolescent
violence.

'I hope not,' said Melville to Elizabeth as they moved with the
drift of the audience towards the Grand Staircase. 'The Gradwell
Press is the womb of lost causes.'

At the first interval Melville's secretary, Waters, arrived with a
message from Ormston inviting him and Elizabeth to join the
party in the private room next to the Crush Bar where Carpino,
the Italian Prime Minister, was receiving a number of official
presentations.

'Oh, no,' said Elizabeth, 'you know I don't speak Italian. You
go, Geoffrey, and greet him and then come out and meet us here.
It's so much more fun.'

She turned to Broome, who said, 'I must say that I prefer the
intervals to the performances.'

'You're the sort of man,' said Elizabeth, 'who prefers TV
commercials to the programmes.'

'Yes, I am,' said Broome, his bucolic face glowing with the heat
in the box. The doors opened, and they moved like a platoon into
the bar where already groups of men and women were posting
themselves in alcoves and doorways, by the staircase and in the
full light of the chandeliers.

Waters, smiling amiably, made a path for the Minister through
the centre of the foyer. Melville, following, felt at ease. The
turning heads, the women who looked at him shyly and curiously
as he passed, the deference of the men, the compound of human
warmth, faint decay of flowers and enveloping scent, were familiar
and agreeable to him. It was far from the accusing gargoyles of
the early afternoon, the violent faces of the demonstrators – far
from Africa and its problems. He noticed the Ghanaian Ambassador approaching, and he made up his mind to greet him with a
special courtesy. But he turned away, leaving Melville to wonder
whether his aversion was accidental or deliberate.

'Dreadful the way that woman Louise Manley hectored you
today!' said Drayford, stopping Melville at the door. 'I could see

from my eyrie that she wasn't going to let you off without a lecture.'

A knot of listeners quickly gathered around, and Melville, wondering vaguely where Drayford had acquired his double row of decorations, said,

'Louise would consider the day wasted if she didn't give us at least one dressing-down.'

'The way she queens it is really insufferable. They're a flabby lot – our Opposition.'

'"In the country of eunuchs, the virago is queen,"' said Melville. The listeners tittered. 'I remember her as a pretty young woman – fifteen years ago. She's hardened, you know – between the hammer of Yates and the anvil of Newman.'

'Yes,' said Drayford, cocking his ear at the old gossip. 'She's been around a bit . . .' He lowered his voice. 'Any news from Kadowa?'

'Nothing,' said Melville morosely.

'I see you've put Ndala inside.'

'It was automatic. He's the secretary.'

Drayford's pleasant face became dispirited.

'He was very hospitable when I was out there. I gave him a drink at the Settlers' only last Friday.'

'Let's talk about it some other time,' said Melville. 'Carpino wants to talk to me. How's Julia?'

'A bit low,' said Drayford. 'I don't think politics really agree with her. Takes me away a lot.'

'It's a problem,' said Melville gravely. 'Politics makes a hard mistress.'

He moved with Waters to the reception-room where the Italian Prime Minister, attended by several members of the British Government, was holding an audience. A secretary from the Italian Embassy whispered a biography of each guest in his ear, and Carpino, his dark eyes darting over the shoulders bowing in front of him, was muttering his congratulations on books he hadn't read, performances he hadn't seen and achievements he didn't grasp.

To Melville, who spoke to him in Italian, he was more explicit. 'You have some troubles tonight,' he said. 'The glory of Italy is to have lost her empire.'

'We, too,' said Melville, 'have lost our empire – and gained a

82

Commonwealth.' Then, feeling pompous, he added, 'It's much more trouble.'

Carpino waved his hands.

'No,' he said. 'That is only politeness, Melville. You did us a favour when you relieved us of our Empire. Empires are to nations what megalomania is to individuals: a perversion, a psychosis.'

'I've yet to meet an individual who wouldn't fight hard to keep his perversion,' said Ormston who was standing nearby.

'For us,' said Carpino sadly in English, 'these questions are now academic. Our obsession is simply to survive. We are for the comfortable life.'

He drew Melville towards the door, and said,

'How do you see the outcome of all these affairs?'

'Africa?' Melville asked.

'Yes.'

'I think,' said Melville, 'that we're still trapped in a nineteenth-century myth. We once believed that Empires – imperialism – could last for ever. And now we see that they can't. But we've accepted the other myth –'

'The myth that imperial nations can survive without empires?'

'Oh, no – I believe that is the only way to survive. No, I'm thinking of the myth – it's a liberal-Marxist myth – that the nation-state is a progressive development in the second half of the twentieth century. Consider the paradox. We suffered for the first fifty years from the disease of European Balkanism. And now, we're deliberately cultivating the African Balkans.'

'But they want it, Minister,' said Carpino, smoothing his brushed-back hair. 'They want it – their little armies, their little customs posts, their little postage stamps. They want to say, "Good-bye, Belgians! Good-bye, Italians! Good-bye, Englishmen! We've grown up too!"'

'It's our fault,' said Melville. 'Africa's woken up into the nineteenth century. But we're living in the twentieth century when everyone depends on everyone else – when you can't fly in a jet without the equipment to receive you at the other end – telephones, water, atomic energy – the world has become too small. There aren't any viable States any more – only viable continents.'

'But they want it, Melville,' Carpino said sadly. 'We taught them. Their political leaders want power. They want to bully the tribesmen – perhaps have colonies, like everyone else. They first taught us the slave trade. We taught them colonialism.'

'Perhaps,' said Melville, 'now that we're discovering the merits of federation –'

'Perhaps,' said Carpino, 'perhaps they'll learn quickly and teach us . . . Ah, Mrs Ormston, how beautiful the line of your dress is! I had hoped to tell it to you the whole evening.'

Mrs Ormston, who had joined them, smiled appreciatively, and said,

'I bought it at Marello's *boutique* in Rome last year. I think you're advertising, Prime Minister.'

'I could have mistaken you for your daughter,' Carpino went on.

'I have no daughter,' Mrs Ormston said, her face clouding. 'Come, you mustn't let Mr Melville absorb you with African affairs. You'll adore the next ballet – do you know *Les Patineurs?*'

As they moved away, Melville wondered why it was mandatory to provide galas of ballet and opera for visiting Prime Ministers. Perhaps they hated music. Perhaps they'd rather go to a strip-tease show. He gave the Italian Prime Minister a second glance, and decided that it might well be so.

The ballerina, encircled by an ice-blue light, traversed the stage in a glissade, and disappeared into the wings. Immediately, the whole *corps de ballet* repeated the movement, the violins of the orchestra feathering their way in rhythm. With her chin propped on her left hand, Elizabeth, sitting between her husband and Broome, looked on with an air of ecstatic concentration. Broome had his usual relaxed, half-amused expression. Beyond the pillar in the Royal Box, the Italian Prime Minister was sitting next to Ormston, his two hands resting on the red plush, his eyeglasses reflecting the carnival streamers which had begun to fall from behind the proscenium on to the dancers. Ormston looked satisfied.

Melville took out his watch, and looked surreptitiously at the time. He was tired, and wished the ballet over so that the exhausting day might come to an end, and that he could take off the stiff collar that was chafing his neck.

Behind the music, there was the aftersound of the voices and arguments of the day – 'On a point of order, Mr Speaker', followed by Parsons' logic-chopping. And Ormston had said to the Press at the Thursday Lobby briefing, 'The Colonial and Commonwealth Secretary may or may not have used the words complained of, but . . .' Anderson, a political correspondent whom he trusted, had told him about it. It would certainly appear tomorrow as a doubt cast by a colleague on his denial. 'But, my dear fellow,' Ormston said when he had protested, 'I was merely dismissing the suggestion that you might have said it. Perhaps it was infelicitous. I'm sorry if it was. I'll try and put it right.'

Ormston's 'infelicities' were notorious. He had said recently, 'Provided the Prime Minister is given the strength to resume his duties, I have every confidence that he will lead the nation to new achievements till the end of the present session.' And he always expressed his 'infelicities' with the pious look of a bogus clergyman. They were repeated with delight by the Ormstonites. It wasn't surprising. Melville thought, that in the last few days the Press had been talking more and more of Ormstonites and Melvillites. He hadn't encouraged the term 'Melvillites'. He had no desire to lead a fragment of the Party. Yet, on balance, he hadn't disliked the label. In any case, Ormstonism had an aura of failure; it conjured up an elderly Crown Prince whose father refuses to die. Melville reviewed the Melvillites in his mind – the business men like Evans, Cantrell, and Robinson-Craig, the young men from the Party's Headquarters, Seabright, Harrison, McAndrew, rising lawyers like Protheroe, Cable-Grant, Baddeley and Clark-Meadows – they were a better lot in every way, he felt, than Ormston's colonels, disappointed ex-Ministers and former coal-owners. The music seemed to have become gayer, and he smiled to himself and then to Elizabeth whose face, in the changing roseate light, had the radiance which he sometimes uncovered in their privacy at night when her face glimmered beneath his and they spoke to each other in whispers. He smiled to her like an accomplice, and she took her left hand from beneath her chin and briefly touched his cheek.

Shortly afterwards the door of their box opened as Waters arrived with a telegram sent from Whitehall. Melville, interrupted in his thoughts, turned his head and in the sudden illumination from the open door, saw that Broome's fingers were entangled in Elizabeth's. Her hand seemed to jerk while her features facing the stage remained unchanging. Broome moved his chair, and leaned forward with his chin resting on his hands, now folded over the front of the box.

'I'm so sorry to disturb you,' Waters whispered to Melville. 'They're getting anxious, and would like you back at the office.' Melville rose.

'Oh, what a shame!' Elizabeth said. 'Do you really have to go?'

'Yes,' said Melville in a flat voice.

'Shall I come with you?'

'It's hardly worth while,' said Melville, already at the door.

'I'll look after Mrs Melville,' said Waters.

Broome had risen, and said, 'Don't worry, Geoffrey – I'll see her back safely.'

'No,' said Elizabeth, rising. 'I'm coming with you, Geoffrey.'

Broome held the door, and called 'Good night'. Elizabeth waved to him, but Melville made no reply.

Later that night, Elizabeth was brushing her hair in front of the dressing-table when Melville entered the bedroom. She glanced at him in the looking-glass, and her strokes became slower.

'What is it, Geoffrey?' she asked.

He tugged at his white tie, and tore the stud from his collar.

'You look so funny,' she said calmly. 'Like a drunk who's been in a fight.' She stood up, and went towards him, wearing a pale-blue dressing-gown over her bare shoulders.

'What is it, darling?' she asked. 'You behaved so strangely after we left the ballet – so morose. It's not like you a bit.'

He took off his tail-coat without answering, and threw it on to a chair.

'I know you're awfully worried about M'landa and –'

'I'm not worried about M'landa,' Melville said, brushing her hands away as she went to remove his cuff-links.

'Geoffrey,' Elizabeth said. 'Darling! You must tell me what's the matter.'

'You know perfectly well what's the matter,' said Melville. 'I want you to know –'

'What do you want me to know?'

Melville sat on the bed, and began to take his shoes off.

'I want you to know,' he said without looking at her, 'that – oh, God, it's so bloody undignified!'

'What's undignified?'

Her voice rose, and she looked at him with amazement.

'What's undignified? Why don't you say if you've got something on your mind. Honestly – I don't know what you're talking about.'

'Of course you know what I'm talking about.'

He stood up in his stockinged feet and said,

'I'm talking about you and Broome.'

Elizabeth stared at him in disbelief.

'Me and Gregory? What about us?'

Melville's face became pale. 'It was unfortunate that Waters opened the door when he did.'

'What do you mean?'

'Broome had his hand on yours – like some fat teddy boy holding a teddy girl's hand in the cheap seats in the cinema.'

Elizabeth returned to the dressing-table, and began once again to brush her short springy hair. After a few moments, she turned back to her husband and said,

'It's no good. I can't see the looking-glass.'

And then he saw that her eyes were brimming over with tears. He sat on the edge of the bed without moving.

'I think you're mad, Geoffrey – quite mad,' Elizabeth said, and wiped her eyes with a corner of the sheet.

'I'm not the least bit mad,' said Melville. The recollection of Broome's large hand with the hairy-backed fingers on Elizabeth's white wrist aroused in him a new wave of resentment. 'Why don't you reserve your episodes with Broome – for when you drive him home in your car?'

'How beastly of you!' said Elizabeth, standing again. 'How can you be so utterly mean! You know very well I gave him a lift to the hospital.'

'I've noticed,' said Melville, 'that you choose your charities very carefully. I've never seen you . . .'

'Please don't,' said Elizabeth, sitting beside him on the bed. 'Don't let's quarrel. It's ugly to quarrel. I swear to you, my darling – Broome – he's – he's like a sort of father – yes, really he is.'

'He was fondling your hand –'

'No, Geoffrey, dearest, he wasn't – he truly wasn't. You imagined it.'

And Melville looked at his wife with the hope that in the

moment when the door opened he had indeed superimposed the image of Broome's hand on her arm.

'Please, Geoffrey,' said Elizabeth, the tears running down her face, neglected and ignored. 'Don't let's quarrel. I like you sometimes to be jealous – a little – but not for long – and not when you're unhappy.'

'He was holding your hand,' Melville said doggedly but his anger had begun to fade in contact with his wife's misery.

'No, Geoffrey, he wasn't,' she said patiently. 'He really wasn't.' And now, feeling her husband's hostility disappearing, she put out her hand to touch his. As she did so, her dressing-gown fell from her bare shoulders, and Melville looked at her right arm.

'What have you got there?' he asked in a sharp fear.

She went to cover her arm, but Melville pulled the dressing-gown away.

'How did you get that?' he asked.

Below the shoulder on the fleshy part of her arm, a bruise formed a red ellipse with a violet margin, lacerated at the edges as if about to bleed; it stared at him, an angry and ugly intrusion on her skin.

Instinctively Elizabeth covered it with the palm of her hand, but Melville pulled her arms away.

'Where did you get this?' he said, lowering his voice.

For a few seconds, she didn't answer, looking straight ahead.

'I got it,' she said at last, 'when we were going into the Opera . . . that man with the stick and the beard – he tried to hit you and I put my hand out to stop him.'

Melville put his arm around her shoulders, and she laid her head on his chest.

'He was trying to hit you,' she repeated. 'There was all that jostling. I really didn't want you to know. I'm so tired. I asked Gregory not to tell you – it hurt so much at the Opera. He tried to reassure me.'

Melville took her hands, and kissed them, and kissed her arm till his mouth reached the bruise.

'I didn't want to add to your worries,' Elizabeth said in an exhausted voice. 'I knew how anxious you were.'

Melville kissed her shoulders, and said, 'I'm terribly sorry, Elizabeth – terribly. Please forgive me.'

She put her fingers in his hair, and said,

'We must go to bed, darling. It's very late.'

Again he put his mouth on the bruise, and then kissed her breast, and she said,

'I've always loved you, and I will always love you. You mustn't be jealous. There's never been anyone else – never, never – and there never will be anyone else.'

Afterwards, she said to him, 'It's like drifting in a warm pool. And when I shut my eyes, I can see lovely, coloured mountains.'

And he said, 'I love you because you are everything that's good.'

'No,' she replied, holding his head tightly against her breast, 'I'm not good – don't say that.'

He fell asleep as she spoke, and dreamt a short, tangled dream of M'landa, laughing, pointing at a bruise on Elizabeth's arm which had turned into a grimacing mouth, and shouting, 'It's red all right'. He awoke with a start, his heart pounding. The dream was still vivid, and he turned to Elizabeth to reassure himself that her bruise was not, in fact, a mouth. The laceration around its edges were like teeth-marks, and Melville pressed his face into the pillow to smother the thoughts which had begun to arise in him.

Elizabeth, who had been sleeping with her mouth slightly open, suddenly whimpered and turned on to her back.

'Does it hurt?' he whispered.

'No,' she answered. 'Go to sleep, my darling.'

But Melville was no longer able to sleep, and at half past three when he looked at the clock, he saw that Elizabeth too was awake, staring in the darkness at the ceiling, her arms behind her head.

8

Greystoke
Personal *July 3rd*
My dear Geoffrey

I've had excellent reports of yesterday's tilt. O. telephoned me to say that 'everything went off passably' from which I concluded at once that you

had done very well. These are, of course, anxious days for you, but I want you to feel strengthened by the knowledge that you have my unreserved support.

The charm of lying in bed, I find, is that one has the occasion to think about ideas and not simply, as is the case with all practising politicians, about things. I've been wondering, for example, what there is in nationalism which makes men ready to die for their nation. What, in any case, is a nation? If you look at a map of Africa –

Melville instinctively turned to the map of Africa hanging from the study wall, and then back to the small, neat, legible handwriting of the Prime Minister's bulky letter, and read on.

If you look at a map of Africa, you'll find that the geographical boundaries for which every African national party is fighting – the Kenya Africa National Union, or the Tanganyika African National Union, or the National Democratic Party of Southern Rhodesia, or the United National Independence Party of Northern Rhodesia or the Malawi Congress Party or M'landa's National Rally of the African People – all were created by Europeans in the last century. Seventy years ago the Matabele and the Mashona were deadly enemies; today, their tribal hostility has been submerged by a nationalism whose territorial boundaries have in fact been drawn by Europeans.

Nationalism isn't an absolute although we sometimes attribute to Joan of Arc, Gandhi, M'landa and the other mystics of nationalism the quality of dedication to the absolute. Nationalism in its modern political forms is merely a system for demanding and securing the absolutes of liberty, individual dignity and the rights of human personality.

Now, if this is true, it would follow that any other system of organization which secures those absolutes would be as valid – and perhaps, even as popular – as nationalism, which has the ugly concomitants of violence and hatred.

'Raising the standard of living of backward peoples', to quote the jargon, is clearly not enough. I can well believe that in the Rhodesias, where the average African wage is £75 and the European £1,100, the African would be happier if he were better fed, housed and clothed. But, the fact remains that in multi-racial societies there is a legitimate demand for equality of rights which can't be frustrated indefinitely. What we must try and get in Africa is a synthesis of economic, social and political organization which will at once serve the absolute of liberty and

90

the rights of human personality while aiming at a more equitable economic order.

I have, as you know, little sympathy with the Opposition abstractionists like Newman — does he still speak with his hand on his liver? (I do miss him) — or Yates — is he still quoting de Tocqueville? — who condemn white racialism because 'Look at the way we treated them.' Indeed, I think that the great treason of our intellectuals in respect of Africa has been to encourage the very forms of political organization which have convulsed Europe for eighty years. 'Hooray!' they cry every time some new African state comes on the scene. They make a patchwork and call it a design.

For my own part, I remain convinced that to serve the interests of continents, we must use world *institutions — and the best we have for the time being is the United Nations with its specialized agencies for economic development. But to apply them, we must prepare the field. The problems of Africa are so inter-related that we in Britain must encourage with all our power a federal or even a confederal organization for Africa with joint functional bodies which will knit together the multi-racial and multi-economic interests of the continent.*

You, my dear Geoffrey, can play a major part in such a project. You have devoted yourself to working not simply for British interests in Africa but for the interests of Africans as such. I should like you very much to renew as soon as possible your personal links with M'landa — a man whose vision of the New Africa, nationalism apart, I greatly respect.

Pray allow me, too, to offer you some counsel in the present situation. Your personal qualities inevitably attract enemies as well as friends, and those who have associated themselves with you in the past may well tend to fall away as the complications of Kadowa grow. There is a form of guilt by association in politics just as there's a form of advancement by association. Don't be unduly distressed by defections. Be patient. Remember that 'time and tide run through all things' — and, above all, bridle your temper.

Melville smiled to himself, and turned the page. The writing had become less legible as if the Prime Minister had become tired.

One last piece of advice — secure your base. Your Constituency Party is the place where you draw your political sap. Go back and tell them all about it. With the endorsement of your Constituency Executive, you're ready to fight the world.

Tell Elizabeth (how lucky you are to have her!) not to distress herself.
The Opera's a favourite place for assassination, and you got off lightly.
Give her my love – from the pseudo-Serjeant-at-Arms!
                                        Yours ever,
                                        Andrew Collard

P.S. – *I am feeling much stronger and hope that the excellent Broome (I'd*
prefer a doctor who looked slightly *ill) will release me in about three*
weeks. Yesterday, I walked as far as the lake. A.C.
P.P.S. – *I dislike Chequers and propose to remain here.* A.C.

Melville put the letter next to the pile of morning newspapers
whose pages he had hurriedly turned. The reports on the whole
were favourable. Most of the editorials congratulated him on his
firmness, censured the Opposition for making Party capital out of
a national misfortune, criticized Yates for what one writer called 'a
marked reluctance to assume that his country might possibly be
justified', and urged that there should be no further negotiations
with M'landa until he had positively denounced the terrorist
activities. In the chorus of support, there were only a few
unharmonious notes. One newspaper which called itself 'independent' had a front-page story from its political correspondent,
Philip Anderson, which had the headline, 'Cabinet Dissension
Over Kadowa'. Each sentence that followed had the cautionary
disclaimer, 'It is thought . . .' 'It is understood . . .' 'It is believed
. . .' 'Informed circles say . . .' Its theme was that Ormston had
been disturbed by the Colonial Secretary's 'indiscretion' at the
Lancaster House dinner to M'landa, although he was putting up a
show of monolithic solidarity with Melville as the Governmental
spokesman. He had, in fact, either written or was about to write
to the Prime Minister to protest against a general policy which, in
his view, would undermine British prestige in Africa through
vacillation between an undue appeasement and 'panicky measures
of pacification'.

It was a typical Ormston 'leak'. He wanted it both ways – the
support of the 'Flog-the-Wogs' as well as of the liberals. Patience!
The P.M.'s advice recurred to him, and Melville stretched himself
in the deep velvet armchair. The sun flowed through the open
window, touched the roses on his desk with an orange halo, and
warmed his chest where his pyjama jacket had fallen loose. The

session was interminable, and he longed for it to be over so that he and Elizabeth could have a few weeks of privacy somewhere where there was sea and sand and idleness. Lord Danby had invited them to Scotland in August, but he had no wish to go.

He remembered old holidays with Elizabeth when Sylvia was a child. He had often chafed at his domestic scene when he had watched gay pairs of young men and women of his own age, apparently uncommitted and free from the responsibilities of marriage and children. Then there had been his political life – much travel in fascinating places – but the flunkeys were always there. The protocol. The secretaries. The ambassadors. And in the last few years since he had been concerned with Colonial Affairs, the private detectives – Mulliner with his pince-nez and revolver, Hepburn with his delinquent's face and revolver, Coles in his business man's suit and its bulging pocket. They were warders as well as guards. He had been to Paris perhaps thirty times in the last ten years, but he had never walked down the Boulevard Raspail alone.

Melville shrugged his shoulders. Perhaps it was too late now. After all those years during which, outside the framework of his career and domesticity, he had only rarely been beckoned by excitements and exhilarations, what he now felt most was the desire to be calm, to be at rest, to enjoy with Elizabeth the security of a mountain climber who from the pinnacle surveys the plain.

He caught sight of his face in a small eighteenth-century looking-glass set in the wall. His eyes were pouchy, his jowls had begun to sag, his hair was grey above his ears and straggling, and a rime of beard stubbled his chin. It wasn't the face in the portrait that had smiled from a thousand hoardings in the last Election. Melville took a comb from the pocket of his dressing-gown, and combed his hair. He plugged an electric shaver in a light socket, and shaved. Then, he looked at himself again in the glass and smiled.

'That's better,' he said to himself.

Dramatically, his appearance had changed like that of an actor who puts on a mask. Here were the steady Melville eyes, the well-groomed hair, the taut chin (he raised it a little to take up the sag), and the confident but somewhat enigmatic smile which made the women at Party Conferences squeal at him with a joy which their daughters reserved for pop-singers.

'Much better!' Melville said to himself, and smiled at his image without restraint.

'A letter from your daughter,' said Elizabeth, entering the study. 'And why are you looking so pleased with yourself?'

'The P.M. sent me a friendly letter,' said Melville. 'He also sent you his love as the pseudo-Serjeant —'

'Oh, God, not again!' said Elizabeth. 'He is an old bore.'

'How's the bruise this morning?' Melville asked.

'It's nearly gone,' said Elizabeth.

'Let me see it.'

'No,' she said, withdrawing her arm. 'I'm going out soon. When are you leaving?'

'In about an hour. Would you like to come to Oldsbury next week?'

She kissed his cheek and said, 'Why do you ask? You know I always go to those things?'

'I just wondered,' he said. The doubts of the night had dissolved with the morning as if they had never existed. He watched her walk to the door in her printed dress, and he wanted to detain her, but she waved and was gone, leaving him with the recollection of her legs and her gait. Her legs were rather plump; she walked with a busy lurch. Yet all these things which once had slightly repelled him, had developed in time a special charm, a special appropriateness to Elizabeth in tune with comfortable feelings of security which she had given him during the years of their marriage. He stretched himself again, and opened the letter with the college coat of arms on the envelope.

Darling Daddy [it began]. *I was terribly sorry to read about what happened outside Covent Garden. I know how you hate that sort of thing, but I hope that you weren't too upset. For the time being, I'm consoling myself with the thought that the newspapers always make life seem even worse than it is.*

I can only tell you that when some idiot from B.N.C. said at the Africa Campaign meeting this evening — I'm writing this at half past one — that you 'deserved what you got', I stood up and left. This was extremely imprudent of me because I have to come to the House next week to lobby you, and he's on the Committee.

I'm still being badgered by the Press. The day before yesterday, I was

94

having a tutorial when there was a message saying that a friend of yours wanted to talk to me on the phone. I did speak to him, and he said his name was Rowland and could he call at my rooms. Naturally, I said he couldn't, and when he said he wanted to talk about Akebo and whether it was true that you were opposed to our getting married — the absolute cheek of it — I hung up on him.

A few hours later, I was in the middle of tea with Henrietta — you met her, she's the girl with the long, fair hair you rather liked — when there was a knock at the door, and who should be standing there but some miserable-looking youth in a raincoat who said his editor had asked him to call. When I asked him why he had claimed to be a friend of yours, he said without a blush, 'If I hadn't, you wouldn't have come to the phone.' I then said to him, 'I've nothing to say, but as you're obviously hard up — you couldn't possibly do these errands otherwise — here's half a crown!' This time he did go red — red and white to be exact — and went away.

Melville, who'd been skimming through the letter with a frown, laughed out loud.

I'm afraid [she went on] *I didn't stick literally to the No Comment line, but I feel that if they're going to be swinish, they will be, however forbearing we are to them. There are some people who can't be appeased by politeness — gossip-writers least of all.*

You'll be glad to know that I've finished my essay for the Chesterfield Prize on 'The Place of Sociology in Modern Society' and have sent it in. I don't expect to win, but I'm pleased that I've gone in for it.

One other thing, Daddy darling! will you please see if you can find my G.C.E. certificate? I need it very urgently — otherwise I can't be admitted to the Diploma Course I told you about the other day at the Zoo. You must promise me, too, that you won't tell mother about it. I don't think she quite understands what I'm trying to do, and while I don't mind being a 'permanent student', I'd rather she didn't keep reminding me of it.

I know it isn't in my room. It is almost certainly in the scrap-room where all my old books and stuff is stored. I seem to remember having put it with my old diaries for safety. You'll get a little dusty, but please, *Daddy dear, will you bear in mind that I need it* at once!

Don't let them be too horrible to you.

Hugs and kisses,
Sylvia

'Hugs and kisses, Sylvia.' It was the schoolgirl ending to her letters when she was at boarding-school which hadn't altered when the timid, shut-in child whom he now recalled had changed into a resolute and articulate young woman. There was nothing in the letter about Elizabeth, and when she asked him what Sylvia had to say, he would reply, 'Oh, the usual talk about her work and the state of the world.' And Elizabeth would say, 'I wish she didn't take everything so seriously! It must be her Elektra complex!' And he would say, 'That's flattering but untrue. She loves you very much. You simply don't recognize it.'

He decided that he would go to the attic before he had bathed to see if he could find Sylvia's certificate.

It was an ugly room with a fanlight, chilly in winter and stuffy in summer, which he almost never entered. Suitcases, an easel, a punch-ball, school books with titles like *Elementary Geometry* and *The Story of the Tudor Kings*, a heap of framed photographs which clattered when he stepped on a loose board, a tangle of photographic equipment including a projector, and the bound volumes of Hansard for the past six years, all littered the room in a haphazard rejection. Melville picked up an album of photographs of himself and Elizabeth taken at Baalbek when he had attended a meeting of the Inter-Parliamentary Union. They were standing by a broken column of the temple, Elizabeth was holding his arm, and they were both smiling happily. That must have been at least ten years ago. For half an hour, Melville distracted himself by examining old photographs, chiefly of himself taken on many official occasions, usually with Elizabeth standing at his side or just behind him.

The fourth album he took up was neatly labelled 'My Holiday Pictures', and had the date of the last year when Robert had stayed with them. Reluctantly, and yet compulsively, Melville opened the album to look at the photographs of himself, Elizabeth, Sylvia and Robert, his dead brother.

Some were of the summer when they had taken a villa at Fécamp. Sylvia couldn't have been more than thirteen, but with her serious face, at ease with the French girls in a bikini, she already seemed an adolescent. Robert with his fair hair and handsome face. Lazy. Unable to keep a job for more than four months. Always in trouble or on the verge of it. Always with some woman or other in tow. Robert – the younger brother –

coming and going. Always tired whenever he himself returned late at night from the House. Exhausted by idleness, Melville used to say when Robert's inertia irritated him beyond endurance. But never too tired for parties or first nights or long conversations with his girl-friends on the telephone. He had stayed with them for two years, and looking at his brother's face, laughing back at him from the photograph, Melville felt his throat tightening as he remembered their childhood and the familiar voice that he would never hear again. He closed the album, shook his head vigorously, and started sorting the papers on Sylvia's shelf.

After five minutes of unsuccessful rummaging, he took a stack of exercise books from the top of a basket filled with Pony Club rosettes, horse brasses and picture postcards. The books had a label on which was written in square, schoolgirl handwriting, 'The Diary of Sylvia Jennifer Melville' with the date. He took each exercise book, and shook it in the hope that the certificate might have been one of the papers with which Sylvia had interleaved the diaries. There were gymkhana programmes, school hymns, lists of prize-winners, a number of school reports and a supplement from a magazine with photographs of a popular actor. When he came to the last of the diaries, it fell open in the middle and Melville, without any feeling that he was intruding into Sylvia's secrets since she had asked him to look in the diaries for the certificate, began to read.

In the afternoon Robin came to tea, and daddy and mother liked him very much. We played table tennis, and he beat me. He says there is a bit of bother about the party, as Colin thinks it beneath his dignity to go with Sawbridge, who is only in the Upper Fourth . . .

Melville turned the pages to Saturday, May 5th.

I think I met Robin outside New Hall, but as usual I was running and it did not register till I had passed him, but I looked back and he looked back at the same moment. I don't even know if it was him. All English schoolboys look alike apart from their faces.

May 17th
They have started emptying the swimming pool again, so I am hopeful of starting again. Talked about 'Brighter Britain' in discussion. Miss

Throssell was complaining that restaurants and food shops in England are dirty. I wanted to suggest she should begin to remedy the situation at school – the food is always left uncovered and the knives and forks are always dirty – but I did not dare. It poured with rain so there were no games. Orchestra in evening was rather feeble as the seconds did not know their part. Mother telephoned to say that she has tickets for Stratford, and we are all going on Thursday. Uncle Robert is coming too. Good!

The well-known names of Sylvia's childhood conversation recurred in the pages – Margaret and Judy Wheeler, Jill Maddox, Liz Chambers, Miss Ambler, Miss Cundell, Miss Driscoll and the Throstle.

June 21st
. . . umpired for the final of the House tennis matches. Made the mistake of giving Jill and Margaret one game too many, but they would have won anyhow. It was jolly good being an umpire. I got two glasses of lemonade.

June 27th
There was a dreadful dust-up this morning. There was a hammer and sickle flag flying from the flagpole. The Throstle was livid, but actually it was the Boys' School House. In the afternoon, Daddy collected me to go to the Bishop's Tea Party. We drove through very beautiful countryside, and sang lots of songs together. It was lovely being alone with him.

Monday July 3rd
There were lots of visitors, the Crawfords, the Jephcotes and a man from the American Embassy with a pretty wife. I think they were called Vandervelde or something. They have two little boys called Peter and Alex. We played tennis and clock golf. Uncle Robert and Mrs Vandervelde played Daddy and me, and we beat them. But Uncle Robert was joking with Mrs Vandervelde all the time, and I do not think he was trying. Missed the last performance of Captain Hornblower *on television, much to my annoyance and went to bed after a tepid bath. Nanny had left the water running in the basin. I think Mrs Vandervelde is dim.*

July 4th
Woke up early and read Boswell's London Journal. *It is very unsuitable, and rather disgusting in parts, but it gives a very interesting picture of life in London in the middle of the eighteenth century.*

Melville laughed, shook the book from its spine to see if any papers were stuck inside, and turned to the pages of the fourth diary.

June 4th – The Very Worst Day of My Life.

Melville smiled indulgently and sat on the ledge by the attic window to read about the 'Very Worst Day' of Sylvia's life. It was strange, he thought, how sure one could be at the age of thirteen that this was the very extremity of unhappiness, that there was no other depth to be plumbed – no greater misery than to be rebuked by a school-mistress in front of the whole form or to be snubbed by a boy in the school bus or to fail in the school sports.

Today was the very worst day of my life [he read]. *He said that he would take me to the cinema if I would take Barbara Solway to Penelope's party. He told me not to come back before half past five. I took the bus to Kensington with Barbara but Penelope had a temperature and Mrs Medlicott said that we had better have some tea and go home. We walked through the Park, but in the end we took a bus back. I knew it was no use getting home too early because she was going to have tea with Mrs Jephcote and Nanny and Solange were going to be out.*

Melville puckered his brow as he tried to follow the complexities of Sylvia's narrative.

I wish Daddy was not away so much. He never has time to talk to me. She didn't give me a key but I know the way in over the buttress wall that leads to my window. I got into my room end all the curtains were drawn to keep the house cool because she's so fussy. After a while, my heart jumped into my mouth because I heard an awful sound of groaning. So I went on to the landing with my knees shivering, and thought I would go to the telephone and dial 999.

Melville stopped reading as his heart quickened its beat. Suddenly he felt that by continuing to read he was preparing a disaster for himself. His fingers made wet stains where he held the paper. The careful writing had become a scrawl, and his grip tightened on the paper as he held it close to his eyes.

99

The noise was coming from the other bedroom which I had to pass, and the door was half-open, so I stopped for a moment before going down to the telephone. Her head was lying over the edge of the bed, and her hair was hanging down, and she was making terrible choking noises as if she had been running and couldn't breathe. And on top of her something white was going up and down, up and down, up and down, and I couldn't see at first what it was because the curtains were drawn. I was rooted to the floor. My legs were trembling, and it all happened at once. It was like animals fighting. Then, suddenly, she gave a terrible scream, and seemed to heave up in the air, and I saw she had no clothes on at all, and she exclaimed 'Oh darling, darling, darling.' And over her shoulder I could see Uncle Robert's face looking terrible and sweating as if he were dying. And then I must have screamed, because his eyes looked straight at mine.

Melville rested his head for a moment on his hand, and continued to read.

After a bit he came into my bedroom, to which I had retired, and told me to stop crying, and said that when I was older I would understand. He sat with me for ages, and gradually I began to stop crying, but the sobbing wouldn't stop. And then I hiccuped a bit, and he laughed. He said that I was his very favourite person in the whole world, and I told him that I loved him next to Daddy. He said in that case I must never tell anyone not even Daddy, because it would make him very unhappy.

In the evening we went to St Giles, where I swore with him on the cross that I would never, never, never, not even to save my own life, tell anyone what I had seen. Today was definitely the worst day of my whole life.

Melville sat motionless holding the diary in his hands, for about five minutes. At the end of that time, he heard Elizabeth calling, 'Geoffrey! Geoffrey! Darling!' and slowly walked down the stairs to his study. She was tugging at her white gloves as she came in, and said, 'Not dressed yet? It's glorious outside – wonderful!' Then she saw his face, and said, 'Is anything the matter? You're looking ghastly.'

He threw the exercise book on the table, and said quietly, 'You slut! . . . You filthy slut!'

The direct line telephone to his office had begun to ring but he ignored it. He stood at the centre of the room and stared at his wife as if he wished the scene imagined, the place unreal, the

100

whole a nightmare which would be dissolved in waking. Elizabeth looked at him in astonishment, and went to put her arms around him, but he pushed her away.

'You're mad,' she said. 'I really think you're mad. I thought so the other day.'

'Read that!' Melville shouted, his fingers tearing at the pages of the diary.

Elizabeth, her face white like that of someone who has had a haemorrhage, took the book from his hands.

'How disgraceful,' she said, as if to herself, 'reading Sylvia's diary!'

'Read it!' he shouted again.

The telephone insisted, and automatically Melville picked up the receiver, his eyes fixed on Elizabeth's face.

'Waters here,' said a deep voice. 'Can we expect you, sir? There are some urgent telegrams.'

'In half an hour,' Melville answered, and replaced the receiver.

Elizabeth was reading the diary with a concentrated frowning expression, the edges of the book trembling faintly as she held it. When she laid it down, she looked calmly into Melville's eyes and said,

'It's very unattractive, but I'm not surprised. It was almost impossible to keep a foreign maid with your brother about. Poor Solange! And how awful for Sylvia!'

He looked at her face, scanning its expression, searching for the truth behind the words, examining her steady glance. Then she turned away, and put the diary on a table.

'You must never tell Sylvia you've read her diaries,' she said firmly. 'I would think less of you if you did.'

And at the door, she said quietly, 'I'm not a slut, Geoffrey. Please don't ever say that again.'

9

Beneath a large sign which read 'Your M.P. at your service', four women and three men were sitting in the waiting-room of the Party Headquarters at Oldsbury. They were the remainder of a long queue which had passed like patients in a doctor's surgery into the main office where Major Danwell-Spicer, the agent, presented them to Melville.

'Next, please!' said Danwell-Spicer cheerfully. He glanced at his watch, and said to Melville, 'We'll have to speed it up a bit. Time's getting on.'

An elderly woman, panting slightly, came into the room, and Melville rose and beckoned her to a chair.

'What can I do for you?' he asked, smiling to her.

'Well,' she said, trying to catch her breath, 'you must excuse me – I get bronchitis.'

'There's no hurry,' said Melville. 'Have a rest.'

'No,' she said, fumbling in a shabby bag, and taking out a retirement pension book, 'I know you're a busy man, and there's still a queue outside.'

'What is your name and address?'

'Mrs Rose Walker, 42 Glenison Road, Barwell – I'm a widow and I live alone – it's about my house – it's damp even in summer – and the landlord wants to put up the rent but won't do the repairs. I went to see Mr Gordon down at the Council offices, but he wouldn't do anything – so I thought I'd come to see you. What I wanted to know was if there were some of those flats for old people. Mr Berry had one when his wife died –'

Melville listened patiently to her, observing her anxious, lonely face, and said,

'I'll do what I can to help you, Mrs Walker. I'll write to the Town Clerk, and get the Housing Manager to look into your case.'

She stood and said,

'Thank you, Mr Melville – thank you. I hope you didn't mind –'

'Oh, no!'

'– they told me at the Advice Bureau to call –'

Danwell-Spicer had come in, and was edging her away, but Melville went to the door and said,

'Write to me at the House of Commons if you have any more difficulty,' and she smiled to him gratefully and left.

'Next please!' said Danwell-Spicer. A man entered briskly, bowed and said,

'Gorodek. I am a Pole. They have refused my application to be naturalized.'

He sat down, and explained to Melville the details of his arrival in Britain as a survivor of Vlassow's army who didn't want to be returned to Poland since it had fallen under Soviet rule. He became indignant and began to say that perhaps he would have done better to have stayed in Germany in 1945.

'I'll go into your case,' Melville said coolly. 'The Home Office, of course, never give reasons in these matters.'

Gorodek stood.

'You will answer me quickly?' he asked.

'As soon as convenient.'

'Next, please!' said Danwell-Spicer. And in the interval before the new arrival, he said,

'Some people have a bloody cheek!'

'It's the price of democracy,' said Melville. 'How many more?'

His agent consulted his sheet.

'Just the effluent smells – interference with TV from Baggott's drills – and a family case. You know, I think you ought to give these surgeries up. It's bad enough they've made back-benchers into welfare officers – but Ministers! I'd say you're about the only one who does them.'

'I don't know,' said Melville. 'But I don't dislike it. It keeps me in touch.'

He stretched himself in weariness. The effort of disentangling the involved narratives of his constituents was an exhausting one; but although he was sometimes perplexed and frustrated by problems which required the attention of a psychiatrist rather than of a politician, he always felt a great and rewarding elation when he was able to help. 'Those who come in tears shall go rejoicing.' That was what he had seen for many years from his seat in the office, as the door opened and among the aggressive, the resentful and the untruthful who came in, there entered also the humble, the defeated and the victims. It was a special and private joy which he had never spoken of, not even to Elizabeth, when those who sat in front of him in discouragement and sometimes despair, left fortified with hope.

He dealt with the complaint about the stench from the river; reassured his constituent who was troubled by nocturnal devils; and was closing his briefcase when Danwell-Spicer called out, 'Last one!' and a man of about twenty-four in a blue suit entered and stood politely in front of him.

'Do take a seat,' said Melville. 'Can I help you?'

His visitor gave a quick glance at Danwell-Spicer, who said, 'I'll be back in five minutes, Minister. We'll have to hurry if we're going to be on time for the Hydro.'

'I won't keep you all that long,' said the man. 'My name is John Westercote.'

'Address?'

Westercote hesitated. Then he said, 'I've been living at 7 Hither Lane, Oldsbury – but I'm in the Navy, see.'

'Well, what's the problem?'

'I want to get out of the Navy, now.'

'I see. Why?'

There was a pause, and Melville waited patiently.

'It's like this,' said Westercote at last. 'Before we sailed on our Far East cruise, my sister went to live with the wife.'

'Yes,' said Melville, his mind on the afternoon's conference. The meeting of his Executive the previous evening had ended with a unanimous endorsement of 'Mr Melville's line on Africa', and the Regional Conference would as usual be a demonstration of confidence. He was anxious to get it over, and he began to feel some impatience with the uneasy man in front of him who wanted to return to civilian life.

'Well, it isn't that simple,' said Westercote. 'My sister's married to a fellow called Purves, and they both had the back room . . . So one day, she notices that Purves is carrying on with my wife.'

Melville picked up a ruler, and began to read its markings.

'What happened?' he asked without looking up.

'She wrote and told me,' said Westercote, 'so I got compassionate leave – it's up tomorrow – and that's how I came to be here.'

'Where's your sister – and her husband?'

'That's where the funny part comes in,' said Westercote. 'When I got home, everyone shuts up like clams, and says nothing. My sister says she wrote it because she quarrelled with Bill, and she's sorry, and they've made it up. He says it's all tommy-rot. My wife says she hates the sight of Purves and wants him to get out with my sister. So where are we?'

'Yes, indeed,' said Melville, nodding his head. 'Where are we? That really is the question. Why do you want to buy your discharge? Are you sick of the service?'

'No,' said Westercote, shaking his head. 'I like the Navy. It's only that – Beattie – that's my wife – she's a good girl, but all on her own – it's hard, like. The other two used to like going dancing – to the Hydro,' he said as an afterthought.

Melville offered Westercote a cigarette which he accepted gratefully, and lit one himself.

'It's an interesting problem,' he said.

Danwell-Spicer opened the door, and Melville said, 'Not yet.'

He watched the smoke drifting in a beam of sunlight, and said, 'How do you feel about your wife? Did this – rather mischievous gossip distress you?'

Westercote said,

'On board ship? . . . I wanted to kill him.'

'You wanted to kill Purves. But your wife?'

Westercote said,

'No – I didn't want to hurt her. She was lonely – all alone –'

'You felt you wanted to protect her?'

'Something like that.'

'You didn't feel that she shared the responsibility in any way?'

'There was no responsibility,' said Westercote, putting his large hands on the table. 'I told you – there was nothing in the story. It was just blab-blab from my sister.'

'Of course,' said Melville. 'Of course there was nothing to it. I'm glad you had the chance to see for yourself.'

He rose and went around the table, and patted Westercote on the shoulder.

'There are some people whose only joy is the unhappiness of others. They are the frustrated people who don't want others to have what they can't get themselves.'

'Dog in the manger,' said Westercote.

'Exactly – Aesop put it much better than I can. If you write to me at the House of Commons with your particulars, I'll drop a note to the Civil Lord of the Admiralty, and see what can be done. I'm sure your wife will be happier with you nearer home.'

Westercote stood to attention, and said,

'Thank you, sir.'

As he turned to go, Melville said,

'By the way, what about your sister and her husband? Are they going to go on living with you?'

'Oh, yes,' said Westercote. 'It helps with the rent, like.'

'Yes,' said Melville. 'Those arrangements are sometimes very convenient.'

He shook hands, and watched him go.

'What's up?' asked Danwell-Spicer. 'He's gone off bright as a bird, and left you with a face like a fiddle.'

Melville half-smiled, and said,

'I'd like some air. Let's walk down to the Hydro.'

The Hydro Ballroom, once part of a hotel on the outskirts of Oldsbury, had been surrounded first by the villas of the city's industrialists and later by circles of council houses, grouped around green precincts, so that with its nineteenth-century pinnacles topping great walls of glass it looked like a cathedral with a vast conservatory, overlooking terraces of happy villages. But the business men had, in fact, moved outward, as the factory workers accumulated in the centre. Their villas had been broken down into flats and, despite their local greens, the council estates had become great dormitories where the husbands and their working wives only returned at night.

For the rest of the county, the Hydro Ballroom had a special significance. Except for the Drill Hall, it was the only building within fifty miles able to seat more than a thousand people, and on the occasions when a symphony orchestra or a revivalist or a leading politician came to Oldsbury, the Hydro Ballroom, nationally famous because of its frequent appearances on television as the site of the Eastern 'Let's Have a Dance' finals, would shake off its new 'regulars' and recover its pretensions as the centre of the social and cultural life of the county. The earth car park, stiffened with ashes and clinker, would then change its motor-bikes and bubble cars for the more solid cars of men and women who looked like foreigners in the city which they and their families had helped to build.

Waters stood at the entrance to the main hall, watching the queue as it stood patiently waiting for the doors to open. The organizers of the Regional Rally had received reports that the mass meeting would be infiltrated by members of the Africa Campaign Committee, and to forestall trouble they were having a check both at the main door and on the inner door of the blue tickets which had been issued to known Party supporters.

Although it was a blazingly hot day, the hall was certain to be packed out, and they had arranged for loudspeakers to relay the speeches to the 'overflow' which would be left on the steps.

Waters said to Danwell-Spicer, 'Well, Gerald – what d'you think of it?'

'They're very good, you know,' said the agent. 'We can always get the troops up when there's trouble. We've got a lot of the young ones too.'

'Stewards all right?' asked Waters.

'Excellent,' said Danwell-Spicer. 'All briefed and posted.' He hesitated for a moment, and said, 'There is one thing I want to ask you. Is there anything wrong with Geoffrey?'

'Wrong?' asked Waters blandly. 'I haven't noticed anything.'

Danwell-Spicer took out his pipe and began to fill it, his gaze following a girl wearing a badge who was running up the stairs.

'Perhaps I imagined it,' he said. 'He just looks a bit under the weather. I thought so at his interviews. I've often noticed it – they get a sort of twitch near the corner of the mouth.'

Waters followed his glance, and said, 'I bet that's not where you get yours.'

They both guffawed and went through the officials' turnstile into the main vestibule which was already filling with a shuffling, excited crowd.

An organist was playing a *pot-pourri* of tunes from Gilbert and Sullivan, Coleridge-Taylor and Ketèlby. Pealing tones swelled through the vast hollow before subsiding into playful cadenzas and trills, only to rise again in massive challenging chords. The organist had been specially imported from the San Remo chain of cinemas whose chairman had recently asked Waters to recommend him for a knighthood. With an inkling of his proprietor's ambitions, the organist threshed his arms and feet, dedicated to furthering their goal. Loud diapasons made the hall vibrate in an accumulation of fervour seeking an outlet.

Waters stood on the platform to give the scene a final inspection before reporting to the official party which was assembling in the private room behind the dais. The hydrangeas, red, white, and blue, were stacked from the floor to just below the row of microphones. The audience, perhaps two-thirds women, was a blur of Anjou pink, the fashionable colour of last season. The Press box below the hydrangeas was full. The television cameramen, testing, occasionally turned on an artificial sun which swept sections of the hall with a special benevolence. The stewards were at their stations. The minor officials were on the platform. Everything was splendid.

'What's the processional order, Minister?' asked Sir Walton Brown, the Chairman. He was immensely proud of his thick white hair which gave him at the age of sixty-seven the appearance of a professional sage although he was, in fact, a distiller; from time to time, he passed one purposeful hand along the side of his head. The organ had already begun to play 'Greensleeves', which was the cue for the assembly at the door. Played *piano*, it lulled the audience into the contemplative mood necessary for the gladiatorial entry in march-time.

No one answered the Chairman. He braced himself, called out cheerily, 'Fall in!' and advanced on to the stage followed by Melville, Lord Gorlay, the Regional President, and twelve Constituency Chairmen. Behind them came the wives who filed into the second tier, their hats a patch of colour behind the black and grey suits. As they shuffled to their places, the audience stood and began to clap. 'Greensleeves' faded away and changed into 'Land of Hope and Glory'. The organ pealed, the voices rose and for two minutes, platform and delegates confronted each other, throat to throat, in a unison of exaltation. When Sir Walton Brown bowed his head and said, 'Thank you. You may sit!' the slow subsiding had a post-cathartic quality. Everyone felt better.

As the Chairman finished his introduction '. . . your splendid leadership on the African question which has confirmed the esteem in which your Party has always held you . . .' the delegates applauded with the frenzy of those who, having listened to a boring speech, welcome the opportunity for exercise. But when Melville himself rose, slowly and with his brow puckered, the applause turned into a genuine ovation. Someone began to cheer, and suddenly, the audience rose to its feet. A woman's voice quavered, 'For he's a jolly good fellow,' everyone else joined in so loudly that the huge glass windows began to rattle. Elizabeth smiled, and flicked the corner of her eyes with one finger.

In his booth near the roof, Merrett, the Independent Television commentator, began to talk into his tape-recorder.

'The Minister has undoubtedly received one of the most remarkable receptions I have ever witnessed. I feel, myself, that this is due not only to the way in which he's been handling the very tricky business of Kadowa – although from my conversations here, I can say that this is regarded as masterly; it's also due to a personal popularity which I think hardly any other political figure can equal today.

'Delegates are very conscious, too, of the great strain which Mr Melville has been under since the trouble in Africa began two weeks ago. Bearing in mind his own efforts to bring about a happy, constitutional settlement, they can well imagine how he must feel in the face of the latest outburst of terrorism. He is standing, a rather lonely figure, with a battery of microphones in front of him – a man of striking appearance, yet haggard, and I would say, rather unhappy about the way things have gone.'

Merrett began to follow the speech from the handout in front of him.

'If anyone expected a Party political speech today, he will be disappointed. The Minister has been making the sort of speech which I can only describe as statesmanlike. But whereas that term usually means a speech that says nothing, this one really does cover some of the major problems such as the economic aspects of political independence in Africa, social changes, multiracialism, African nationalism and above all, the idea of the United States of Africa which is very much Mr Melville's baby.

'The delegates have settled down receptively' (Merrett observed that in the somnolent afternoon some of the audience seemed to be lulled into a doze by Melville's steady delivery), 'and are following the speech thoughtfully and undemonstratively. I have the feeling that the Minister is deliberately trying to damp down the passions which the Kadowa affair have aroused . . .'

At the end of Melville's speech, Merrett, after noting the sustained applause which followed it, switched off his apparatus, and decided that he would listen to a few speeches from the floor before leaving. These, for the most part, were ceremonial and congratulatory. The Conference received them with a spontaneous indifference registered in an equal and cordial handclapping. But just as Merrett was preparing to leave his cubicle, a young man with black hair and an equine face went to the rostrum and announced his name and constituency – Allan Risbury-Jones, Hadley.

'Mr Chairman, sir' (he began hurriedly but his voice was confident), 'we've listened to a lot of interesting speeches today, but strangely enough, no one has spoken about the ten Britons who've been killed in the last few days.'

A growl of agreement came from the delegates, and the whole Conference pricked into attention.

'What about thinking of them – their mothers too?'

Again the growl.

'We all approve of the way that the Secretary of State has tried to help M'landa and company. Some of us may even think that he has gone a bit too far with his concessions.' (He waved away a burst of applause.)

'What's been M'landa's reply?'

Merrett telephoned to the producer asking for the camera crew to get to work on the challenging speaker, and the television arc-lights blazed up again, as if a new planet had entered the scene.

'What's been M'landa's reply to our concessions?' Risbury-Jones went on. 'I'll tell you. Ten British soldiers dead. Ten mothers weeping. That's M'landa's reply.'

The growl swept through the Conference again but this time loudly.

Risbury-Jones stood back from the microphone, waiting for anger to heat up the audience. Then, unexpectedly, he smiled, 'A lot of the Ormstonites –' (the delegates began to open their mouths in sympathy, and the Chairman, despite an incipient smile, tried to assume a neutral expression), 'a lot of the Ormstonites are blaming Geoffrey Melville for the massacre of our people in Kadowa. But there's only *one* man to blame and that man is M'landa. M'landa – he's the nigger in the woodpile.'

A woman shrieked with laughter, several members of the platform smiled, and in an instant, the laughter, licensed and uninhibited, became a roar until the audience observed that Melville hadn't joined in but sat, scowling, and gradually the laughter was reduced to a few left-over titters.

'You will observe, sir,' said Risbury-Jones, 'that my views on Africa are not shrouded by any sophisticated considerations. I don't feel any great compulsion to call the black members of our Empire our coloured brothers. I want to make it clear that when I speak of M'landa and his ilk, I believe in calling a spade a Spade.'

He raised his voice to a shout which was followed by a tremendous outburst of hand-clapping and foot-stamping from the audience.

110

Merrett spoke into his tape-recorder.

'Raven-haired Mr Risbury-Jones is in serious danger of stealing the Conference. At the moment, he's got the delegates jumping. His tough, I-stand-no-nonsense attitude is just the kind of talk which they've been looking for after the Minister's somewhat academic discourse. But he's saying the sort of thing which may prove a boomerang. It is the heady stuff which is liable to leave a political hangover. In the middle of all these junketings, Mr Melville is sitting with his arms folded and a curiously remote, detached, almost a dissociated look on his face. You might almost think it's all got nothing to do with him.'

'There was a time,' said Risbury-Jones, 'when the greatest compliment you could pay a man was to say, "You're a white man." Nowadays, there is a tendency to apologize for being white. As the Americans say, "Pardon us for living".'

Risbury-Jones paused, and scanned the audience, which had fallen into silence. Then he seemed to brace himself as if for a leap before he roared,

'That's – got – to – stop.'

'Hear! Hear!' said the Chairman, beginning to clap.

'I'm not ashamed to say,' said Risbury-Jones, his voice subdued again, 'that if it's true that a statement on,' he paused, '– eugenics, sparked off this crisis, then I don't regret it.' He hurried on. 'I hope the Conference will affirm its support in no uncertain manner for the Secretary of State in resisting the knock-kneed, sob-sister, yellow-bellied fellow travellers – in the Government as well as in the Opposition – who have raised their lilac flag of surrender as a substitute for the Union Jack.'

He finished his speech amid a storm of cheering which grew louder as he felt his way down the polished steps from the dais. When he reached the floor, he was surrounded by a group of journalists who had left the press table to question him, and on the way back to his chair, to the accompaniment of rhythmic clapping, he had to shake hands eleven times and was twice asked if he was already committed to a candidacy.

'What a splendid speech!' the Chairman whispered in Melville's ear.

Melville took out his cigarette case, and put it back in his pocket. The hall seemed far away, and Sir Walton Brown with his thick white hair appeared to be addressing him from the end of a

111

vast gallery in a dream. During Risbury-Jones' speech, he had been thinking of Sylvia playing on the sands at Fécamp with Elizabeth. With a peculiar precision, he had conjured up the images and sounds, even the scent of that day on the beach. He had been very happy.

'Yes,' he said to the Chairman. 'Yes.'

They were all looking at him; the meeting was over; and he rose and led the way out as the chatter rose from the hall and the organ began to play the triumphal March from *Aida*.

IO

The pain at the back of his head persisted, and he asked Waters to draw the curtains to exclude the shaft of sunlight which lay across the table. Briefly the phantasy recurred of being alone in a green primeval forest with long groves of towering trees, a place without sound or movement where the sky was shut out by architraves of branches. Main Road. Police Station. Road Block. Rough grass. Mesh fence. To Chisluka. The diagram on the table with its blue and red shading was beginning to lose its sense. In front of Melville, Sir Rupert Benning, the Governor whom he had recalled to report, was waiting for him to continue the questions which he had already been asking for over an hour and a half. He sat on the edge of his chair, bulky, alert, his sharp blue eyes keenly studying the Minister's expression as he formulated his questions.

'The report of the arrests –' Melville went on. The haze of the sleeping-pills which he had taken at three o'clock in the morning was beginning to lift, and like a boxer who after receiving an unlucky and staggering blow, suddenly recovers and counter-attacks his surprised opponent, Melville who had hitherto been submitting passively to the Governor's replies, began to force the pace of his questions.

'I've been looking at the report of the arrests – Nos. 53 and 72 for example – after the incidents at sub-chief Maudi's court and Chief Kunda. I see that in about a dozen cases there were head wounds – four men died of fractured skulls. Why?'

'The arrests, Minister, took place at night,' said the Governor.
'In the dark and confusion, it's what you might expect.'

'None of the arrested was armed. Is that so?'

'Pangas were found in some of the huts.'

'Those are also agricultural implements?'

'Yes, but in riot areas they're classed as weapons under the Emergency.'

'What about the drill for the use of batons?'

'They had no alternative —'

'I'm not asking that. I should like to know the drill.'

The Governor referred to his papers on the table, and said in his even, unruffled voice,

'In case of resistance, blows are to be aimed at the collarbones, the arms and the legs — not usually at the head — and in a given sequence.'

'That is the drill?'

'Yes, but —'

'I hope that the aim of the police will improve after your visit, Governor.'

The Governor looked up with the beginning of a smile, but seeing Melville's expression, he merely said, 'I will bring it to their attention.'

'That,' said Melville, 'isn't quite good enough. I want the drill to be observed. I will not permit detainees to be beaten up.'

He spoke crisply. With the discipline of many years, he had brought his mind fully into focus on an administrative problem.

'Now let's deal with the second outbreak at Kadowa,' he said. The two secretaries turned the pages of their books, and prepared for a long session.

'I have the summary here,' said the Governor, 'and I will, if I may, read it in order to get the chronology right:

'After the major trouble at Kadowa, there were large numbers of gangs operating chiefly in the Mbela district. On this particular day, a crowd of between 500 and 1,000 had assembled at a road-block, made by a felled tree at the junction you see in the diagram. They were carrying sticks and spears, and the D.C. accompanied by a police party told them to disperse.'

'How many were there in the police force?' asked Melville.

'About a dozen men all armed with rifles and one Sterling gun.'

'What happened then?'

113

'The D.C. read the Riot Act both in English and in the vernacular. The crowd still didn't budge, having lined up in front of the police platoon. Some of them were excited. They bared their breasts and said they'd come to take away the prisoners.'

'When did the rioting begin?'

'The crowd refused to move.'

'I'm asking when the shooting began.'

'Inspector Rolbart raised his rifle and kept it in position for a full minute. He then fired at a man in the front rank who was waving a stick.'

'Waving a stick,' said Melville, looking up. 'That was the extent of his riotous behaviour?'

'That is so,' said the Governor. 'I am reporting to you, sir. The African was shot in the chest, and died shortly afterwards.'

'The crowd then dispersed?'

'Not at once. A sniper was ordered to pick off a ringleader who was waving a flag. This he did, and the crowd dispersed.'

'There were, however, five wounded, I see.'

'At close quarters, a single shot can do multiple damage.'

Melville pondered for a moment, and then he said,

'I'm interested in your technique of crowd dispersal, Governor. Both these men were killed at close quarters. What is the general relationship of the police with the military in these matters?'

'Well, Minister. You'll see it illustrated later in the report. After the incident I've already described, the crowd reassembled near the prison at Kishengu, and Inspector Rolbart, finding himself outnumbered, decided to obtain military aid. The D.C. had meanwhile gone to argue with the crowd, which was pressing up to the perimeter gates of the prison. At this stage, he only had the support of four Riflemen who had formed into line with fixed bayonets. The Africans were brushing the bayonets aside, and gradually edging forward with the line giving ground the whole time.'

'Was the crowd violent?'

'No – but hostile and excited.'

'What was the District Commissioner doing while all this was going on?'

'He was arguing and reasoning – if that's the word – he was reasoning with the mob which was being incited from behind. At any rate the sergeant in charge finally ordered his men to retreat fifteen yards, and had a bugle sounded. He then gave the order, "At the crowd in front, present!"'

'Did the crowd begin to scatter – or as you would say, disperse?'

'No,' said the Governor coldly. 'The crowd didn't move. The sergeant gave his men an "As you were". The Africans then advanced in a menacing manner, and the sergeant, without further warning, gave the order, "Present and fire!" He himself gave three bursts from his Sten gun, and his men fired a few volleys. When it was all over, it was found that there were sixty-three casualties of whom twenty-seven were killed outright or died soon afterwards.'

There was silence in the Minister's room which had become excessively warm because of the drawn curtains.

'Excuse me, sir,' said one of the secretaries, 'did you say sixty-three or fifty-three?'

'Sixty-three,' said the Governor, smiling to her. She smiled back at him, and thought how attractive an older man could be.

'Why are men killed at such short range?' Melville asked in a sharp voice which interrupted the Governor's ruminations.

'The drill,' he replied, 'is that a selected individual should be killed, not maimed, first because if you shoot into a crowd you may miss the target and hit a less guilty individual, and secondly, if you miss or only slightly wound the individual, it might be regarded as a sign of impotence which would encourage the crowd.'

'It is, in effect,' said Melville thoughtfully, 'a form of execution. The sniper is ordered to execute an individual nominated, I suppose, by the sergeant.'

'In a sense, yes,' said the Governor, 'although, of course, Emergency conditions are war conditions.'

'Except that in most of these cases, the Africans have been unarmed?'

'That is so,' said the Governor. 'But you must remember that in Africa prestige is the basis of authority, and that goes with a show of strength.'

'Would you accept that sound administrative reasons justify breaches of the law?'

'I don't understand,' said the Governor.

The Permanent Secretary who had been sitting silently at the end of the table, said,

115

'*Inter arma silent leges.*'

Melville said,

'That, Arthur, is the ugliest of all Latin saws.'

'It's an observation – not a recommendation,' said the Permanent Secretary.

'How do you account for the extreme bitterness of the Africans?' asked the Minister, turning to the Governor again.

'For the time being,' said the Governor, 'I attribute it to the aftermath of the disturbances. Three weeks ago there was only friendliness. But in the first instance we have to go back to M'landa. He is looked on as a sort of Messiah. What he says goes. I'm obliged to tell you, sir, to complete my report' – and he looked Melville firmly in the face – 'that the origin of this outbreak springs from M'landa's resentment at the remark attributed to you about mixed marriage. He has successfully interpreted it to the Freedom Party as an attack on the African's human dignity.'

'It's absurd,' said Melville.

'I'm only reporting,' said the Governor. Then he added, 'Of course your prestige with the European population – leaving out the missionaries – has never stood higher.'

Melville stood, and asked,

'When are you returning?'

'Tomorrow afternoon, sir.'

'Well, between now and tomorrow, will you give your attention to changing the rule which obliges snipers to shoot to kill when breaking up crowds?'

'Certainly – if you will accept the responsibility of the police and military being overwhelmed.'

At that moment, Melville decided that as soon as it was convenient he would ask the Governor to resign.

When his visitors had gone, the Minister sat in his chair, listening to the clack of typewriters from the secretarial office; his gaze settled on the Tudor roses of carved oak which formed a frieze to the panelling. A man left his hut in the morning and joined a crowd. Five hundred others did the same. But one particular man went a few minutes earlier or a few minutes later than the other, and the crowd moved first in this direction, then in another. The morning was hot. There was singing and shouting, and by noon, the man is face to face with the Mobile Police Force or a platoon of soldiers. At last, a sergeant looks at him, appoints him as the dedicated sacrifice, summons a sniper who leaves the man in the dust with a hole blown in his chest. The guilty individual left his hut in the morning on a bicycle and joined a crowd. Five hundred others did the same. But one man was dedicated to death – the guilty individual who went singing with a stick in his hand. What is guilt? He would ask the Governor tomorrow.

Waters stood at his elbow and said, 'I've got the Africa Campaign lot in the Central Lobby. They've sent in a wad of Green Cards. I imagine you don't want to see them.'

Melville said, 'You're quite right. See them for me, but don't get involved in long arguments. Blow a bugle. Read the Riot Act. And if they won't disperse send for a sniper. Shoot the first one with a beard.'

'What's that?' asked Waters in bewilderment. 'Oh – sorry I'm rather slow.'

'If Sylvia's there,' said Melville, 'tell her that I'd like to see her when she's finished lobbying.'

'Righto,' said Waters, 'I'll try to get rid of them. There's a huge queue stretching into Parliament Square, but luckily they've got the names of all our Colonial and Commonwealth Affairs Committee. That'll keep 'em busy!'

The Central Lobby was full with the Africa Campaign Committee, most of them young, a few Africans among them, who were standing with their gaze fixed beyond the policeman's barrier at the heavy doors leading to the Chamber. A few M.P.s had come out in response to the Green Cards, and had been immediately surrounded by groups who stated their case. Within the permanent twilight of the lobby, there was a reverential hum of conversation; the visitors spoke in lowered voices as if they had entered a church. Even the Inspector of A Division, walking about with a pious smile, had the look of a verger in fancy dress.

After a long wait in the queue, the lobbyists, who had arrived in a militant mood, felt that something had vanished from their inspiration when they were finally admitted in batches by the two policemen at the door.

'You sign your name there, sir,' said the policeman at the barrier to the Nigerian secretary of the North Kensington Section, explaining the Green Card to him. 'Name of M.P. and your business.'

'What then?'

'Then – you just wait, sir.'

Waters stood by the policeman, and said, 'You'd better give the name of the Minister.'

'Mr Melville,' the policeman called out at the top of his voice.

At first the lobbyists didn't grasp what he was shouting; the name had become distorted in the reverberations from the cupola.

'Mr Melville,' the policeman called again.

This time, like the crowd scene in a film, the small groups disintegrated, then re-emerged in a single drift towards Waters.

'I'm the Minister's P.P.S.,' he said. 'The Minister has asked me to apologize – I'm afraid he can't see you but he has asked me to have a chat with you.'

There were mutters of discontent, and Waters retreated a pace from the group, some in open-necked shirts, which was pressing against him. 'I like democracy,' he had once said, 'but not too close.'

'I'm Chairman of today's deputation,' said a tall, fair-haired young man who spoke with a slight stutter.

'Perhaps you'd tell me your name.'

'It's Halebrook – Brasenose, Oxford. There are two major points, sir, we want to make. The first is that we want the Secretary of State to put clearly his position on racial discrimination in Africa – and elsewhere for that matter.'

'His position is quite clear,' Waters murmured.

'The second matter really arises from it. The Regional Conference passed what amounted to a vote of confidence in the Minister –'

'Indeed, it did.'

'– which was moved by an out-and-out fascist called Risbury-Jones.'

Waters frowned, and straightened himself in an attempt to reach eye-level with Halebrook.

'Before you go on,' he said sternly, 'have you examined the bona fides of the members of your committee?'

'We're all united – we belong to a number of different parties and some of us to none – we're all united in our attitude to Africa.'

'You yourself, Halebrook,' said Waters, pressing his point. 'Do you know how many of your members are Communists or crypto-Communists?'

'Stop smearing,' somebody called from the back of the group, which had steadily grown in size.

'I'm not smearing,' said Waters angrily. 'You come here, and make charges against the Minister because his policy has had the unanimous, democratic – I stress the word – democratic endorsement of a Party Conference – and you have the effrontery to allege –'

'That's not the point,' said a woman student who had been standing behind Waters. He inclined his head to her – she was short and snub-nosed and wore no stockings – and changing his tone of scorn to one of gracious condescension, said with a light smile,

'Well let's hear the point you have to make.'

She had taken a First, and having formed the impression that Waters was probably a Pass felt at ease despite the grey-green gloom of the unfamiliar surroundings.

'A number of Africans have been killed,' she said crisply. 'An even larger number have been insulted and degraded. Mr M'landa and others are in prison under the Emergency Regulations. Mr Melville as Secretary of State has been responsible for the policy which has led to these results. The other day, he sat at a conference, and accepted a vote of confidence moved in a speech – leaving out the personality of the mover – which was based on the principle of racial discrimination, and urged, in effect, the denial of human rights to Africans. As a member of the S.C.U., I'm here to protest against it. We are affiliated to the Africa Campaign Committee, and we want your Minister to know that we oppose him on moral grounds.'

Waters, who had been listening to her declaration with a frown, echoed her last words.

'On moral grounds,' he repeated ruminatively. As a barrister in his professional life, he believed in the sudden and changing question.

'And what connexion have you with the Chairman of the deputation?'

She glanced rapidly at Halebrook, and, flushing, said, 'What do you mean?'

'I see,' said Waters, at ease now. He wasn't very good, he had

119

to confess to himself, in dealing with abstractions, but when it came to dealing with people he was what Yates had once called 'the Westminster Vidocq'.

'What is your name?'

'Hazel Rogers.'

'Mrs or Miss?'

Her flush deepened, and she said, 'I don't see the relevance –'

'You are asking me to report your views to the Minister. Are you Mrs or Miss?'

'Mrs Rogers.'

'I see,' said Waters. He pondered. 'You were at the International Conference of Students for Colonial Liberty last month in Prague, I think.'

'Yes – what about it?'

'I'm trying to get the picture clear,' said Waters. 'You – and Mr Halebrook – are lobbying the Minister, I gather, on moral grounds in conjunction with your friends.'

'My grounds are political,' said Halebrook.

'I see,' said Waters for the third time. 'Your grounds are political but not moral – and yours –' turning to the woman, '– are moral but not political.'

'Oh, come off it!' someone called out.

'I can only tell you, sir,' said Halebrook, 'that we feel ourselves to be representative of a strong movement in the country which has been sickened' – he had acquired confidence – 'and disgusted by the massacre of unarmed Africans by troops. We protest against it. That's why we're here. In a matter of that kind, there's no room for argument – only for feeling. We feel that Britain's traditions have been dirtied –'

'I think that will do,' said Waters. 'I will tell the Minister your views.'

He pressed his way through the crush around him, stood for a moment to survey the full lobby, muttered, 'Scruffy lot!' to the policeman and returned with a feeling of relief to the emptiness of the Members' Lobby.

Near the Lords' Corridor, a student had spotted Ormston who had appeared as if by accident to examine the lobbyists. Surrounded, he accepted the situation with a tolerant air.

'Well,' he said, shaking hands with a few of the students, 'what's it all about?'

120

They began to tell him simultaneously, but he raised his hand, and said,

'I will perhaps tell you. We want to see this trouble in Africa settled as soon as possible. We want to continue our former happy relations with Mr M'landa as soon as possible. We detest racial discrimination. I speak,' he added with a private smile, 'for the great majority of our Party.'

'Which Party?' a coloured student asked. 'The Ormstonites or the Melvillites?'

'We recognize no such distinction,' said Ormston, with his smile broadening. 'In our Party, we are a happy band of brothers.'

The students laughed. They liked Ormston. He seemed different from his public *persona*. Despite the melancholy bags under the eyes, he was gay and friendly, not like that stuffed-prig Waters.

'What I say, of course, isn't for quotation,' he added, examining the unfamiliar faces around him. 'The responsibility for public statements is naturally the Colonial and Commonwealth Secretary's. All I want to say is that I want the Emergency to end as soon as possible even if it involves changes. I want Mr M'landa to rejoin our discussions. I want our own lads back home as soon as possible. And no more killings.'

There was a murmur of approval, and with a friendly wave Ormston hurried away.

Half an hour later, a message on the tape describing the mass lobby had the headings: 'No more killings; Ormston. Deputy Prime Minister foreshadows changes.'

At five o'clock, Elizabeth put her head around Melville's door, and said, 'May we come in?' Melville rose, and said, 'Of course, Elizabeth.' She was wearing a neat hat, trimmed with white petals, and she said, as she entered with Sylvia,

'I've just come for the National Association tea-fight downstairs. You must come and meet some of them. I captured Sylvia in the lobby.'

Sylvia kissed her father, and said, 'Do tell mother that I positively don't want to go to her tea-party, and that if I did I'd be sure to say something ghastly like –'

'Like what?' Elizabeth asked severely.

'– like I can't stand women's tea-parties anyhow. I'm not really

121

dressed suitably. I haven't got a funny hat.'

Before Elizabeth could comment, Melville put his arm in his daughter's, and said, 'I think you look absolutely adorable. I'm told that gingham dresses are very fashionable.'

'They were three years ago,' said Elizabeth.

'I happen to like gingham,' said Sylvia.

'Well, why don't you wear stockings to go with it?' her mother interposed.

'Because,' said Sylvia, 'I also happen to dislike stockings.'

'Come on,' said Melville, 'let's all go down. I'm going to hang on to Sylvia, and try to get some credit by association.'

'Not with our ladies,' said Elizabeth, cheerful again. 'They've just moved a resolution deploring young people – and, incidentally, approving of you, Geoffrey.'

'Where's the party?' Melville asked. 'In the Harcourt Room?'

'No, on the Terrace,' said Elizabeth. 'They wanted a nice cool breeze after Church House.'

Melville walked towards the summer marquee on the Terrace with his arms linked in Sylvia's and Elizabeth's. The sun had fallen behind the Houses of Parliament, and the Terrace was in shadow. But the river and St Thomas's Hospital were still bright with sunlight. The steamers and barges glowed gaily as they passed the parapet where Members and their friends who had finished tea were idling in conversation. Melville's walk was interrupted with greetings.

'It's the sort of domestic scene that gives M.P.s a good name,' said Lord Ardrossan, the Lord Privy Seal, stopping Melville near the marquee. 'Wife on one arm – daughter on the other. How are you, Elizabeth? And Sylvia – you've grown!'

'It isn't surprising,' said Sylvia, 'if you bear in mind that the last time we met I was twelve.'

And when Lord Ardrossan had left them, she said,

'Pompous fat bore! All piety and wind!'

'It really must be the Africa Campaign –' Elizabeth began.

Sylvia stopped walking, and disengaged her arm.

'You don't know what the Africa Campaign is about, mother, and if you did know, you wouldn't understand it.'

'I'll see you, Geoffrey, at seven o'clock,' said Elizabeth, detaching herself in turn. 'I have to help with the drafting of a resolution.'

'Aren't you going to have tea with us?' Melville asked, standing unhappily between his wife and his daughter.

'No, darling, I won't – I think you'll do better with Sylvia alone.'

She looked at Sylvia, and kissed her husband carefully on the cheek in full view of the delegates at the tables. Sylvia watched her with a half-smile.

'Why do you smile?' Melville asked his daughter when Elizabeth had gone.

'Why?' Sylvia repeated. 'Because she's funny. You know, Daddy, she finds it hard even to be polite to me.'

Melville shook hands with a number of women who were finishing tea 'before returning for the evening meeting of the National Association. At last, they all rose in a spontaneous movement, gathering their handbags and agendas from the litter on the tables, and leaving Melville and Sylvia to their table alone near the corner of the marquee.

'They spoil everything,' Sylvia said. 'They've even put cigarette ends in the geranium pots.'

'It was that or the Terrace,' said Melville. 'We must learn to be tolerant.'

'You taught me to be intolerant,' said Sylvia. 'And I'm glad. Why should we put up with the third-rate?'

After tea, they walked on the Terrace near the House of Lords end which was almost deserted. Sylvia spoke of Oxford and a novel by Turgenev which she had read in translation as *Premier Amour*.

'It's about a boy,' she said, 'who falls in love with his father's mistress. It's terribly moving. I adore Russian novels that take place in the long summer evenings. You can almost smell the lilacs and hear the crickets.'

'There's always someone sitting on the verandah with Aunt Varvara.'

'That's right. But this is written from the point of view of the boy. It's an adult myth that children can't fall in love – and can't suffer terribly.'

Melville guided her towards the parapet from which they looked down at the fast-flowing river.

'Were you ever in love as a little girl?' he asked, watching her profile closely.

'I was always in love when I was a little girl,' she said.

'With the boys in School House?'

'Oh, no!' she laughed. 'I was always in love with someone much older – Mr Osborne, the riding teacher, Lopinski – you know, the violinist – I simply adored him for a whole week.'

Melville smiled too, with a faint retrospective disapproval of the man who had occupied his daughter's mind.

'Who else?' he said.

'I think you're jealous, Daddy.'

'Of course I am,' he said. 'Who else?'

'Well, there were all the ski instructors – and Marjorie's father who was in the Navy –'

'Anyone else?'

'No, I think that's the lot.'

Melville looked towards a red bus in the distance that seemed to be creeping over Westminster Bridge.

'What about Uncle Robert?' he asked in what he tried to make into a natural voice, but his gullet had contracted as he mentioned his brother's name, and he had to clear his throat.

'Robert?' said Sylvia, as if to herself, 'Uncle Robert?'

'Yes,' said Melville, and he tried to force a casual smile. 'What about Uncle Robert?'

'Oh,' said Sylvia quietly. 'Uncle Robert was different. Don't you think the river gets wonderful colours at this time of the evening?'

'Yes, wonderful. Sylvia, I want to ask you something –' he hesitated, and she turned to face him.

'Go on, Daddy,' she said, 'you often tell me not to begin things and then stop.'

'All right – I will go on. Do you remember a housemaid we once had – a Swiss girl called Solange?'

'Yes, of course I do.'

'What did you think of her?'

Sylvia looked at him with a pucker of bewilderment between her brows.

'Why do you ask?'

'I have a special reason for asking.'

She thought for a moment, and said,

'Typically Swiss-French-Calvinist, always talking about God and hellfire. I couldn't stand her. Why do you ask?'

124

Melville lit a cigarette before he answered.

'I always had her on my conscience. She was very young, and I sometimes wondered if there was anything going on —'

Sylvia looked at him in astonishment.

'Solange?'

'Yes — Solange and Uncle Robert. She left suddenly — you may remember.'

Sylvia began to laugh, at first quietly and then loudly till the laugh became uncontrolled, and Melville seized her wrist.

'Sylvia!' he said sharply.

She stopped laughing.

'I'm so sorry, Daddy,' she said. 'It's so ridiculous. Solange was the most terrible prude. I never saw her and Uncle Robert exchange two words. Is anything the matter?'

Melville had put his elbows on the parapet, and was supporting his head with his hands. He didn't answer, and she said again,

'Daddy, dear, is anything the matter?'

'No,' he said without removing his hands, 'there's nothing the matter. It's been a worrying day, that's all.'

After a few moments, he stood up straight, and smiled into her frightened eyes. 'There's nothing the matter, Sylvia,' he said. And as they walked back to the entrance, through the strolling Members and the waiters carrying drinks to the tables, he said, 'I want you to be happy'.

I I

'Could we have a window open, sir?' a Member called out. The Chairman of the Private Members' Committee, James Lockhart, peered angrily at the blur of faces in the crowded room. To keep out the noise from the river and the Terrace, he had ordered that the windows should be kept shut, but in the course of the Chief Whip's long speech the smoke and the heat had become palpable.

'We'll try it,' he said, and Scott-Bower, the Chief Whip, stood in stiff silence as the windows clanked open.

'I was saying,' he said when the long room had become silent, 'that the Opposition will make as much political capital out of the

125

bother with M'landa as they possibly can while at the same time paying lip-service to national unity. Yates has been under pressure from his Colonial Affairs Committee, which is virtually in the hands of fellow-travellers. Their amendment next week is, in effect, a vote of no confidence and we must make quite sure —' he paused and looked sternly around '— that we go into the Lobbies as a united Party. We have eight Members sick; and our nominal majority is down to thirty-six. Committee Room 14 has seen many Party meetings. It has also seen many Parties go to bits, just because the chaps haven't had the right spirit. We've got to have a full vote next week, and there can be no "pairing" in any circumstances at all. That's all I have to say.'

He sat down and wiped the sweat from his forehead. 'Was that all right?' he said, turning to Melville.

'Excellent,' said Melville absently. 'Excellent.'

From his seat on the dais, he had been looking at a picture called 'The Flight of the Five Members'. Where, he wondered, had they flown? A boatman was bending anxiously over his oars at the bottom of Westminster Steps, the sky was bright blue, and the Members had the easy manner of men with the whole day before them. How far could you get before you were caught?

'. . . the Sexual Offences Act.'

Dr Paynter, a heavily-built, middle-aged general practitioner, who was a persistent questioner on all matters of morals, was developing a familiar argument.

'It seems to me,' he said, 'that once we hand over to the Africans, we are also delivering up to them the whole of the protective legislation which we've built up for our kinsmen and kinswomen. The Sexual Offences Act was some guarantee; and with great respect to the Secretary of State, I can't help feeling that he should have made it a condition of the handover that the Sexual Offences Act which expressly forbids mixed marriage between white women and black men should be preserved. The Secretary of State is the guardian of public morality in the Commonwealth. I am not concerned with whether he used the famous words at Lancaster House. If he hadn't said them, I would have said them for him. What does the Act say? I've got it here.' He put on his glasses, and read from the paper in front of him.

'"Any white woman or girl who voluntarily has illicit sexual intercourse with a native shall be guilty of an offence," and here,

126

"Any native who in public or private commits an act of indecency towards any white woman or girl shall be guilty of an offence, and be liable to receive . . . two years . . . fifteen lashes or strokes with a cane."'

'Sexual offences . . .'

The pain in Melville's head was still there. He had gone to bed soon after he had returned from the House. Elizabeth had spoken to him about Sylvia's bad manners, her insolence towards her, and her determination to disagree with anything she said. Melville had made no reply, and his wife had undressed without speaking. Then instead of embracing her in bed, he turned away from her, and fell almost at once into a heavy sleep as if in flight from his preoccupations. In the early hours of the morning he awoke, and in an old habit drew her towards him, their bodies awake before their minds, entangled in warmth and touch, firmness and softness.

Afterwards, the half-dream gave way to a waking, and they lay quietly holding each other's hands.

Melville said,

'I'll be glad when all this is over. I'm tired of Emergency Orders and Removal Orders.'

She put her fingers on his neck, and said,

'Go to sleep. You've been sleeping terribly badly. Don't think about them. Go to sleep, darling.'

And Melville felt her head beneath her hair and its weight on his shoulder, and watched her profile silhouetted against the window. He could hear her heart-beat, slow and steady like a metronome, and he felt at peace in the comfort of her presence.

'I'm anxious about Sylvia,' he said.

'Oh, don't worry about anything,' she answered languidly. 'She's a very big girl, and can look after herself.'

Melville lay watching the lights made on the ceiling by passing cars.

'Elizabeth,' he said.

'What?'

'I asked Sylvia today —'

He felt her stiffen in his arms, and detach herself from him. She sat up in bed, and said,

'Well, if you're not going to sleep, I'm going to read.'

'I asked her about Solange,' said Melville, raising himself too.

'Really – Geoffrey! You asked her –'

'No, I didn't mention the diary. I just asked her about Solange.'

He switched on the light, and turned his face to her.

'You shouldn't look at me with all that light,' she said, putting her hands over her face.

He drew them away, and she said with a sudden anger, 'What is the matter with you? Why have you become so strange in the last month? What are you trying to do?'

'I want to know the truth,' said Melville.

'What truth? What on earth are you talking about? You make me feel like something in Kafka. You seem to be accusing me all the time, but I don't know what the real charge is. What am I supposed to have done?'

She had pulled up her knees, and clasped her hands around them, and was talking without looking at him.

Melville got out of bed, and put on a dressing-gown.

'I don't know what I'm accusing you of,' he said, sitting on the stool by the dressing-table. 'I think I don't want to know. I am afraid to know.'

She burst into tears.

'I think you're losing your reason, Geoffrey. You're quite mad. No man in the world has ever had a more devoted and loyal wife than you have – none. And you've always known it's true!'

She threw back the covers, and said,

'Come to bed, darling. You'll catch cold sitting there.'

'I've become uneasy,' said Melville. 'Yes – uneasy.' He stared at her round outstretched arms which a few minutes before had enclosed him like a womb, and said,

'I'm uneasy about you, Elizabeth.'

'But why?' she said. 'Why?'

Her tears began to flow again.

'What else can I do to make you know that I love you? You began it all – this wild, ludicrous jealousy of Broome and him – it's just too sordid to speak about.'

She instinctively touched the bruise on her arm which had become a multi-coloured smudge, and said,

'Even this – you had some grotesque –'

'It wasn't Solange who was with Robert that day. Who was it?'

'It wasn't Solange – you mean, what you read in Sylvia's diary?'

Her sobbing had stopped, and she wiped her red eyes with the corner of a sheet.

'I wonder what Ormston – or your constituents – would say if they knew that you read little girls' diaries.'

Her expression and her voice had become taunting.

'It wasn't Solange,' said Melville, his voice becoming lower. 'Who was it, Elizabeth?'

She reached for her dressing-gown, and put it on rapidly.

'Geoffrey,' she said firmly. 'I'm afraid I can't stay here. I think you're ill.'

'I want to know,' he said.

She opened her eyes wide as he stood facing her.

'Are you suggesting,' she said, 'you – that Robert – your own brother –'

'I want to know,' he said slowly and carefully, like a sleepwalker who speaks, 'I want to know if you and Robert –'

'I can't bear it,' she said as if to herself. 'It's vile. I can't bear it.'

And then with a sudden motion before Melville could stop her, she reached for a small cut-glass powder bowl on the dressing-table and dashed it against her forehead. The skin seemed unbroken for a moment of horror in which it happened, and then suddenly it bloomed into a red gash with blood lacing her face and trailing over her breasts and staining her white nightdress like blotting-paper absorbing ink.

'Elizabeth!' Melville cried out. 'Elizabeth!'

He tried to hold her in his arms, but she screamed,

'Don't touch me! Don't come near me!'

Her knees sagged, and she slid to the floor near the foot of the bed. As Melville picked her up, she kept saying, 'Don't touch me! Don't touch me!'

He telephoned Broome as if he were an accomplice, each turn of the dial an act of defiance to himself, a penance and a wound.

When Broome came half an hour later, he said that the injury was superficial and told Melville to say that his wife had fallen in the dark.

'I've calmed her down a bit,' he said, 'but you know, Geoffrey – you must go lightly with her. I'm an old friend. That's why you sent for me, and that's why I've come. What's behind it all? What's the trouble?'

They sat together in Melville's study watching the first pearl light of daybreak flecking the sky, and Melville said,

'I don't know. Perhaps I'm overstrained. I sleep badly. You know, once upon a time I used to feel that everything was secure – my work, my family, my ambitions – and now, suddenly, I'm uneasy – as if there's no solid base anywhere – religion, politics, family – nothing – I feel as if it's all crumbling away.'

'Why don't you take a holiday?' said Broome.

'It's impossible.'

'A week?'

'It's impossible.'

'Well,' said Broome, taking his hat from the table, 'it's a long time since I've walked along the Embankment at dawn. I'm glad I took a taxi here.'

Melville shook hands with him in a gesture of gratitude, and Broome said,

'She's under great strain too, Geoffrey. Don't press her too hard. I had a quick word with her when I was waiting for the injection to work. She's got the idea firmly in her mind that you're persecuting her for something that she doesn't grasp. She's worried about you, and is beginning to feel she might be better out of the way.'

'Why should she want to hurt herself?' Melville asked.

'To get your sympathy,' Broome said in a hearty voice. 'Give it to her. I'll drop in tomorrow.'

When Melville returned to his wife's room, she was sleeping deeply with her head swathed in a bandage like a turban. He stood contemplating her for a few minutes, feeling above all a mild surprise that the quietness of his life was gone. Elizabeth was breathing evenly, her mouth was open, and she had an expression of contentment.

'. . . the Sexual Offences Act . . .' Dr Paynter's voice was being submerged in a rising murmur of boredom. '. . . the Act of Sexual Offence . . .' Nobody appeared to be listening. A passing tug hooted twice, and laughter interrupted the speaker.

'Order! Order!' said the Chairman. From the river a voice crackled in an unintelligible commentary like the incoherent fragments of remembered conversation in Melville's own mind. Another Member was on his feet – Lawrence Gore, a thirty-five-year-old barrister, the leader of a group of back-benchers who sat below the gangway and were collectively known as the New Africa Group. He was a tall, good-looking man who had recently been appointed to the Board of a mixed company for African development.

'. . . I think I speak for some of the newer Members,' he was saying, 'when I say that we came into the House as supporters of the Party, but now we're beginning to wonder if we've got one Party or three. Nowadays, you're not asked if you're a member of the Party but if you're an Ormstonite or a Melvillite.'

There was a murmur of agreement and Gore, encouraged, went on,

'When I say I'm neither, I'm told I must be one or the other. It's like having to be either male or female.'

The laughter grew louder.

'It makes it difficult. Who'd admit that he's neither male nor female? But honestly, I don't quite know the difference.'

A voice called out, 'Between male and female?'

'The Secretary of State, as I see him, takes a moderate view on Africa, but he's backed by a lot of extremist cranks who want to beat up the blacks or segregate them. The Chancellor of the Exchequer is another man of moderate views – who seems to have the support of a different lot of cranks. Their slogan is "White is never right". All I can say is that between them they're alienating a lot of moderate opinion – in my view, the majority of the country – which would like to see the Secretary of State take charge of events and not be pushed around by them.'

He turned to his neighbours, and said,

'The immediate question is how do we look to the country – for that matter to the world – on this issue? The African bloc has already put down a motion at the U.N. condemning the "massacre" –'

There were shouts of protest, accompanied by banging on the desks, and he went on.

'– all right, I used the words in quotes – the *events* in Africa. The total of casualties is rising. The Governor has made a Deportation Order against M'landa. Our African connexions are all feeling the strain – there's even talk of boycott in Ghana. What does it all spring from? Frankly, I've never been worried by the attitude of Godfrey Paynter. It's an antediluvian point of view which we can understand even while we regret it. What I'm worried about is the indiscretion attributed to the Minister. I don't accept that it's trivial. We're still the centre of a world-wide Commonwealth. We still are a world force in our material and moral power. The African-my-brother-but-not-my-brother-in-law jibe belongs to a different age – almost a different century.'

He looked at some of the frigid faces around him and added, 'I'm not arguing today in favour of raising miscegenation to a principle. We are not doctrinaire reformers.'

He felt the need for the support of his associates, and began to speak in the plural.

'We are conservative pragmatists who believe in taking things as they come – modifying tradition in the light of experience and tempering change in the light of tradition. The world is not what it was. The old slogans – the old jibes – are no longer valid in connexion with Africa.'

He had seized the attention of his audience, and now felt confident.

'Sir,' he said, turning to the Chairman, 'there are some of us, loyal members of the Party, who have the gravest doubts about the way the Secretary of State has been handling African affairs. Verbal ineptitude, premature violence and finally, the tragic impasse which we are witnessing today have all been the features of his administration.

'Can we in honesty resist all the strictures of the Opposition? We know that their motives are merely political. We know that the shootings are just another weapon to attack the Government with. But it would not be enough merely to win a paper victory – a prefabricated majority – in next week's vote.'

He paused, and the crowded room waited for him to continue.

'What I now have to say,' he continued, 'I say with reluctance. But' – his voice rose – 'I'd rather say it here than whisper it behind my hand in the Smoking-Rooms or in the Lobbies as some people have been doing. I believe that events have gone too far. With over a hundred Africans and twelve Europeans dead, M'landa and hundreds of others in gaol, the Secretary of State can never regain the confidence either of Africa – or for that matter, of Britain.'

Amid cries of 'Shame!' and 'Sit down!' and an aside of 'You

132

little rat!' from Granger, followed by protesting cries of 'Order! Order!' Gore shouted,

'That is my view. It would be dishonest of me to conceal it.

'I am not prepared at this stage to say that I will go into the Lobby in support of the Government's policy as interpreted by the Secretary of State – and I venture to believe –' he stared defiantly at Granger, who looked up at him with an angry, flushed face '– I believe that I will not be alone in abstaining under present conditions.'

A few 'Hear! Hears!' muttered for the most part *sotto voce*, and unidentifiably, marked the end of his speech. After it was over, the discussion went on in a predetermined manner because most of those who spoke had arrived with speeches prepared in support of the Government.

When it was nearly half past twelve, the Chairman said,

'We've invited both the Chancellor and the Secretary of State to attend our meetings, and the Chancellor will now sum up. Mr Ormston!'

Ormston rose and said, in a quiet voice,

'It's been a very valuable and interesting discussion. Its frankness has added to its value. And if I reply rather than the Secretary of State, it's because I have been perhaps less directly involved in these matters and therefore am under less strain.'

'Every word a leer,' someone muttered.

'The Secretary of State' – he inclined his head towards Melville, who was sitting with his hands covering his head 'deserves all our thanks for his heavy labours in recent days.'

There was a burst of applause and some Members banged on their desks.

'I am not going to discuss the merits of the various arguments which have been put forward today. The Prime Minister has asked to be kept informed of what was said today, and naturally the Secretary of State and myself will undertake to do so.

'Mr Gore –' he smiled a cold smile with his teeth closed – 'Mr Gore has made an interesting suggestion which I take to mean that he recommends the reconstruction of the Government. I will, of course, communicate his advice to the Prime Minister.'

There was a murmur of amusement, and the tips of Gore's ears reddened.

'If Mr Gore has any specific recommendations for these changes perhaps he will let the Secretary of State have them when the meeting is over. I am, Mr Chairman, most grateful to you for the opportunity of listening. We don't want Mr Yates or Mr Newman as a *tertius gaudens*. I hope that we will have a full vote next week.'

He sat down, and turned to Melville.

'Did you want to say anything?' he asked. Melville shook his head.

After he left Elizabeth, he had returned to his study, and sat in an armchair till six o'clock. A worm crept through his brain. Elizabeth. His wife's name was an essence that had inspired him through half his life with trust and faith. And Robert. He had loved him, and sheltered him. And that was over too.

Melville had gone to the bathroom, and looked at his face in the looking-glass – haggard-eyed and pallid. Downstairs, he could hear the sounds of the house-maid moving about. Solange. There'd been many servants since then. What had they seen? Robert – Broome – perhaps a dozen others? Every man who had ever visited the house? During his absences. Perhaps even Waters – the attentive Waters. She had smiled to them all, spoken to them all in the same cordial, flattering voice. In the summer afternoons, when he was at the House. When Sylvia was away at school. The hair trailing over the bed. The white shape above it. He remembered. There was a fashion of long hair. Her long, wispy hair, the hair that he touched so benevolently because she could 'never do anything with it' at a time when other women drew his attention with their fashionable *coiffures*. How often when he was away? Who were they? During the period of Helen Langdale, she had been restrained and tolerant, as if she'd known.

She had her own distractions. They had gone to Stratford, Fécamp, other places. He had cooperated. Go on – take Robert. Robert will look after you. Someone he could trust. I'll take Robert. Robert will come and help. We'll take Sylvia. Never mind, we'll have Robert. Dead. Years ago. Seven, eight. But the pain was like yesterday's, and today's, and tomorrow's. An amputation. A new death. The limb was hacked off and nothing could rejoin it. And the pain continued.

Yet, he might be wrong. A hope began to rise in his viscera. Perhaps he was mistaken. Perhaps the entry in Sylvia's diary – she hated her mother; she had been jealous of his attentions to her;

perhaps it was the hysterical invention of a child who herself in puberty had fallen in love with the nearest, familiar man. Perhaps that was the origin of her hatred which had then led him by her subconscious design to the diaries. The memory of Elizabeth, greeting him with her outflung arms, soared into his mind and with it the recollection of the bloodstained towel which he had held to her forehead.

'Oh, God,' he thought, 'perhaps I'm wrong,' and with the thought came an unexpected hope like that of a man who, told that he has an incurable disease, hears that the pathologist had made a mistake in examining the tissue. Perhaps I'm wrong. The hope became a music, and with it a compulsive need to see Elizabeth again, to hold her and to feel again their old safe love.

'That ends our proceedings,' said the Chairman, and the Members rose with a shuffle and scraping of chairs. They began to leave the Committee Room like a pattern of the trends in the Party. Ormston stepped down from the dais into the central aisle, taking the longest route through the room to the Public Exit. He was greeted on all sides with friendly smiles. Members made a path for him, and he was quickly surrounded by a number of ex-Ministers who had retired to the back benches, a few knights of his recommendation, and a rank-and-file of younger Members whom he had encouraged with advice and expectations.

Gore and a few of his associates in the New Africa Group became involved in this stream as it pressed towards the door like a debouching cinema audience, and they were regarded with the same indifference as members of cinema audiences reserve for each other.

Melville moved towards the platform exit, together with some of the Party officials and Waters. He was followed by about half the Members in the room as if he were leading them into a plebiscite. They grouped themselves around him, smiling and demonstrative as if to show where their sympathies and loyalties lay, though no one addressed him personally. In the Corridor, the Chief Whip caught up with him, and said,

'I thought the Chancellor settled Gore pretty well.'

'Did you?' Melville said. 'I had a different impression; I rather thought he was goading him.'

'To abstain?'

135

'Yes,' said Melville. 'There's nothing he likes more than to frighten the Party. That's the first step. Then he likes to come along and kiss it better.'

He outdistanced his attendants with Waters, and said, 'I'll have to talk to the P.M. Will you telephone and arrange for me to go down to Greystoke tomorrow?'

'Yes,' said Waters. 'Are you lunching in the Members' Dining-Room?'

'No,' said the Minister. 'I want to walk across the Park.'

He walked briskly without hat and coat, and soon felt himself sweating under the hazy, copper-coloured sky, heavy with the storm which had begun to rumble and crack beyond Buckingham Palace. The ducks had retreated to the reeds, and the water had black reflections. On the grass, couples lay stretched out, the men in shirt-sleeves, the women in sleeveless summer dresses, some engaged in what otherwise would have seemed coital prelimi-naries, were such activities not the normal convention of London crowds in hot summers. Others picnicked close by – the whole a picture of domestic living in the open air.

As Melville walked, a thunderclap awoke the prostrate figures as if by the alarm signal of a gigantic clock. They rose. The women smoothed the creases of their dresses. The men languidly put on their jackets. And to the accompaniment of the first fat raindrops, they began to move swiftly away in pairs. The lake started to become dappled with rain, there was a dazzling flash, followed by a massive roll, and soon the Park began to scurry with figures running for shelter from the storm.

As Melville walked, he heard steps splashing behind him.

'Like a share of my mac?' a voice said.

He turned with the rain purling down his face to see Armstrong, who had quickened his step to keep pace with him. For a moment, he didn't recognize him. Then he said,

'That's very civil of you. No, thanks. I'll just imagine I'm doing a cross-country run. I'll change when I get in.'

'As you like,' said Armstrong, and was about to turn into a side path but Melville, thinking that he might have felt snubbed, said, 'Come this way – then you can cut across.'

'I used to play rugger,' said Armstrong. 'I missed it when I gave it up.'

'How old were you?'

'Thirty-six,' said Armstrong. 'I'm fifty-four now.'

To make conversation, Melville asked a few questions about his family and South Wales. He liked his cadenced voice, his easy, undeferential manner and his pleasant, open face with the blue scar at the side of his head.

'You're having a bad time,' said Armstrong.

'In Africa?'

'Yes.'

'It's pretty bad.'

'Well, I'm sorry for you, lad,' said Armstrong.

They walked along without speaking with the rain streaming down their faces, and Melville wished that he had learned to know the Opposition back-benchers better. He wanted to talk to Armstrong, but he had difficulty in finding the language and so they walked in silence. But the leaves gave off a warm, soaking smell, the pain in his head lifted, and he felt refreshed.

He changed his suit in his dressing-room into which a bed had been moved, and then knocked on the door of the main bedroom. Elizabeth was sitting propped up against the pillows, wearing a pale blue bedjacket over a white nightdress. Broome was sitting at her bedside, and greeted Melville with a broad smile.

'She'll live,' he said. 'Don't let the head-dress worry you. She likes wearing it. Thinks it makes her interesting. I'll look in tomorrow.'

When he had left, Melville stood by the window, looking out at the street, and Elizabeth turned her face into the pillow. After a minute of silence, Melville said,

'Elizabeth – I must talk to you.'

She didn't answer, and he faced her. On her bandages, there was a trace of blood; her cheeks were pale; and her eyes had heavy violet shadows beneath them. She was looking straight in front of her as she answered in a flat voice,

'I have nothing to say to you. You are a very wicked person.'

'I have something to say to you,' he said savagely, sitting on the bed and taking her wrists in his hands. 'I want to know – I've got to know –'

She turned her eyes on him, and said in the same flat voice,

'If you say again what you said last night, I'll kill myself as soon as you leave the house.'

He slowly let go of her wrists and rose from the bed. His gaze still held her expressionless eyes, and he withdrew to the door.

Then he went to his study, his certainties complete. It was done, and nothing could ever change it. Nothing. Ever. He looked at a photograph of Elizabeth and himself taken on the Terrace a few years before, and suddenly, covering his face with his hands, he began to weep, the tears trickling through his fingers as they had done in his childhood when his father had died and there was no comfort in the whole world.

12

After lunch two of the Prime Minister's grandchildren who had sat, rather intimidated by Ormston and staring at the Grinling Gibbons carving around the fireplace, rose gratefully from the table, leaving the two men together. A nurse came in, and asked the Prime Minister if he wanted to be helped out on to the lawn, but he waved her away impatiently. The Prime Minister was wearing a grey suit and a white shirt with a soft collar, but his neck had become thinner and the collar stood away from it as if it had been bought haphazard. His face had a jaundiced colour, and his cheekbones were red, touched with a feverish cosmetic. Only his voice was unchanged; it was slow and thoughtful with its familiar, rehearsed calmness. He crumpled his table napkin, and laid it on a plate.

'I see no urgent anxiety,' he said at last.

'Perhaps I can put it this way,' said Ormston, 'and now I'm seeing the situation purely as Chancellor. Our reserves are low, and are getting lower. I feel rather like a father whose child is bleeding to death.'

His simile disturbed him; it evoked other associations, and he hurriedly drained the glass of water. The Prime Minister said nothing, and Ormston continued,

'Let's leave out the political merits of the situation.'

'Is that possible?'

'For the sake of my hypothesis – yes, I'm thinking for the moment in plain, economic terms. We can't afford to increase our costs in Africa – we simply can't afford it. I don't mean just our direct military costs. I'm thinking of the African Boycott which is already working up. I'm afraid, Prime Minister, you're not going to like the trading position when you see it.'

'I never do,' the Prime Minister commented wearily. The Chancellor was repeating an argument which he had already developed for an hour before lunch.

'It comes at a bad time,' said Ormston. 'A singularly bad time. The Party's very restless, you know.'

'It's a sign of life – very encouraging!'

'The younger men –'

'Which ones?'

'The younger ones like Gore, Vaughan, Hadley, Prebble, Lambert-Price – the New Africa lot –'

'Do they confide in you? Have you spoken to them?'

'Only at yesterday's meeting – they're very restless, Prime Minister. They feel that it's very old-fashioned – shooting down mobs of natives. They're very much afraid that if the Opposition get a Commission of Inquiry some rather dismal stuff is going to come out.'

'Young back-benchers are always restive when they're bored,' said the Prime Minister, and for the first time since his grandchildren left the table, he smiled. 'Why don't you give them something to play with?'

'They've found their own toy,' said Ormston, 'and this is it. They want to abstain next week.'

The Prime Minister continued in his flippant tone,

'Tell the Chief to give them a talking-to.'

The Chancellor closed his eyes, and then said,

'I think it's gone beyond that, Prime Minister. They feel pretty strongly about Africa. They are greatly disturbed by the new and rather ugly image of the Party which our African policy is creating. On the whole, the country is still in favour of moderation and common sense. Melville has in a curious way made us look old-fashioned – extravagant – nineteenth centuryish – almost cranky.'

'Don't you think the British public has reveries of Britannia's strong, firm hand?'

'I think the British public doesn't dislike force provided that it's short, sharp and rewarding.'

They both laughed and felt relaxed. Then Ormston frowned and went on,

'What the British public doesn't like is violence that's protracted, messy and expensive. At that point, you get a moral revulsion against force – especially if it makes taxation rise. I must tell you, Prime Minister – we're heading for an ugly crisis – and I'm obliged to say this – Melville has a very heavy responsibility in this matter.'

'What could Melville have done to avoid all this?'

'Well, obviously,' said Ormston, taking up a pair of nut-crackers, 'he boobed by talking to Julia Drayford – and that was the start of the whole thing.'

The Prime Minister looked puzzled, and said,

'Julia Drayford? How does she come into it? I can't follow these complexities –'

'It isn't quite that. The whole business blew up from Melville's disgraceful indiscretion to Julia Drayford in Mrs M'landa's presence. I don't know the exact chain of gossip or who told who what. All I know is that it was lamentable of the Secretary of State to engage in loose talk. He's completely alienated liberal opinion in the country.'

'It would have happened anyhow,' said the Prime Minister. He made as if to rise, but he lacked the strength, and sat back, unwilling to reveal his weakness.

'No,' said Ormston decisively. 'It's not my view, nor is it the view of the Foreign Secretary or of half a dozen others. We feel that Melville has – in your absence – involved the Government in very grave difficulties. Worst of all, perhaps – and I'm reluctant to dwell on this – there's been little of importance till recently which hasn't reached Yates by way of Julia Drayford.'

'That,' said the Prime Minister, 'is a singularly unpleasant suggestion.'

'It is indeed,' said Ormston drily. 'Quite frankly, Prime Minister, there seems to have been a curious deterioration in Melville lately. People are noticing it. Even his manner at Question Time –'

'What about it?'

'It's strange – almost manic-depressive – one moment up-in-the-air, next moment sullen. He leaves the office without accounting for his movements – Ledbury was telling me – in confidence, of course – that there are unread telegrams – and the other day, he was singularly rude to the Governor in the presence of various secretaries. I do say most earnestly, Prime Minister – I don't want to intrude personal considerations because fundamentally I like Melville –'

He cracked a walnut, and crumbled the shell.

'– I like Melville – and I've tried to help.'

The Prime Minister was observing him with eyebrows pursed ironically.

'He seems to be under some private strain,' Ormston went on, speaking faster. 'I was told the other day that all isn't as it should be between him and Elizabeth –'

'Elizabeth?' the Prime Minister asked sharply. 'That seems very unlikely. She's the most devoted wife I've ever known.'

Ormston shrugged his shoulders, and looked over the Prime Minister's shoulders at the hills which the afternoon had turned into a primrose mist. He wanted to end the interview, and leave the foody vapours which hung in the room.

'One never knows these things for certain,' he said. 'I must say this though, Prime Minister – and I've been delegated to put this point to you. Many of us believe that if Melville continues as Secretary of State, it will be disastrous for the Party. M'landa will never renew negotiations.'

'Never is a word that doesn't exist in politics.'

'Never,' said Ormston, 'is a word that exists for individuals.'

He saw Collard's frown deepen, and felt sorry.

'It exists for us all,' he added. 'We believe that if the Opposition were able to establish in the face of Melville's denial that he had in fact made his statement on miscegenation to Mrs Drayford, not only Melville but all of us will stand condemned in the eyes of a broad section of ordinary decent Englishmen. And our own abstainers will underline our responsibility. There's a world of difference between feeling something and saying it.'

'How can the Opposition establish that Melville made this – this statement?'

'I've been told by a journalist – a trustworthy one – Anderson – that Mrs Drayford has confirmed it to Yates, and that she is prepared to stand by her statement in public if challenged.'

141

The Prime Minister moved the plate in front of him and studied the portrait of Sir John Copeland before he replied,

'And if Melville went –'

'It would save us an embarrassment – perhaps a defeat – and certainly, some millions of pounds.'

The Prime Minister rang a bell concealed beneath the Aubusson carpet and his secretary came in.

'I'm going to stay here a little longer, Charles. Mr Ormston is leaving. Will you see him off?'

He looked up at Ormston who was standing.

'Thank you for your visit, Gerald,' he said. 'I've taken your point, and I'll brood on it. It needs thought. I'll have to reflect. It's very important – very.'

When Ormston had gone, his two nurses came and helped him to the hammock on the terrace. His youngest, two-year-old grandchild, who had been playing on the lawn, came stumbling and picking himself up, closely followed by a nanny, who said,

'No, Anthony, you must leave grandfather alone.'

The Prime Minister waved her away, and for a few moments the old man and the child contemplated each other gravely. At last, the child said something unintelligible.

'What did he say?' the Prime Minister asked the nanny who was standing awkwardly near by.

'He said, "Music".'

'Music?' the Prime Minister asked. Then he said, 'No, my boy. I can't give you music. The Duchy of Lancaster, the Chairmanship of the Coal Board, a Governorship, perhaps a bishopric – but not music – not music.'

The boy continued to look at him with serious eyes, and repeated,

'Music.'

'The time for music is over,' said the Prime Minister. 'Why should he want music?'

'He likes music,' said the nanny. 'He calls the television music.'

'You've given him the impression that I'm a television set?'

'Oh, no, sir – perhaps he thinks you look like one of the announcers.'

'You are seeking preferment by flattery,' he said to the bewildered nanny. 'Where are my daughters?'

'They're walking by the lake.'

'Well, tell them I don't want to be disturbed, and take this myopic child away.'

He picked up his grandson, and kissed him, and nanny and child hurried away like fugitives.

'When you come into Parliament, your reputation as a speaker will depend much more upon your words than upon the subject. The same matter occurs to everybody of common sense, upon the same questions; the dressing it well is what excites the attention and admiration of the audience.'

Collard began to read one of Lord Chesterfield's Letters from the pile of books at his side. The name of his father, who had given him the Letters long ago, was on the flyleaf, and for over half a century he had enjoyed and been guided by their worldliness. Was it true, he wondered, that 'the same matter occurs to everybody of common sense'? Before the days of political parties, it was perhaps true. But even in the twentieth century, there was nothing more harrowing for a back-bencher than to be called by the Speaker at the end of the day when all the men of common sense on his own side had disposed of all 'the same matter'.

He read the letter, dated December 19th.

'. . . we need not suppose that because a man is a rational animal, he will, therefore, always act rationally, or because he has such or such a predominant passion, that he will act invariably and consequentially in pursuit of it.'

'That,' said the Prime Minister aloud, 'is most certainly true.'

His father had underlined in pencil the next paragraph as if in warning to his own son.

'I will suppose ambition to be (as it commonly is) the predominant passion of a Minister of State, and I will suppose that Minister to be an able one. Will he, therefore, invariably pursue the object of that predominant passion? Sickness or low spirits may damp this predominant passion; inferior passions may at times surprise it and prevail. Is this ambitious statesman amorous? Indiscreet and unregarded confidences made in tender moments to his wife or mistress may defeat all his schemes.'

The Prime Minister laid the book aside, and shut his eyes. His father's emphasis had never been relevant to his own indulgences. But to others? He reviewed his Cabinet in his mind, and thought of three colleagues to whom the sententious warnings of Lord

Chesterfield might apply. And Melville. He had rarely known so considered and rational a man. Till recently at least. Yet how could you know a person whom you only met on his public occasions, wearing the qualities and the demeanour of his public personality? What could you know of that man who at night closes his door, switches off the light and with clenched eyes turns his face to the pillow? And what were Lord Chesterfield's precepts of conduct except a private system of public conformity which, as it proved, was ill-adapted for his own son? The Prime Minister felt exhausted. After his operation, he had been encouraged first by the surgeons and later by Broome to believe that he would be able to return to Westminster within a few weeks. A gastrectomy. What an ugly word! He had always disliked thinking of medical terms, and he had chosen to accept without analysis the assurances of his doctors. But this was endless. The days and weeks, almost months; the constant changes of programme – he had been due to visit the German Chancellor in June and the French President in the first weeks of July. All that had to be postponed. No cricket this year either. His visits to Lord's used to give him a genuine pleasure which the journalists and cartoonists had distorted into an affectation as a counter-blast to Yates the Batsman. But this year the only cricket he had watched was on the television set which from time to time was brought out with a long, snaking lead from the drawing-room and put in front of the hammock. Sometimes, his three daughters would visit him with their children – fortunately without their husbands, Vice-Admiral Peskett, Lord Barden, and Sudders. Sudders. The worst of the lot. A natural remittance man; Mrs Peskett – Goneril; Lady Barden – Regan; and Mrs Sudders – Jane – his Cordelia. The Prime Minister was feeling exhausted, and the thought occurred to him that his chief objection to dying was that Sudders would share Jane's inheritance. That was a private problem. There was the balance of payments. He hoped the trading position would improve this quarter. He had intended to talk to Ormston about Bank Rate, but the fellow had gone on and on about Melville. What Ormston really wanted was to get rid of Melville in order to make himself king. A man may fish with the worm that hath eat of a king, and eat of the fish that hath fed of that worm. The predominant passions all came to the same end. And if ambition wasn't thwarted by amorousness, in the end it was frustrated by the

144

worm. 'The worthy gentleman who has been snatched from us at the moment of the election and in the middle of his contest whilst his desires were as warm and his hopes as eager as ours, has feelingly told us what shadows we are and what shadows we pursue.' The Prime Minister dozed in the melancholy of the quotation, and then woke feeling stronger.

The lavender bushes were stirring with an incessant motion of bees, and the grass, recently cut, gave off a sharp scent that reminded him of a time, long ago, when he had stood on that very lawn early on a summer's day, listening to a cock crowing, and feeling an ecstasy which he had never known since. He could only have been six or seven, but occasionally the poignant memory still came to his thoughts, and for a fraction of a second he was able to recapture the crystal bliss of an untrammelled spirit. He breathed in deeply, and felt the morning mood return. Then he rang a handbell, and its echoes started a flight of birds beyond the fountains. Like a chorus of extras from the wings, his secretaries, nurses and grandchildren came hurrying towards him.

'I'd like tea,' said the Prime Minister, 'and when Mr Melville comes, ask him to see me in the library.'

His chorus dispersed, and the Prime Minister composed himself in preparation for Melville's arrival.

'The appetite,' he said later to Melville when they sat in the library, 'is slow in returning. They make me Lucullan banquets but I can't eat them. Do have some of these cucumber sandwiches. I can't bear to think of the nurses eating them all. Why is it that nurses always seem to eat cucumber sandwiches?'

He seemed to be waiting for an answer, and Melville made a helpless gesture with his hand. The Prime Minister had been talking to him for the past half-hour about trivialities like a doctor who distracts his patient with conversation while he studies his symptoms, prolonging his anxieties in order to make their origin more manifest. Melville scutinized in turn the yellowy eyes of the Prime Minister. Since he had last visited him, Collard seemed to have shrivelled. The intervals between his sentences were longer. Occasionally, in mid-statement, he would wander off into a fugue of silence, staring over Melville's shoulder through the windows at the hills with their constantly changing colours. Yet, from time to time, the old Prime Minister whom Melville had known in the

House would reappear – taunting, incisive, dogmatic and, despite everything, robust.

·The Prime Minister lit a cigarette and said,

'My doctors forbid me nothing except locomotion. "Eat what you like, drink what you like, smoke what you like." It sounds like the regime of a condemned man.'

Melville's eyes met his, and seeing in that second that the Prime Minister, for all his levity, was saying, 'Reassure me,' he said,

'It seems to be doing you good. You haven't looked so fit since your operation.'

And the Prime Minister repeated,

'The appetite is slow in returning.'

He paused, and added, 'Now tell me about it.'

Melville rose, and went to the window.

'There's not a great deal to say, Prime Minister,' he said, looking out. 'I've come to ask you – to accept my resignation.'

The Prime Minister's features remained impassive. With the discipline of long experience, he assumed what he called his omnibus expression.

'Why?' he asked.

'I have a twofold reason – a public and a private one,' Melville answered.

He returned to his armchair, facing the Prime Minister, and said, speaking rapidly,

'I find it hard to say this – but I have a profound sense of responsibility – guilt is the word – about Kadowa.'

The Prime Minister went to speak, but Melville said,

'Let me perhaps tell you this straight so that you can understand my feelings. When M'landa was over here, the new Constitution was virtually settled. I had done what I could for it. And that was that. Then came the dinner at Lancaster House. There's been a lot written and spoken about it – most of it lies but some of it true.'

Melville stopped, and looked at the Prime Minister's watchful expression. Then he went on,

'There are times when a man who has everything in front of him – an open goal – a sympathetic audience –'

'Or a willing woman –'

'Yes, even that – says or does something that destroys everything that he has painfully and laboriously built up. What I

146

said at Lancaster House at the end of my speech –'

'You said it to whom?'

Melville hesitated, and said,

'I said to Julia Drayford –'

'And then the gossip – I can only call it gossip – was relayed to Africa –?'

'That's how it happened, and I must take the responsibility for making a careless and odious quip in order to amuse an untrustworthy woman. That is all there was to it.'

'But the quip? Where did it come from?' the Prime Minister asked, and his eyes were ironical.

'Where did it come from?' Melville repeated. 'It was a jest – meaningless – a verbal jest, and that was as far as it went.'

'Can you say,' said the Prime Minister, 'that it was quite meaningless? That something at that moment – when you were looking at M'landa – that you didn't feel something stir in your unconscious – some old prejudice?'

Melville said,

'I am not without prejudices. I try to subdue them, and my conscious mind rejects them.'

'Of course,' said the Prime Minister, 'we all have them, but it's the characteristic of a civilized society to tame its prejudices. No, if you hadn't said what you did – and at this stage I positively do not wish to know exactly what you did say – someone else would have said something or other to put M'landa in a paddy. And don't you believe that Mr Yates and Mr Ormston don't know this as well as anybody else. There's a time for violence, and time for keeping quiet. This was M'landa's time for violence. He wanted to go out with a firework show.'

He spoke in a jovial tone, but Melville listened to him unsmilingly.

'I would like to believe that – it would make it easier for me – but I can't. In any case, there is more to it than that. I'm afraid I must talk to you about my personal affairs.'

'Are you ill?'

'No, I am well. But I must talk to you for a few minutes about something personal that reinforces my decision to resign. . . . I am going to divorce my wife.'

'No,' said the Prime Minister, looking up sharply. 'No. That's quite absurd. You're going to divorce Elizabeth?'

Melville didn't answer.

'Why, Geoffrey – for heaven's sake? Why?'

He rose unsteadily from his armchair, declining Melville's gesture of help, sustained himself half-way against a Buhl cabinet, and put the latch on the door.

'Why?' he said, returning and settling himself down with relief in the chair.

'You'll forgive me,' Melville said, 'I don't want to say any more about it.'

'A little more,' the Prime Minister coaxed him, 'a little more. Is she divorcing you?'

'No – I propose to divorce her.'

'There's somebody to be cited?'

'Yes, but it wouldn't be like that.'

'Who is he?'

'He's dead.'

'And how long ago?'

'Seven – eight years – I'd really prefer not to say any more.'

They sat without speaking, the sounds of the late afternoon sharpening the silence between them. At last, the Prime Minister said,

'You will listen to me, Geoffrey, for only a few minutes – and you'll open your mind an inch or two to what I've got to say, because at this moment it's shut tight. I've known you and Elizabeth now for a number of years. I've known you, and have great affection for you both. Elizabeth and Geoffrey! – that was always a pleasant and happy thought in my mind. It meant a couple who were well fitted to each other – who gave joy to everyone who met them together.'

Melville propped his forehead on his hand, and looked down.

'Well, it was like that,' said the Prime Minister, 'and that's how it was when I saw you together. Now you say that something that happened years ago cancels out everything else –'

'Yes – it cancels everything.'

'I see – you mean all the devotion and the experience you shared – everything cancelled?'

'Yes – it's a bracket that encloses everything and cancels it. I don't ask you to understand –'

'Oh, but I do understand,' said the Prime Minister. 'I know nothing about the episode – naturally I don't – but you say the

148

man's dead – it's all past and over – why do you want to rake it up and destroy a marriage which after all is the greater part of your life? How do you know it's true?'

'It's true,' said Melville, raising his voice and standing. 'Excuse me, Andrew, I don't want to discuss it any more.'

'No, wait a minute,' said the Prime Minister, motioning him back to his seat, 'you've told me today about two unhappy experiences with women. Come now, Geoffrey – two untrustworthy women – Julia Drayford and Elizabeth. I have an idea – let me put it to you.'

The Prime Minister's eyes had brightened with his interest in the problem.

'Don't you think,' he said, 'that perhaps you yourself create a pattern of behaviour in women that makes them untrustworthy?'

Melville shook his head.

'It goes beyond that.'

'You mean that you require your women to take responsibility for their actions – but you won't take responsibility for your own?'

'I accept my responsibility – and we must both accept their consequences.'

He looked at the Prime Minister, and added,

'I was very happy with Elizabeth.'

The Prime Minister contemplated him gravely, and said,

'Your own conduct – has that been immaculate?'

'No,' said Melville. 'But this isn't an equation – it isn't a case of wrongs cancelling each other out. It isn't even a question of abstract justice or what we deserve. It's a matter of feeling.'

'Yes – but ought you to feel like that?'

Melville shifted a signed photograph of the Turkish Foreign Secretary which stood on Collard's desk, and said reflectively,

'Ought to feel . . .? I only know how I feel.' Then, firmly, 'I'm sorry. I've made a firm resolution. I'm going to divorce Elizabeth.'

'Just one minute,' the Prime Minister repeated, and he put his thin white hand on the table. 'You can't disregard your situation in the Party and the Government.'

'I'm sorry about it,' said Melville. 'It's an unhappy accident that my personal problems coincide with the Party's.'

'That's not the point. The point is whether you're going to put

149

your personal problems at this moment before the Government's interests. A few hours ago, Ormston came to see me.' The Prime Minister was scowling, and his frailty became transmuted into visible strength. 'He wanted me to get rid of you, you know.'

'I've saved you the trouble. He'll be gratified.'

'Oh, no – he's not going to be. What he would like is to get rid of you by resignation – or if that doesn't work, he'd like just enough abstentions to get rid of us both. I can assure you he won't succeed. I'm bound to you, Geoffrey, like a Siamese twin because if you go, I go. And that's not simply because I like you but because I'm stuck with you. I've backed you on Africa. And Mr Yates isn't going to have it his own way. And I'm backing you against Ormston . . . Do you want to know why? Help me up!' he said to Melville, and Melville hurried around the table to give him his arm.

'I'll tell you why,' said the Prime Minister as they edged together towards the door. 'I think Ormston as Prime Minister would be a tragedy for the Party and the country. If I go – and I can't go on much longer – perhaps till the General Election – the man I want is you. You have great qualities and a unique opportunity to serve the nation. You're the one I've pinned my hopes on for the last two years. You're the one I'll recommend to the Sovereign.'

He stopped at the door, unlatched it, and said,

'We're going to fight them on Africa – and until then I want no more talk of resignation or of divorce. You must consider releasing M'landa and making a new start.'

'The Lancaster House speech –'

'– will be dealt with,' said the Prime Minister firmly. 'I have arranged to see Mrs Drayford.'

In the corridor a nurse hurried to offer the Prime Minister her arm.

'Not a word about either matter,' said the Prime Minister. 'Not a word.'

'I will leave the arrangements till after the Debate,' said Melville. 'I can't change my mind.'

The nurse listened with curiosity.

'We'll see,' said the Prime Minister, 'we'll see. Don't make hasty decisions. There'll be nothing about it at the Cabinet tomorrow.'

Melville looked quickly at the nurse, and said,

150

'I will discuss it with you again.'

He walked from the house through a sun-dappled avenue of poplars to the circular drive where his car was waiting. He tried to imagine the Speaker saying in his casual voice, 'Prime Minister', and himself rising to the Despatch Box; but another image obtruded itself. The summer afternoon. The darkened room. The dangling hair. And the pale sweating forms moving on the bed in sympathy.

13

In the evening, the Prime Minister received his third visitor of the day. A single lamp was lit on his library table, and he himself sat in an armchair with a plaid rug on his knees.

'It's a mistake,' he said, 'to imagine that we're living in an entirely philistine age. I would say that there is more scribbled, daubed and hacked today than at any time in history. More literacy to begin with. The individual patron has gone, but the collective patron has taken over. The artist nowadays is weighed down with scholarships, grants and commissions. We live in an age of credulity, not of philistinism. *Omne ignotum pro magnifico est.* Our deference to culture has become so excessive that we accept any exotic mannerism as art. And the fraudulent thrives.'

Mrs Drayford sat listening to his mumbled monologues waiting for the Prime Minister to explain his sudden invitation. She had known him long enough to understand his discursive table talk which he would suddenly interrupt with a harsh statement of some political purpose while his listener's attention was straying. But he was taking longer than usual to come to the point. She had already smoked four cigarettes in succession. It was nearly dinnertime, he hadn't invited her to stay, and she was wondering how she could get the old man to say what he intended.

'I bought a small Loiseau the other day,' she said.

'A much underrated artist,' the Prime Minister observed.

She waited for him to continue, but he seemed to sink into a doze. She watched him with a rising anger. He made her feel ill-at-ease, and she didn't like the unfamiliar sensation. She looked towards the door, hoping that a secretary would come into the room to interrupt this rather dismal *tête-à-tête*, but there was no sound except for the emphatic ticking of the slim eighteenth-century clock in the far shadows of the room. There was still some sherry left in the bottom of her glass, and she finished it, putting the glass back on the table with a decorous noise in order to awaken the Prime Minister. He didn't move, and she half-rose, seeing that one of his eyes was closed, the other half-open.

'No,' he said suddenly like a waxwork that speaks. 'I'm not dead yet.'

He opened both eyes and smiled to her, a frank, illuminating smile which uncovered the changeless essence of his face.

'Pray, Julia, take a little sherry.'

Mrs Drayford poured herself another glass of sherry, but the decanter trembled in her hand and the wine spilled over.

'It is nothing,' said the Prime Minister. 'I like the smell of the sherry cask. I like it to permeate my surroundings.'

'I'm afraid,' said Julia, lowering her face to take a quick sip of the sherry, 'you are making fun of me. Why?'

'Not fun,' said the Prime Minister, his face becoming grave. 'I want to help you.'

'To help me?' she asked cautiously. 'I'm not aware that I had need of help.'

'I think so,' the Prime Minister said slowly. 'I think you do. I believe you know a fellow called Anderson – the political correspondent.'

'Yes – slightly. My husband knows him better than I do.'

'That is exactly the point,' said the Prime Minister. 'I have a lot of regard for your husband.'

'I'm afraid I don't understand,' said Mrs Drayford stiffly. 'I believe Anderson is dining with my husband in the next few weeks or so.'

'Yes,' said the Prime Minister quickly, looking at Mrs Drayford from under his grey eyebrows, 'Anderson came to see me yesterday.'

'And –'

'What I'm going to tell you, Julia, is of course strictly confidential. It's simply this. The Gradwell Press has got on to the idea – it's too far-fetched for words, but you know what they're like – that you are having improper relations with Mr Yates.'

His gaze didn't move from her face, and she returned his glance steadily.

'It's an absurd lie,' said Mrs Drayford.

'Of course it is,' said Collard. 'I told Anderson that I couldn't imagine you having anything to do with a man who is notoriously unreliable – the sort of man who is probably as promiscuous and squalid in his private life as he is in his political attachments. I told Anderson I couldn't believe it.'

Mrs Drayford rose, and said,

'This is a very distressing conversation. I hope you'll allow me to leave.'

'Please sit down,' said the Prime Minister. 'I have a little more to say. My concern is to protect you.'

'I have no need of protection,' said Mrs Drayford sullenly, still standing.

'Yes, you have,' Collard said sadly. 'You have indeed. Gradwell, who dislikes Yates –'

'What has that got to do with me?'

'– with a fervour which probably has a personal origin, has been keeping a dossier of your meetings with Yates, reinforced by photographs – almost respectable, I hasten to say, for young lovers – less so for – for less young ones. He wants to publish it all.'

'How beastly!' said Mrs Drayford. 'How unutterably beastly!'

'How beastly, indeed!' said the Prime Minister cheerfully. 'It is typical of my friend Lord Gradwell.'

'I don't mind – I really don't mind for myself – I'm only sorry for him.'

'For Gradwell?'

'No.'

'Ah, Yates – it would be ugly. It would have a sad effect on his public image – very sad. And it's a kind of political warfare I dislike. Then, of course, there's your husband –'

Mrs Drayford put her gloves in her handbag, and said quietly, resuming her seat,

'What are you asking me to do?'

'That,' said the Prime Minister, 'I will tell you later.' His voice became stern. 'But in the meantime, keep away from Yates till after the debate. Don't talk to him even by telephone.'

He hobbled around the table with his shawl trailing on the

153

floor, and patted her on the shoulder.

'And don't worry about Gradwell. I have spoken to him severely. He has promised me – and in these respects he's a man of honour – not to whisper a word or publish even a snapshot of you and Yates. Not without my permission –'

She looked up at him with a frown, and he added,

'– which naturally I withhold.'

In an easier tone, he said as she rose,

'Tell me, Julia, how would Edward like to be an Ambassador – or some such thing?'

She said,

'This is the hot and cold treatment.'

'Yes – that's it,' said the Prime Minister. 'I have an idea which I must discuss with your husband. I think he can help me with M'landa.'

'In Africa?'

'Yes – both of you. I think that on the banks of some steamy African river you might see Mr Yates in a different perspective.'

She smiled ruefully as he pressed her hand.

'I hope you will stay and dine,' said Collard, smiling happily and pressing a bell, 'but before we do so, there's something I would like you to put in writing for me.'

Palethorpe, one of his secretaries, entered the room, and the Prime Minister said, 'Mrs Drayford is going to write me a letter. Perhaps you'll stay to refresh our memories if necessary.'

They were walking along an endless shore. Melville could hear Sylvia's voice from afar and then Elizabeth began to recede like a figure seen from a liner as it leaves the quay, her lips moving, soundless, and in his sleep, held down by a powerful hand, all his limbs paralysed, he tried to shout to her and he knew that it was a dream from which he had to waken himself. He tried to shout but the huge weights pulled him down like a corpse into waving weeds. He tried to fight his way free, and he groaned, as he rose into light with the hand on his naked shoulder.

'Wake up, darling, wake up,' she spoke urgently, though she was shaking him gently. 'You were having a bad dream.'

He was sweating and he dug his fingers into the pillow while he felt for the lamp switch of the unfamiliar room.

'What is it?' Helen said in her soft voice, and its sound calmed his terrors and the panic of the blackness.

She stretched across him, and he felt her breast against his face, its heavy curve and hyacinthine smell stirring a new desire.

When she switched on the bed-lamp, the pale grey curtains, the blue carpet, the Daubigny on the left-hand wall, the white Regency looking-glass facing them came into his consciousness as the *décor* of a new existence. She pillowed his head against her shoulder, and said, distracting him,

'Look how sweet they are – the *putti* – rocking up and down on the see-saw.'

He gazed idly at the plaster frieze, and said,

'It's a playful frame. We look like a French engraving.'

In the looking-glass, he could see her inclined over him with her hair drooping a little over his face, her short nose just visible, and her bare arms encircling his dark face and shoulders.

'I like to look at you,' she said.

'No – you. You're the most beautiful woman I've ever known.'

'You're a flatterer,' she said conventionally. 'But I like to hear you say it.'

'I don't want to leave you,' said Melville. 'What time is it?'

She reached for the travelling-clock at the bedside, and he drew her on top of him.

'You mustn't,' she said, laughing. 'I can't tell you the time if you behave like that. In any case, it's unsuitable for a Privy Councillor.'

'Privy Councillor smothered by actress!'

'Yes,' she said, 'it would make an interesting headline . . . It's nearly one o'clock. What are you going to do?'

'I'd better go, Helen,' he said. 'I don't want to.'

He lay back with one arm behind his head, while with the other he drew her against his chest. They rested for a few minutes, till he said wearily,

'I'd better get dressed.'

She didn't move, and he felt her quick heart-beats beneath his hand.

'You know I love you,' she said.

Melville kissed her head, and said,

'It's a word I hate.'

'Love?'

'Yes – love.'

155

'Why do you hate it?'

'I hate it because it's like an inflated and bogus currency. It's used by too many people.'

'I love you,' she repeated thoughtfully. 'I loved you since I first heard you speak at the Royal Society – I loved you when we went away to Cap Estel – that was the happiest part of my whole life – and I loved you when I married. I loved you when I made love with other men, and I love you now.'

'You loved me when you made love with other men? Explain that to me, Helen. I want to understand.'

He turned to her eagerly and kissed her mouth.

'Explain it to me – how could a woman possibly love one man and sleep with another?'

'In my case,' she said simply, 'there was no option. You dropped me – without warning after we came back. You wouldn't talk to me when I telephoned. You didn't answer my letters – except to ask me not to write. All that humiliation – but I didn't really mind it. I had no pride or anything like that in relation to you.'

'But you slept with others?'

'In the end – yes. When I saw it was all hopeless. It was a kind of self-destruction. I wanted to debase the things I had valued with you – everything including our love-making and our secret words and private things – I wanted everything to be blotted out and spoilt – all my memories and myself as well.'

'And then?'

'Then,' she said, and looking up, he saw that her face had become youthful and bright, 'all of a sudden, it was like recovering from an illness. It was sometime after my divorce. One day in early April, I was walking down Dover Street – and I suddenly thought, "Why am I wasting my life on these dreadful, second-rate people?" And I was like someone who decides to give up drink – and really does. It had all been so joyless. And I felt free – and as soon as I felt free, I felt happy.'

'And you forgot me?' Melville asked, and his vanity urged him to hope that she would deny it.

'No,' she said, 'I went on loving you. But it had become better, less painful. I read about you in the papers, as if you were a person outside myself. But sometimes, when I saw you on television – everything you did – the movement of your hands –

the way you say "indeed" – that was a pang. And then, I used to yearn for you and think, "If ever he wants me, I'm here." It's shameless – but I'm not ashamed.'

'But if you love someone, how –?'

'Have you really never loved, Geoffrey? All the women you've known – never, never?'

The vague faces of the past presented themselves to him as for an inspection. He'd forgotten most of their names. In France, South America, London – a long time ago. Once upon a time there had been women who had troubled him briefly. For a few weeks, a few months. The places, the voices, the scents – he couldn't even remember them. They'd come and they'd gone. Until he'd seen Helen at the party, he'd forgotten her too.

'No,' he said, 'not what you mean by it.'

He sat for a few moments on the edge of the bed, and she asked,

'Can I get you anything – a drink, cigarette?'

'No, darling Helen,' he said, 'nothing at all.'

'Are you sure you want to go? Won't you stay and leave early tomorrow?'

Melville gave a half-smile.

'I'm shackled to a detective,' he said. 'He's waiting outside to make sure I come to no harm from M'landa's friends. I can't have him shivering all night.'

She joined him on the covers, drawing her long legs beneath her.

'I've been very good, haven't I?' she said. 'I didn't ask you any questions.'

'No,' he said.

'I don't know why you're so unhappy. I hate you going out like this.'

'It's all right,' he said, and began to dress. 'I'm not complaining.'

'No,' she said, taking his hand, 'you're not complaining. But there's something terribly wrong. Won't you tell me?'

He disengaged his hand, and said,

'No, Helen, I can't tell you. There are some things I'll never tell anyone.'

She put her arms around his waist, and laid her face against his back, and said reflectively,

'I wonder, Geoffrey – have you ever thought of giving up Parliament? Do you think you might be happier if you did something else?'

'No,' said Melville. 'I love the House of Commons – I've been there so many years – much longer than I was at school – much longer than I've belonged to any club – or anything else.'

He paused, and then said,

'It's strange – when I came into the House as a young man, I had never even attended a debate. At first, I thought I was in a cathedral.'

'It's the dim, religious light,' said Helen.

'And then in the Chamber, I thought the House was a bear-garden. And after that, I sometimes felt that it was like Versailles in the eighteenth century – a great court full of intrigue and hangers-on revolving around the sovereign.'

'How do you think of it now?'

'Now,' said Melville, bending to tie his shoe-lace, 'now I think it's unique in the world – there's never been anything like it before and no one can imitate it now.'

'That's rather superior, isn't it?' Helen said, lazily kissing his shoulder.

'Yes, it is,' said Melville, 'but it's true. You see, we have the ingredient of time. We had our revolution centuries ago, and since then we've been working with history. Parliament has somehow created itself. It has adapted itself as we've gone along.'

'I like being taught history, like this. Come and lie down again.'

'No,' said Melville, following his thought. 'I will tell you one other thing about Parliament. It has a lot of ordinary men and women – most of them intelligent in some way, most of them hard-working and sincerely devoted to their causes, and all of them with ordinary human strengths and weaknesses. But there's some mysterious quality about Parliament as an institution that elevates those who belong to it – certainly when they carry out their public duties.'

'And their private ones?'

Helen released her arms from his waist, and Melville said,

'Those we have to debate with ourselves.'

She put on a dressing-gown and walked slowly with him to the door, his arm around her shoulders.

'You'll see me again?' she asked timidly.

'Yes,' he said, kissing her. 'I'll see you again soon.'

But they both knew that what he had said was untrue.

The detective fell in behind him at a distance of about fifty yards, and as he walked through the deserted streets he could hear the echo of his footsteps. Melville had driven straight from Greystoke to Helen Langdale's house in Swan Street. They had gone to bed in the evening, and had stayed there till the early morning. In the darkness, the agonized nerve had been soothed. But before he left her, the torment had already come awake.

Elizabeth! He had condescended towards her. She must have been amused. He had patronized her. He caught a glimpse of himself in a shop window, and repeated aloud to his image, 'She must have been amused'. He leaned for a few moments with his forehead against the cold plate-glass window, and the detective moved closer and halted.

She was always limping behind last year's fashions or floundering to keep up with the other wives. He had laughed at her affectionately. She hadn't cared. She was always self-deprecatory, but always brash. 'Don't *care* so much,' she had always recommended when he was troubled. She must have been amused. She used to run to meet him when he came from journeys – yes, run. All those years, all those years.

He walked back to the detective, and said,

'Well, we might as well walk together. What a lovely summer night. Are you a keen gardener?'

The detective said he was a keen gardener, and for the rest of their promenade he spoke to Melville about frost and composts. For camellias, he recommended a mixture of sandy peat and loam, and Melville agreed.

There was a light in his study, and he pushed the half-open door, wondering who had been using the room. From behind the green leather armchair, he could see the top of a woman's head and a dangling hand over the arm rest and he had an access of fear.

'Elizabeth!' he called out.

The figure stirred, and a voice, half-asleep, said,

'It's me, Daddy.'

Sylvia stood up, put her arms around his neck and kissed his cheek.

'You look so tired,' she said, still with her arms around his neck. 'Why do you let them work you so hard?'

Her face was pale, even her smile was pale.

'What are you doing up so late at night?' he asked. 'And why aren't you at Oxford?'

'Because this is my usual bedtime and because term is over. Don't you ever read the papers?'

'Would you like tea or something?' Melville asked.

'Something,' she answered. 'I'll have a small whisky and soda with you.'

Melville looked at her quickly, and poured out the drinks.

'I'm staying home for a bit.'

'I see.'

'You don't look pleased.'

'I'm very pleased,' said Melville. 'It's what I always wanted. Have you told your mother?'

'Yes – that's one reason why I've decided to stay. She told me you want to divorce her.'

She had crossed her legs in a matter-of-fact, sophisticated position, and she was answering his questions as if they had been put in an examination paper.

'Does that disturb you?' he asked.

'Not if that's what you want,' she said. 'I've given up my idea of going to Africa,' she went on. 'I want to go to America instead.'

'That's excellent,' said Melville, adopting her own easy tone. 'Can I do anything to help you?'

'No. Lady Faucher is recommending me for a travelling studentship under an exchange scheme.'

'What about the Africa Campaign Committee? How will they manage without you?'

'Don't be silly, Daddy. We change officers every term.'

'And Mr William Akebo?'

'He's gone back already. He's going to be a Minister – they have them young in Africa – and after all, he's a frightfully good economist.'

Melville looked at her gravely. 'I'll probably meet him in the course of my duties.'

'Not as things stand,' said Sylvia. 'I couldn't persuade him that you insist on showing the worst side of your character to people. . . . She's desperately miserable.'

Melville didn't answer.

'I'm sorry for her,' she went on. 'I always wanted her to go away. But now, I no longer do. But I'm more sorry for you.'

They drained their glasses, and Sylvia said,

'Daddy.'

'Yes.'

'Can I come to the debate next week?'

He looked up in surprise.

'But you've always loathed debates. Why do you want to come to this one?'

She hesitated, and said,

'I want to hear you speak. And I want you to know – it wasn't that I didn't like debates. It's just that whenever there was an important one, you naturally gave the ticket to her – and so I pretended, I suppose, that I wasn't interested –'

'Of course I'll get you a ticket – and besides, this is a very important debate.'

'Is it true that if the majority falls below ten the Government will have to resign?'

'I don't know about ten,' said Melville. 'A lot of abstentions would mean that the Opposition's vote of no confidence would be reinforced from our own Party's.'

'But the situation itself,' Sylvia asked. 'That *is* better, isn't it?'

'It's uneasy,' said Melville. 'There's been a sort of truce till the debate's over. Then, something different will start up.'

'Something worse or better?'

'It depends on how M'landa views the debate – what sort of mischief the Opposition and your friends make.'

'I can't help it,' Sylvia said, standing. 'I agree with them more than with those frightful people at your last conference. But that isn't what I'm concerned about.'

'What are you concerned about?'

'I'm concerned about you. You're not looking well, and you're unhappy – there's mother – everything all coming together – and I want to be of some use, but I don't know where to begin. Please help me!'

She picked up a book, opened it and put it down.

'Please help me!' she repeated. 'It's so bewildering. I feel that I'm to blame in some way for all this –'

161

'In what way?' Melville asked sharply.

'I don't know,' she answered miserably. 'I really don't know. Perhaps something I said or wrote – I want you to be happy, not like this.'

'Tell me,' he said reflectively, 'tell me –'

'What?' she said, and her eyes had begun to brim with tears. 'What do you want to know?'

'I want you to tell me' – she looked at him in a rising panic, and he ended – 'I want you to tell me what time you want the tickets for.'

She put her arms around him, and her face against his chest, and held him closely while he laid his hand on her head. The clock chimed the half-hour, and he held her away from him and wiped her eyes with his handkerchief.

'You must go to bed,' he said.

They smiled to each other, and he said, 'I like it when you're home.'

14

'Hats off, strangers!' the policeman shouted, simultaneously removing his own helmet.

The turmoil of the Central Lobby fell into an orderly hush, and the semi-circle of spectators narrowed in curiosity as the platoon of the Speaker's Procession advanced in step from the Library Corridor on its way to the Chamber – first the Usher, then the Serjeant-at-Arms, proudly carrying the mace, then the Speaker, bewigged, erect and dignified in his eighteenth-century dress, with his train-bearer, his secretary and his chaplain in attendance. Their feet trampled the stone floor like those of a guard going on duty, and the inspector of police raised his arm to prevent the crowd from pressing forward too closely.

When the procession had passed, the visitors, who included an awed party of schoolgirls, a group of German journalists, guests of the Central Office of Information, a dozen American tourists, three African chiefs in native dress, and numerous lobbyists from the Africa Campaign Committee, relaxed into eager conversation, and moved up to the barrier where another policeman was inspecting the signed admission orders with their assurance that the visitor would not introduce a camera or a musical instrument into the Chamber or interrupt the proceedings or create any other form of disturbance.

'Spea – ker at pray – ers!' a policeman wailed from the Members' Lobby.

'What's that, sir?' a schoolgirl asked Parsons who was conducting the party. Parsons stuck out his belly, and smiled. He regarded himself as an authority on Parliamentary institutions, and no honoured jest had ever escaped him.

'It's prayers, my dear,' he said. 'The Speaker takes a look at the assembled Members, and then he prays for the country.'

He began to laugh before the schoolgirls understood his point, but soon they too joined in, their soprano laughter rising above the arrival and departure sounds of the Lobby.

'There's always the next Election but three,' said Anderson who had approached the group.

'Yes,' Parsons muttered, spreading his legs. 'I attach great importance to the rising young voter. Besides they've all got a parent or two.'

'You might be busy soon.'

'Electioneering?'

'Yes.'

'I wouldn't be surprised,' said Parsons. 'I've been doing some arithmetic, and I reckon that if Gore does his stuff, the majority might be down to six – perhaps even less.'

'I don't give it so little,' said Anderson. 'My guess is twenty-three.'

'Nothing like it,' said Parsons. 'You mustn't under-rate your young men, you know. They've got nothing to lose. They weren't included in the Government changes. They're too young for baronetcies. Life peerages don't interest them. All they want – and I'm leaving out their convictions – is to do something – and do it fast!' He chuckled. 'You ought to hear Gore in the Library. Livid with Ormston. Furious with Melville. He goes about quoting Burke.'

'That's very dangerous,' said Anderson, shaking his head. 'When a politician starts quoting Burke, it can mean only one thing. Trouble with his constituency party –'

163

'– or with the Whips.'

'I can tell you,' said Anderson in his confidential Lobby voice, drawing Parsons away from the schoolgirls, 'Scott-Bower's had them in one by one this morning – I watched them coming out with tears in their eyes. But whether that's because the Chief Whip spanked them or appealed to their better selves, I wouldn't know.'

They were joined by Lovell, of 'Behind the Talk'. He had an excited air, and asked, 'Heard anything?'

'Nothing,' said Anderson.

'The Cabinet's still sitting – they've been sitting for four hours.'

Parsons shrugged his shoulders.

'They've had it coming to them – Melville especially. . . . Oh, well, back to the constituents. Keep it under your hat,' he added, with an admonitory wink to Anderson.

The two journalists followed Parsons with their eyes as he assembled his party of schoolgirls, and led them with a satisfied air in the direction of Westminster Hall and the crypt.

'He's not very pleased with me at the moment,' said Lovell. 'He told me a secret the other day, and I didn't leak it.'

'Actually,' said Anderson, 'he isn't as stupid as he sounds. The manner's a bit shaggy, but the bite's rather dangerous.'

'Treats journalists like lamp-posts,' said Lovell, carried away by the metaphor. 'Can't pass one without stopping.'

'All right,' said Anderson, raising his hand. 'We're beginning to sound like a couple of grave-diggers in Shakespeare.'

Lovell turned cautiously around, and said,

'I hear Melville's going.'

'What makes you say that?' Anderson asked.

'Well, you know Ormston went to see the P.M.'

'Well?'

'He gave him an ultimatum. Get rid of Melville – or else.'

'Would you like to bet me a small sum that Melville won't go?'

Lovell grinned, and said,

'A large sum, if you like. I'm making a book on it.'

'Two quid – evens.'

'Right you are,' said Lovell, still grinning. 'You'll lose it. I've seen Yates.'

'I've seen the P.M.,' said Anderson. 'If Melville goes, he'll go with him.'

'That may well be,' said Lovell. 'It's going to be an interesting debate. There's a queue outside as long as the Embankment.'

They walked over to a leather bench, observing the constant movement of Members, guests, constituents, policemen, secretaries, messengers and sightseers.

'It's like Piccadilly Circus,' said Lovell. 'If you stay here long enough, you can see anyone you like.'

They watched a secretary in a tight skirt clicking with short steps over the tessellated floor on her way to the post office.

'Why,' asked Lovell, 'do they wear twinsets in summer? And why do they hug themselves as they walk?'

'It's cold in Westminster Hall,' said Anderson solemnly, 'and they get lonely.'

The wives of three Cabinet Ministers arrived in a group, and the policeman at the barrier ushered them through. They were followed by Mrs Ormston, tall in a flowered dress and accompanied by a nephew. They paused briefly to chat with a Junior Whip, and Mrs Ormston's clipped voice sounded clearly through the murmur of the visitors in the Lobby.

'Well,' she said, 'are they all present?'

'They will be,' said the Junior Whip with some unction. 'We're flying four back from the States, one is coming with a nurse, and Freeborn is arriving in an ambulance.'

'You're not serious,' Mrs Ormston gasped. 'It'll kill him.'

The Junior Whip laughed.

'It's a noble death,' he said. 'Fallen in the Aye Lobby for Whips and Country. What more could a back-bencher want? Actually, he's only got a broken leg. We'll put him on a chair, and I'll walk through the Lobby for him.'

'Like running for someone at cricket,' said Mrs Ormston. 'How British it all is. I suppose Gerald's opening?'

'You've got Newman first,' said the Junior Whip.

'I adore Newman,' said Mrs Ormston. 'He makes me feel such a sinner. I mustn't miss a moment.'

When Newman, the Leader of the Opposition, rose to speak, the Chamber was already fairly full. He passed his hand over his forehead and leant with his elbow on the Despatch Box as he waited for the cheers of his supporters to subside. The Government back-benchers joined ironically in the cheers, and Ormston crossed his legs on the table and smiled. For the last two

165

years, the performances of Newman in debate had steadily become less effective. With his stiff white collar, his silver curls and his aquiline nose, he had the air of an elderly boulevardier, although one commentator had described him as 'an Assyrian bas-relief in action'. In his youth, he had been a trade union official whom a by-election, a safe seat, and the Party's set-back in the 1930s, had steadily prodded upwards. He had no enemies because he never said anything to deserve resentment. And everyone agreed that he was a man of high moral principles. On the Government side, it was customary to say when dissenting from his views, 'With great respect to the Right Hon. Gentleman who speaks with such deep sincerity . . .' To have omitted this tribute would have been like failing to ask for the indulgence of the House when making a maiden speech. He was, indeed, a professional of sincerity, and like the word 'widow' in Finance Debates, the introduction of Newman into any debate on moral principles was always enough to silence the scoffers. Politeness did not, however, extend as far as attention. When Newman opened his mouth, it was usually a signal for a lazy drift to the Tea-Room, the bar or the Smoking-Room. In the Chamber as in the Party, Members assumed that Newman's job was ceremonial until the time when Yates was ready to take over and he himself would go to the Lords.

But after he had been speaking for a few minutes, the Government back-benchers began to become restive. This wasn't the familiar Newman, deferential, exchanging jests with the Government Front Bench, angry with evil and invoking the good 'of which neither side of the House has a monopoly'. Newman was talking about the role of Africa in world affairs.

'Within the last ten years,' he said, 'the map of Africa has changed so that our fathers would not recognize it. And in ten years from now, the Africa we know today will have changed – economically and politically – as radically as it has changed in the last ten years. But there are Right Hon. Gentlemen opposite who, with an obstinacy which is equalled by their obtuseness –'

There were cries of 'Oh! Oh!' from the Government benches.

'– insist on looking at Africa as if it were the Africa of Rhodes. They cling to their Imperial dream as if it still was valid today. But I can assure the House – and I say this from my own experience when I was Minister – too briefly' – he ignored the smirks – 'too briefly, I'm afraid, to realize all the projects which I

166

and my Hon. Friends had for the advancement of the African peoples – I assure the House that the new Africa isn't the old Africa.'

The smiles opposite him grew broader.

'Right Hon. Gentlemen may smile,' he said, pointing an accusing finger at Ormston, 'but what will the effect be in Africa when it is known that during a debate in which we, the Opposition, demanded an inquiry into the massacre at Kadowa' – amid the cries and counter-cries he forged on – 'Yes, there's no other name for the shooting down of over one hundred unarmed Africans, Right Hon. and Hon. Gentlemen opposite sat laughing on the benches?'

Ormston, white-faced and with his lips pursed together, rose to interrupt him. Newman yielded to him at once.

'I'm obliged to the Right Hon. Gentleman for giving way,' Ormston said. 'Let me assure him straight away that if he observed that some of my Hon. Friends were smiling, it was certainly not at the tragic events at Kadowa with which my Right Hon. Friend' – and he indicated Melville sitting next to him – 'will be dealing later tonight. For the time being, I will only say that my Hon. Friends were smiling with satisfaction at the Right Hon. Gentleman's confirmation –'

Newman nodded his head appreciatively.

'– that the new Africa isn't the old Africa.'

'Mr Speaker, sir,' said Newman, turning on his elbow away from the delight of his opponents, 'the Right Hon. Gentleman has responded to these grave developments with an uncharacteristic flippancy . . .'

He then settled down to a protracted analysis of the Industrial Finance Corporation which would help the cocoa, timber, and sisal industries. It would work hand in hand with the Development Corporation and half of its directors should be Africans. Through the Registrar of Co-operative Societies, it would make advances to approved co-operative enterprises setting up secondary industries.

During this economic passage of his speech which was listened to respectfully by the specialists in colonial affairs, the benches behind him started to thin. The Industrial Finance Corporation was one of Newman's favourite themes, and his supporters had heard it all before.

As if sensing that he was losing his audience, the Leader of the Opposition put his notes down, and braced himself for his peroration.

'We meet today, sir,' he said, facing the Speaker, 'in circumstances of great anxiety. I do not speak merely of our trading position which has suffered so grievously because of the Government's inept policies in Africa, and the sense of outrage, translated into the threat of economic boycott, which the Afro-Asian group has already expressed at the United Nations.

'No, sir. There is a greater issue at stake. Nations, like individuals, have to be able to look at themselves in the mirror of their conscience each today with the certainty that they are worthy of self-respect as well as of the general respect.'

Melville, who had listened to Newman's droning voice with indifference to the sense of his remarks, looked up.

'Our national greatness,' Newman went on, 'has always lain as much in our moral strength as in our material power. Can the Right Hon. Gentleman – can the Secretary of State – say that after Kadowa – Kadowa which like Guernica and Sharpeville has entered our language as a term of shame – can they say that Britain's reputation and self-respect has not been dragged down? Sir, I believe that there are Hon. Gentlemen opposite who have grave doubts about the Government's policies. I have heard reports that some, led by the Hon. Gentleman the Member for Bradley' – Gore folded his arms and looked blank – 'will not find it in their conscience tonight to vote against our simple Motion of Censure which in their hearts they must approve.

'Let that be as it will. Tonight's vote will be our demonstration that the discredited policies of the Government in Africa as elsewhere stand condemned by what is best in the nation. Sir, I beg to move.'

The cheers which swelled up as Newman sat down were challenged and at last enveloped by the louder cheers of the Government supporters as Ormston rose to reply. He advanced to the attack quickly, his voice light and unruffled.

'. . . a characteristic speech by the Right Hon. Gentleman the Leader of the Opposition – sincere, and, of course, a little emotional – and that is understandable; factual – which is as it ought to be; and inaccurate, which is perhaps most characteristic of all. Consider, first of all, his figure of casualties. One hundred and twenty-six is a large figure. It is a figure which rightly produces a sense of shock, and that no doubt is what the Right Hon. Gentleman wanted to produce. Indeed, he has used it in the country as the number of Africans slain.'

Newman nodded his head in agreement.

'But those figures,' Ormston went on, 'are what I would call Opposition Truth rather than truth –'

'On a point of order, sir,' said Parsons, rising from below the gangway, 'is the Right Hon. Gentleman under the rules permitted to impute dishonesty to my Right Hon. Friend?'

The Speaker stood, and said curtly,

'I understood the Right Hon. Gentleman to be defining certain categories of truth. Mr Ormston!'

Ormston, who had resumed his seat, rose again.

'I am obliged, Mr Speaker. My purpose is merely to correct the Right Hon. Gentleman's figures which are today being bandied about the world, and are creating an impression detrimental to Britain. The figure of one hundred and twenty-six is the global figure of casualties – including our own.'

He said the last words emphatically, and from behind him came shouts of 'Withdraw! Withdraw!'

'The Right Hon. Gentleman,' Ormston continued, 'may not withdraw today. But I hope that my correction will put an end to the mischief which has been created – not by the Right Hon. Gentleman whose sincerity and good faith I would never question – but by the enemies of Britain, by his own friends and perhaps unwanted allies, the fellow-travellers of the Africa Campaign Committee who are less anxious to help Africa than to injure the Commonwealth.

'Sir, I will turn from the events at Kadowa . . .'

In the Gallery, Anderson wrote on a slip of paper,

'Total casualties 126 – African 116 – Newman tripped on statistics – House relaxing nicely – Ormston on colonial development doing well.'

Nearly three-quarters of an hour later, Ormston, who had spent most of that time in a survey of the Government's financial policy towards the African members of the Commonwealth, said,

'Sir, whatever the future administration may be of that great new state whose birth has unhappily been accompanied by the pangs of Kadowa, I can assure the House that it will have our benevolence. And whatever Minister may be concerned with that future – he will strive his utmost to wipe out unhappy memories, and to work with the young African state for its advancement in step with Britain.'

'Whatever Minister may be concerned . . .' From the other side of the Gallery, Lovell grinned to Anderson, and there were shouts of 'Who is he?' from the Opposition. Ormston sat down to loud cheers, his face paler than usual but a slow smile appearing in his eyes as the Chief Whip muttered his congratulations.

A sheaf of Members sprang up on each side of the House, and stood waiting to catch the Speaker's eye.

'Mr Wellock!' said the Speaker, giving an ageing Privy Councillor and former Cabinet Minister his due priority.

There was a faint groan of protest from frustrated back-benchers, and they sat again, waved away with their papers by the Speaker as if he'd done some conjuring trick.

At seven o'clock Melville made his way to the oval Government Table in the Members' Dining-Room where Forbes, Mabel Walpole, Grantley and Seabourn, two of the Whips, were already seated.

'It was certainly an interesting phrase "Whatever Minister may be concerned!"' Seabourn was saying. 'No one can say that Gerald doesn't make one think.'

'Have you heard anything?' Forbes asked through a mash of salmon.

'No,' said Seabourn, ending his conversation as he saw Melville taking his seat.

Melville ordered cold tongue and salad, and examined his companions who had begun to eat busily. Mabel Walpole who usually engaged him in hearty conversation didn't even raise her eyes. Her light peroxided moustache was glistening with a French dressing, and her broad but bony shoulders were covered with a stain of freckles. Her political achievement had been based on a single principle – loyalty to power. And with the flair of a hunting dog, she knew both the master and the quarry.

Once, Melville recalled, one of his two dogs had been mauled in a fight, and as it lay panting and half-dead he had seen how his other dog, its normally inseparable companion, had approached, sniffed it and then moved disdainfully away. It was a law of nature and of politics. Too bad about the fallen! Who's next? Who's next? He would give up the house and take a flat. He'd sell their small house in the country. Forbes had a glittering eye when he spoke. That was one he wouldn't miss. *Virilissima*. Miss Walpole. She worked hard. But why? She was about fifty-eight, and ambitious.

'Glass of wine?' Waters was asking. 'What's that?' Yes. He'd have a glass of wine. Something light. A *rosé*. How do jugglers keep eight balls in the air all at once? Waters was looking surprised. He liked Waters, and trusted him. Did he? Was Waters one of them? Waters was laughing. He wasn't concerned. Perhaps he knew. He was often at the house. He'd rush to help Elizabeth on with her coat. Light her cigarettes. What time was Yates speaking? Oh, the usual time, about nine.

Miss Walpole was standing. 'All right, chaps,' she was saying to one of the Whips. 'I'm going out for some air.'

'Well, don't go far,' he said cheerfully.

'Ah,' she replied in her mezzo-baritone, 'I haven't missed a division for six months. I'm not starting tonight.'

She avoided Melville's eye, and left the table with a brisk, splayed walk.

After she had gone, the conversation became relaxed, and Melville felt again the warm companionship which he had always enjoyed in the Members' Dining-Room. 'When I was in Morocco,' said Seabourn, 'I was eating spaghetti in Casablanca when two young men – I thought first of all that they were shoe-shine boys with black boxes – rammed the things in my face and then photographed me. I complained to the P.R.O., and he said, "Don't worry. It isn't for the Press. They're from the Archives Department – they want your photograph in case you get assassinated!"'

They laughed and exchanged travel stories, ignoring the debate, till the annunciator started spelling out with its machine-gun rattle, '7.12 p.m., Mr L. Gore.'

'I think,' said Waters, 'I'd better hear what he's got to say.'

'Do,' said Melville.

'Are you coming?'

'Not yet,' said Melville calmly, pronging lettuce with his fork. 'I've heard what he has to say. Let him wait and hear me.'

'How do you think it's going, Geoffrey?' Seabourn asked.

'As you might expect,' said Melville. 'We've had the White Lobby and the Black Lobby – the settlers and –'

'The unsettlers.'

'More or less. But when the vote comes, it'll be a Party vote.'

'What about the abstentions?'

'I hope there won't be any.'

He drank his coffee, signed the bill, and hurried back towards the Chamber.

Watching him go, Seabourn said to Grantley,

'I don't know what's come over Geoffrey. He doesn't seem to click any more – it's as if he's out of touch. How can he possibly believe there won't be abstentions?'

'Well, we'll soon know. And you never know how he'll be when he goes to the Box. "Hanging concentrates the mind wonderfully."'

Melville stood for a few minutes behind the Speaker's Chair in the brown-green gloom of the Chamber as Gore spoke the last sentence of his speech.

'Our purpose is to insist that the Government carries out the African policies on which it was elected,' he said in a hectoring voice, 'and which were explicitly stated in some of our election addresses.'

There was a chorus of approval from around him.

'We seek to help not to obstruct. We will therefore –' he paused and waited for the interest to accumulate '– we will, therefore, decide on the basis of the Minister's reply to the arguments which we have advanced whether we will go into the Lobbies tonight –'

'Who are we?' someone called out from the Opposition benches.

'– the Hon. Gentleman will soon be wiser – or whether we will register a protest by abstention.'

He sat down to the cheers of a number of back-benchers below the gangway, reinforced by ironic cheers from the Opposition.

'On a point of order,' a Government back-bencher said rising. 'It's so dark in the Chamber, sir, I will have some difficulty in reading my notes if I have the good fortune to catch your eye. I beg to move for candles.'

The Speaker rose in turn, and said, smiling,

'I can give the Hon. Member little encouragement as to the first part. But for the second –' He instructed his messenger and the concealed lights gradually rose so that in their brilliant illumination a new mood came over the Chamber. It was now a quarter to eight; most of the back-benchers who would be called had spoken, and only those who would make hurried speeches in the last hour and a quarter were yet to be heard before the final speeches of Yates and Melville.

Yates hadn't stirred from his place for practically the whole afternoon and evening. He had sat, taking notes on his board, listening attentively to every speaker, unlike Melville who after hearing the early speeches had left the Chamber. Now, Members were arriving in ones and twos from the dining-rooms or the Tea-Room or the Smoking-Room. They disposed themselves with a leisured curiosity as if for a spectacle. In the arena that lay between their tiered seats their champions would meet as usual, sandbag each other, and then there'd be a vote, and everyone would go home. But tonight would be different because the vote was no longer predictable. Not everyone would go home as he had come. Neither Yates nor Melville. Nor Ormston. Nor the Government nor the Opposition.

The public gallery was crowded, and behind the Hansard reporters the political correspondents of the foreign as well as of the British Press were beginning to take their seats. Some craned forward to catch sight of Melville who was resting his arm on the Speaker's Chair, and he withdrew to his room, followed by two of his staff whom he had greeted in the Civil Servants' Box to the left of the Front Bench.

He passed through the outer office into his own room where Sir Arthur Ledbury was already waiting.

'It seems to be going quite well,' he said. Melville answered,

'I imagine they're saying the same. It depends, I imagine, on what Yates is going to pull out at the end. Was there anything else we had to run through?'

'The timing – the announcement will be at 9.15.'

'On the tape?'

'Yes.'

'Isn't that cutting it rather fine?'

Ledbury smiled, and said,

'Maximum effect. The F.O. is taking it rather hard – they don't like political appointments.'

Melville picked up the folio of official papers, and said,

'This is one they'll have to get used to. Is 9.15 the time from Greystoke?'

'No – the Press Association have it for release at 9.15.'

Melville stretched himself, and inhaled deeply.

'Well, that's it,' he said. 'Never a dull moment.'

'Not for Yates at least,' said Ledbury.

'Thank you, Arthur,' said Melville, giving his Permanent Secretary a friendly pat on the arm. 'Next time, I think, we really ought to have our Parliamentary Secretary in the Commons, not the Lords.'

They led the way, chatting, along the corridor, followed by a group of retainers with Waters in the rear. The door-keeper pulled open the door of the Chamber, and the members of the Government already on the Front Bench uncrossed their legs in a serial and clumsy motion as Melville, accompanied by a ripple of cheers which became a wave, made his way to his place next to Ormston. The time was twelve minutes to nine, and a young Opposition back-bencher who had recently been to Africa was struggling to make himself heard above the swell of conversation. All the Galleries were now full. Some Members were sitting on the steps between the packed benches. Beyond the bar next to the Serjeant-at-Arms, about twenty Members were standing, the front rank with their arms folded as if in a drill.

Yates lay back with the relaxed air of a boxer between rounds. From time to time, he gave a quick glance to the West Gallery, and then looked away again. She wouldn't come. Yesterday and today until three o'clock he had tried intermittently to reach Julia by telephone, but each time the maid had replied that she wasn't in, and he had rung off without leaving his name. It was unusual for her not to be in the Gallery when he spoke, but if she wasn't coming, to hell with her.

He was feeling confident. On balance, the debate had gone well. Gore, it was true, was so far only a Beta Plus, but the atmosphere had steadily deteriorated as the debate drew to a close. There had been an ugly scene when Dr Paynter introduced his eugenic argument, and someone else had asked Da Silva about his Portuguese origin. That wasn't a bad thing. Rows gave life to debates. It was axiomatic. The Opposition had evoked a few wild observations from the Government backwoodsmen, which would do them no good at the next Election. The Africa Group was looking uneasy. Eleven more minutes. Yates looked rapidly through his notes, dwelt for a few minutes on the page marked 'Kadowa and Lancaster House' and felt content.

At eight minutes to nine, a Whip leaned over his shoulder and handed him a letter marked Private and Confidential. Yates turned it over, frowned, opened the envelope, read the letter, stuffed it in his pocket, took it out again, re-read it, then slowly put it away, his face expressionless. Involuntarily, he looked up at the Gallery to Mrs Drayford's usual place, and his thoughts seemed to stray, but when the Opposition back-bencher finished his speech, Yates rose to his feet as if a gong had sounded.

'Mr Yates!' said the Speaker firmly above the cheers.

'Give it to 'em, Alf!' the loud voice of Bill McCullough called from behind him, and Yates half-turned and nodded amid the laughter.

'Sir,' he began, 'my Hon. Friend has given me an instruction which, in a sense, he and my other Hon. Friends together with my Right Hon. Friend, the Leader of the Opposition, have made unnecessary. For in a long experience in this House, I have difficulty in recalling any debate in which argument and emotion – and we do not apologize for our emotion on this subject – have combined so powerfully to indict a Government. There have been many interesting speeches in this debate on both sides of the House, and I have sat here, practically all day, and heard every one. Perhaps I may be allowed to offer my particular congratulations to the Hon. Gentleman the Member for Barley on his lucid and well-informed maiden speech. I do not expect to persuade him on this occasion to enter the Lobbies with us, but perhaps later in the session –'

His compliment to a Government Member was well received. The back-benchers returned his amiable expression, and Yates examined his opening notes.

'We on this side of the House regret the necessity as well as the occasion for this debate. The Government had our goodwill in accepting the recommendations of the Report on Constitutional Reform presented to Parliament by the Secretary of State in June. Indeed, it seemed that a new and sunlit era of cooperation was opening between ourselves and Mr M'landa after the bitterness of the past. Once again, it seemed that, as has happened so often, an old enemy was to be converted into a new friend.

'But, sir, the Hon. Gentlemen opposite have a curious habit of letting their cloven hoof peep out from under the surplice.'

There were shouts of protest from the Government benches.

'I'm sorry that Hon. Gentlemen opposite are so touchy,' said Yates. 'Why should they be?' he added in feigned surprise. 'If they really believed in the new constitution, why is it that since the terrible happenings at Kadowa, the old arrogant assumptions of colonialism have again burst out among the Right Hon. Gentleman's supporters with a fervour which we thought had died in the miseries of the last war? Why is it, sir, that the Secretary of State whom many of us, for all our political differences, have always regarded as a humane and enlightened man – why is it that he was able to sit at a conference, accepting the encomia of a supporter who – and I'm told that this was loudly cheered – described Mr M'landa as "the nigger in the woodpile"? Oh, yes, some Hon. Gentlemen opposite may smile. But I venture to suggest that that is the state of mind which produced that blood-stained mess of rags – the bodies of the Africans lacerated by machine-gun fire.'

Melville, who had signalled that he wanted to interrupt, rose to his feet, but Yates refused to yield.

'Give way!' shouted the Opposition in a roar.

'Sit down!' the Government back-benchers countered, matching their noise.

Amid the din, Melville could be seen angrily but inaudibly addressing Yates, who stood nonchalantly at the Despatch Box. The Speaker rose, and said, 'Order! Order!' The two front-benchers resumed their seat. 'The Right Hon. Gentleman has possession of the House. If he doesn't wish to give way, he cannot be obliged to do so.'

Yates rose and said, 'Thank you, sir. I will give way to the Right Hon. Gentleman in a moment. I only wished to add that a vote of confidence from a gathering which condones the language of racial abuse condemns those who are prepared to accept it.'

The whole of the Opposition benches united in 'Hear! Hears!' and Yates indicated to Melville that he would yield. Members craned forward to hear Melville's reply.

'I do not seek to defend the indefensible,' he said in a quiet voice. 'That the Right Hon. Gentleman should seek to stigmatize me with holding a point of view and tolerating a language which I loathe and reprobate, is to him perhaps a normal form of debate. Nevertheless, I welcome the opportunity of repudiating totally the views, the sentiments and the language used by Mr Risbury-Jones at our Conference. They are not those of our Party.'

His supporters cheered, and Yates jumped up again.

'No, it is not the language of the Party – that is to say, not the public language. But – and I will return to this before I'm through with the Right Hon. Gentleman – it reflects a mode of thought and a private manner of speech –'

There were murmurs of 'Lancaster House' from behind him.

'But first of all,' he said, indicating Gore, 'let me exculpate those who both inside and outside the House have had the courage to reject the crude violence which the Secretary of State and his supporters have offered as a substitute for policy.

'There is, sir,' Yates went on, 'a tradition of independence in our political system which even the Whips Office is occasionally compelled to admire. For my own part, I welcome in the Party opposite a revival of that spirit which we, on our side, have always encouraged and sustained. We have no Standing Orders which thwart the conscience of Members. We do not speak with one voice and vote with another. But the monolithic unity of which Hon. Gentlemen opposite are inordinately proud has never failed – till the present – to stifle the private Members opposite who have had some stirrings of doubt about the Government's blunders in Africa.

'But now, I see some hope.'

Again he pointed to Gore, who looked back at him dubiously from the crowded Government benches. 'The Hon. Gentleman has had the moral courage to protest. I trust that the other Hon. Friends who have spoken so feelingly in this debate will show that they too have the moral courage not to join the Secretary of State in the lobby in support of the policy at Kadowa. If, despite everything, they were to do so, then indeed they will stand condemned in the eyes of the House and of the nation as men who are both ready to strike the attitudes of sham rebellion and willing to accept applause for the pretence of a moral stand. Sir, I cannot believe that' – he looked at the clock above the Speaker's head – 'within forty minutes from now those Hon. Gentlemen opposite who have the opportunity of helping to record our disapproval of perhaps the gravest blunder and almost the gravest crime in our history as a colonial power, will fail to do so.

'In the short time that remains to me, let me touch on some economic problems before turning to the tragedy of Kadowa itself. We believe –'

A Whip handed him a slip of paper which Yates read as he continued to speak.

'. . . that the Industrial Bank is . . .'

His speech became slower.

'. . . of vital importance.'

He accelerated.

'But this matter is overlain in importance by the report which has just arrived – it is, I understand, on the tape, and to that extent will require confirmation – that the Governor has been recalled on indefinite leave . . .'

There was a stir of surprise in the Chamber.

'. . . that the Prime Minister has appointed Mr Edward Drayford Minister of State in Africa, that the Emergency is to be brought to an end, and that Mr M'landa is to be released and invited to proceed with the constitutional changes.'

From the Government benches came half-hearted cheers.

'Sir, these are developments of the greatest importance both because of their substance and because of the manner of their announcement. At first sight – and I could have wished for more notice in the matter though it is clearly the Government's purpose to deny us that – the Secretary of State appears to have capitulated wholly to the demands of the Opposition that the Emergency should be ended, Mr M'landa released, and normal relations begun. But I observe that the Chancellor of the Exchequer is not as happy as the Secretary of State –'

He paused and looked at Ormston who was whispering earnestly to the Chief Whip.

'Was the Chancellor aware of these changes – the recall of the Governor – the new appointment of' – his voice stuck at the name, and he added, '– the Commission's Chairman?'

Ormston nodded.

'And Mr M'landa – what have been his reactions to this

178

volte-face, to his own commuting between Liwande Prison and Government House?'

Yates' speech was petering out. On both sides, Members had begun to discuss Drayford's appointment, first in whispers and then in a rising clamour of talk which made the Speaker frown angrily and tap the arms of his chair with his fingers.

'That,' said Anderson to his neighbour in the Press Gallery, 'is the nicest bit of sabotage I've ever come across.'

'Melville?'

'No – the Old Man himself. You know his favourite tag – "In politics timing is all".'

At nine-thirty, after a final six minutes in which he was constantly interrupted by barracking Government supporters, Yates ended with the words, 'I ask my Hon. Friends, therefore, to record with full emphasis their disapproval of the Government's policy which by its muddle, its dilatoriness and at last its undignified retreat, has humbled Britain's reputation, imposed on us grievous and unnecessary burdens and left both Africans and Britons with a legacy of guilt, bitterness and mourning.'

The Opposition cheered him loudly when he sat down, but when Melville rose to reply, the applause from his own benches became a roar.

Anderson grinned across to Lovell who was looking down pensively at the scene.

At ten minutes to ten, after he had been speaking for twenty minutes to an attentive and enthusiastic House, Melville felt the physical joy which he had always been accustomed to feel when either in Parliament or at Conferences he sensed the responses of men and women to his mind and his mood.

'Of course,' he said, leaning over the Despatch Box towards Yates, 'of course, the Right Hon. Gentleman is chagrined and discomfited. We have given him what he always professed to want and what we have always wanted. We have provided the means of a new understanding with Mr M'landa. And the fact that it is in the person of Mr Drayford – a gentleman of whom Mr M'landa has said that he is privileged to call him his friend – that fact is in itself a guarantee that we are hopeful – I will put it no higher – of renewing our happier relations with the embryonic African State.

'Sir, I would wish before I end my speech tonight – and this may well be my last speech in this capacity –' he waited for the excited mutter to die down, 'I wish to offer the House very briefly a statement of faith about Africa.

'In Britain, the age of the two nations – the rich and the poor – is happily over. But in the world, the age of two mankinds – the privileged and the fed on the one side, and the deprived and the hungry on the other – that age is still with us. And we in the West, partly for self-interest but wholly for humanity's sake, must take it on ourselves to make the world one as we tried to make our nation one. The deprived and hungry of the world are mainly in Africa and Asia. In both great continents, we have affiliations and interests which require of us that we play our part in so raising the living conditions of our African and Asian brothers that we can eat at our own tables without guilt or shame.

'Sir, I will end by saying this.' He turned and surveyed the House, which had fallen into silence. 'I have served in my present office for over three years. During that time, I have seen the New Africa growing in strength, in dignity and in achievement. I hope I may be thought to have made some contribution to that advance.

'Yet, I confess, that there have been moments of failure – phases of disappointment – regrets for unrealized opportunities. There have been occasions when old and ugly manners and modes of the past have risen up to destroy in a second the patient building of years. I do not reject my blame in these matters. Nor can I stand here without recording my unhappiness at the events at Kadowa. I hope that this debate – this deeply felt, profoundly argued debate – will go out to Africa and to Mr M'landa as an earnest of our wish to purge the past, and enter a new era of cooperation, of friendship and – I repeat the word I used at Lancaster House –' he spoke the word challengingly – 'of brotherhood.'

Melville turned from Yates to Gore.

'Those who censure us,' he said, in a loud challenging voice, 'censure those hopes. I ask the House to reject the Motion.'

Sitting down amid the din of cheers, the rustle of the waving Order Papers, the congratulations of his colleagues around him and the voice of the Speaker putting the question, he glanced upwards to the West Gallery, and caught sight of Sylvia, wearing glasses for the occasion. Then the dark green of the Chamber; the

Civil Servants like witnesses in the Box beyond the Speaker's Chair; he would certainly give Elizabeth the London house; where was she? The crash of Ayes followed by the answering crash of Noes. The Chief Whip speaking in his ear, and laughing. A straggle of papers on the floor – love letters blown over a battlefield. Long ago. His first memory of Parliament included her. It was like a death. Again the roar of Noes. The first death that encloses them all. The Serjeant-at-Arms was standing. Lock the doors! Members were filing out.

'The bastards are still sitting there,' said the Chief Whip.

Gore and a group of his friends were sitting on the third bench below the gangway, some with their arms folded, spurning the clamour of the Division Bells which reached the Chamber from the corridors. Melville turned to look at them, and then looked away. He knew them. They would come.

Then, when the Speaker put the question again, and the Front Benches rose, Gore rose languidly too, and to the accompaniment of ironic cheers from the remaining Opposition Members who were queueing to go into the Lobby, walked dutifully behind Ormston, Melville and the other members of the Cabinet in support of the Government.

Waiting to pass between the clerks who were registering the votes in the Lobby, there was some muttering about Yates' speech. 'Weak,' a Welsh Member was saying, 'we should have chewed him up about Kadowa. And what about the Lancaster House speech? He just muffed it.'

At the entrance to the Lobby, the Deputy Chief Whip said to Yates, who had lingered,

'It was very good, Alf – but why didn't you have a go about the Lancaster House speech?'

Yates took the letter from his pocket which he had been handed during the debate. It was marked Private and Confidential, but Yates said, 'Read it.'

The letter read,

Greystoke

My dear Yates,

In a question addressed to the Secretary of State on the 12th, you asked whether at the Lancaster House dinner to Mr M'landa he had made an

injurious statement to a neighbour (Mrs Edward Drayford), as offensive to Africans generally as to M'landa personally.

I have inquired into this matter, and I have now received a letter from Mrs Edward Drayford confirming that the words attributed to the Secretary of State in conversation were not, in fact, uttered.

Yours sincerely,
Andrew Collard

The Deputy Chief Whip handed him back the letter.

'Clever old devil!'

'Yes,' said Yates reflectively, 'they're remarkable people. They've been governing a long time.'

He thought of Julia in Africa – a modern vicereine, happily queening it and holding court. He felt relieved. They'd both be better off in different continents. He strode on to catch the tail-end of the queue which was about to disappear between the tellers.

15

At Melville's bedside, a cup of tea had grown cold next to a pile of newspapers. He had fallen into a half-doze towards morning, and now awoke with the night's arguments still heavy in his mind. The room was unfamiliar, the bed uncomfortable. The window faced a blank wall of the next-door house, and the red curtains, fringed with daylight, were like drop curtains which would open to reveal an empty stage.

He turned on his back, and examined the bare ceiling of his dressing-room. The day stretched before him, and he didn't know what to do with it. The routine of his life, the morning conversations with Elizabeth, their engagements together, their talk of men and women and politics – that was over; and he thought of her, alone, private and inscrutable, lying in the bedroom which they had shared for so many years. It was strange to live with someone for a long period, to assume that you knew them in intimate detail – their speech, their thought, their mode of feeling – only to find that all you really knew was their speech, their

182

thought, and their mode of feeling towards you yourself. He didn't even know if she was unhappy.

He drew the curtains, and the small room filled with yellow light. It touched the book-case and the asters which Sylvia had put on the table, and the telephone, and Melville rubbed his eyes and took up the newspapers.

'Government Triumph in Colonial Debate.'

'Majority of 36; Drayford for Africa.'

'Rebellion Fizzles Out; No Abstentions.'

He began to read the report of one of the political correspondents.

'The debate which at one time had threatened to produce a clash of personalities as well as of convictions, was remarkable for the speech by the Deputy Leader of the Opposition which, beginning trenchantly, lost its cutting edge half-way through. The Secretary of State who seemed to view the preparations for his execution with some detachment, had no difficulty at all in demolishing both the hatchet-men and the block when he came to reply. Mr Gore and his supporters were taken into the Lobbies by the Whips like carted stags.'

'Melville's great Day'; with the sub-heading, 'Government Trot Home'.

There was a paragraph from 'Our Political Correspondent'.

'A curious passage in the Chancellor's speech gave rise to the belief that the Prime Minister was contemplating changes in the Government. But it was quite clear by the end of the day, that for the time being, at any rate, Mr Geoffrey Melville's mastery of the African situation is such that changes are very unlikely at the Ministry of Colonial and Commonwealth Affairs.'

Melville picked up the wadge of papers, and flung it on the floor. Then he stood in his dressing-gown at the window, staring at the blank wall opposite. After a few moments, he began to see the cracks in the cream paint; cities of ants sent out columns through valleys of cement; birds darkened the plains with a shadow of wings; a piece of stucco crumbled; the blank wall had become a landscape in ferment. Melville lay on the bed again. He didn't want to move. Elizabeth! There was nothing that could ever change it. It was final, like death itself.

The telephone rang, and he let it ring, with his face pressed into the pillow. He had wrapped the sheet around him till it was a shroud excluding the living world. Within its white cocoon, without thought, without feeling and without fear, he felt protected from the bell summoning him from outside.

The telephone bell groaned on, insisting. He flung the sheet away, and reached for the receiver.

'Yes?' he said.

'One moment, please,' a woman's voice said. 'The Prime Minister.'

'Geoffrey? Andrew here. Did I wake you?'

Melville sat up.

'No – this is just my insomnia voice.'

He heard the Prime Minister chuckle.

'I thought you were first-class,' he said. 'I've been for a walk and I've been reading Hansard.'

Melville looked at his unmade bed and felt displeased with himself that he was still unshaved. The Prime Minister's voice was strong and optimistic.

'What happened to Yates?' he asked, and Melville smiled.

'He seemed to have an attack of conscience half-way through.'

'Yes,' the Prime Minister said, 'yes. It comes from youthful indulgence in high moral tone. It catches up on you in later life.'

Melville tried to interrupt him but the Prime Minister continued,

'I want to hold a Cabinet here tonight. There are a few things we ought to talk about, and I've already told Palethorpe to arrange for the assembly and dinner. I'm returning, you know, on Thursday week.'

'I'm very pleased,' said Melville, 'very.'

His delight sprang into his voice, and he could hear the Prime Minister's pleasure when he replied.

'Thank you, Geoffrey. Thank you very much. I have always valued your good wishes. And, by the way, I want you to come with Elizabeth.'

Melville hesitated before answering.

'I doubt, sir, if Elizabeth can come.'

'Oh, yes, she can,' said the Prime Minister. 'I'm having a few of the wives.'

'I'll have to ask her,' said Melville, temporizing.

'Of course you'll have to ask her,' said the Prime Minister. 'But I want her to come specially.'

Melville heard Collard speaking to a secretary, and then he said, 'Seven o'clock tonight – I've got a lot to do. Good-bye, Geoffrey.'

'Good-bye, Prime Minister.'

He heard the telephone click, and he himself replaced the receiver. Seven o'clock tonight with Elizabeth. At seven o'clock he would arrive with Elizabeth, and they would appear in public. They would appear for their last public performance. Positively their last public performance. They would smile, and everyone would say, 'What a happy couple! Elizabeth and Geoffrey!' The telephone rang again, and now, alert, he answered it briskly. The Minister of Education was snarling his congratulations.

For half an hour, Melville drove without speaking, only glancing occasionally at the white unsmiling face of Elizabeth, who sat at his side. He hadn't wanted his official chauffeur to be the witness of their silences, and had taken his private car. He drove with his foot pressed hard on the accelerator, much faster than he normally drove because in the speed of the car he felt partly the illusion of escape and partly a challenge to his destiny. On a turn in the road, he overtook a lorry and cut in front of another car approaching from the opposite direction. Behind him, he could hear the sound of braking and glimpsed the frightened expression of the oncoming driver, tugging his wheel to the left. The sudden acceleration made his heart pound as they reached again an open stretch of road.

'I don't mind if you kill me,' said Elizabeth calmly, 'but don't kill some innocent driver.'

'I'm sorry,' he said. But he was glad that she had spoken, and slowed the car down to fifty miles an hour.

'What time are we expected?' she asked.

'About seven – he wants to dine at eight o'clock.'

'It's quite definite that we'll be back tonight?'

'Yes – he said so.'

After days of avoiding each other, the ordinary words which they had exchanged were like an intimate gesture, a communal act, and when they spoke again their sentences came more easily.

'What shall I do about the tickets for Sadler's Wells next Thursday?' she asked. 'It's for the Combined Children's Appeal.'

'I don't know,' said Melville. 'I think we'd better talk about all those things tomorrow.'

'It's as you like,' she said. 'Whatever's convenient.'

She spoke humbly. The spasms of violence had exhausted themselves, and she was waiting for him to make decisions.

'I imagine,' said Melville, 'there'll be a lot to clear up.'

'Yes,' said Elizabeth. 'If you have a few moments, perhaps we can go through the diary together – and you can let me know what you want me for – if there's anything at all.'

They had turned into a secondary road, and were now driving through long avenues of poplar trees bordering two estates.

'It's so much like France here,' she said in a conversational voice.

'Yes,' he said. 'It's very much like Fécamp – like the road to Fécamp.'

And as he said the words, he remembered his brother Robert lolling in the back with Elizabeth, while he drove with Sylvia, who became car-sick, at his side. Cigarette, Elizabeth? Here you are – have this one. Jolly old Robert! Uncle Bob looks after the picnics. They stop by the roadside under the poplars away from the hot sun and the smell of drying manure. The cicadas are creaking like mad. The grass is hot. Bob looks after the food. He's gone to the back of the car to help Elizabeth with her picnic basket. The Putney Chortle – it sounds earthy and right in the bright sunlight with the sea glittering beyond the dunes three miles away. And Robert laughing and tugging at the cork of the Beaujolais. He himself had spread the table-cloth with Sylvia. And they are all nut-brown except for Elizabeth, who has to protect her skin from the sun. It was a long time ago. Melville had been happy that day.

They fell again into silence, and once again the hand of the speedometer began to creep up as they drove towards Greystoke.

With evening, the day's stifling heat gave way to a faint breeze which blew from the lake. 'We're expecting about twenty in all,' the butler told Melville as they walked in the direction of the lawn where drinks were being served to the guests. Most of the women wore short evening dresses. But Elizabeth wore a long evening dress, red, conspicuous and strangely dowdy against the

186

background of slender fountains which occasionally threw out a spray over the lawn.

'My dear Elizabeth,' said Sir Julian Greenhill, the President of the Board of Trade, 'how very elegant you look!' He took both her hands and examined her.

'Yes,' said Lady Greenhill, 'you make us all look under-dressed.' Elizabeth eyed her slim figure, and said,

'I'm wearing this old thing because the Prime Minister once told me he liked it.'

'Of course,' said Greenhill hurriedly. 'Poor Marjorie's the slave of fashion designers. I think they must give her special prices.'

Melville and Elizabeth walked on to the alleyway of statues where Prebble-Keir, the Secretary of State for Scotland, and Rossiter, the Minister of Transport, had rested their drinks on the podium of Castor and Pollux. After they had greeted Elizabeth, Rossiter said,

'What happened to Yates last night? He seemed to fold up half-way through.'

'I don't think he likes the idea of his friend going to Africa,' said Prebble-Keir.

'Drayford?' asked Rossiter.

'That's the name,' said Prebble-Keir.

They both laughed, but Elizabeth looked at them frozenly.

'Has McIver arrived?' Melville asked, changing the subject.

'He was expected back from Rome this evening,' said Rossiter. 'How did he take the Drayford appointment?'

'He liked it very much,' said Melville. 'If the P.M. likes it, McIver loves it. It's as simple as that.'

They all laughed, and Elizabeth instinctively made to take Melville's arm as they joined a general movement towards the house, but he drew away as if by accident and she walked behind him with Rossiter at her side.

Outside the hall, a group of guests was studying the table placings, and Melville and Elizabeth joined them trying to decipher the names in the plan.

'You're drawn very well,' said the Chief Whip to Elizabeth. 'Next to the P.M.'

She leaned over his shoulder, and saw that she had been placed on the Prime Minister's right hand and Mrs Ormston on his left.

'Well,' said Mowbray, the Minister of Education, in his slow voice, 'someone's got to be on the left.' He smiled to Elizabeth, but she didn't return his glance. Instead, she joined Melville, who was listening patiently as Lady Greenhill explained to him why she preferred Positano to Portohno.

'I hope he's not going to keep us up late tonight,' said Lord Ardrossan, the Lord Chancellor. 'The only consolation for his illness was that we did at least get to bed early. I don't know how he does it. He's got a stamina like a horse.'

'One never knows,' said Greenhill, 'whether he does all that work because he's tough, or whether he's tough because he works.'

'All I know,' said Prebble-Keir who had joined the other guests waiting for the Prime Minister, 'is that two of his secretaries had breakdowns – and another two were on the way. . . . I'm getting hungry. I wish he'd get a move on. It's nearly half past.'

One or two of his neighbours looked surreptitiously at their watches, but the others regarded Prebble-Keir's observation as injudicious, and went on with their conversation. Through the open doors, the long oval table with its brilliant silver and glasses was a tantalizing promise which was underwritten from time to time by a delicate whiff from the kitchens.

'Has anyone seen the Old Man today?' the Minister of Education asked. 'Are we sure he's here?'

There was a murmur of laughter. Outside, dusk was beginning to creep over the hills, and the temperature had fallen. The conversation was still lively, but more and more frequently there were glances at the wide stairs down which the Prime Minister was expected to come.

Suddenly there was the sound of a door slamming, and Palethorpe, one of the Prime Minister's secretaries, came running down the stairs with an intent expression. He didn't stop in the hall, but rushed through the door. They could hear him running over the gravel and then they heard the noise of a car starting up.

'That's one way of resigning,' said Lady Greenhill. 'D'you think the Prime Minister's after him?'

Again there was the sound of a door being hurriedly closed, but this time a nurse came down the stairs. She stopped on the last step but three, scanned the guests, and then went up to Melville.

'May I have a word with you outside, sir?' she asked, taking him through the door on to the terrace. He looked at her anxious face, and said,

'Anything wrong?'

'I'm afraid so,' she said. 'Sister Seddon's with him now, and I've sent the Private Secretary to get Dr Holmes.'

'What's the trouble?' Melville asked.

She looked over her shoulder, and said,

'I can't say – I really can't. He was dressing, and then he rang the bell. I went in, and he was dressed completely but his shoe-laces were undone. "Shall I do them up?" I asked. And then he said with a smile, "Yes – I've been trying for the last few minutes." And then, just as I bent down, he seemed to stand up and change colour. And the next thing I knew he'd collapsed.'

'You'd better go back.'

'Yes – I thought I'd let you know – the dinner – he's unconscious, I'm afraid.'

Melville said,

'I'll tell the others – I think they'd better return to London.'

The nurse smiled, and her smile made her face ugly.

'He won't be eating dinner tonight.'

Melville said, 'Have you telephoned Sir Gregory Broome?'

'The doctor will do it when he comes, I have no doubt.'

'Do so at once,' said Melville curtly. 'Tell him I hope he'll be able to come straight away – and that if there's any difficulty with transport to telephone the duty officer at my office.'

'Yes, sir,' said the nurse, chastened.

When Melville returned, he was immediately surrounded, but he addressed himself to the Chief Whip.

'I'm afraid,' he said, 'the P.M.'s been taken ill. The staff have everything in hand but I'm afraid the dinner must be cancelled. I'm quite sure refreshment will be arranged if necessary, but I think it better that anyone who has to go back to London should do so at their convenience.'

There were exclamations of sympathy and distress from the women; the men looked solemn; and Mowbray said to Greenhill, 'Poor old chap! I think this is it.'

Ormston who, together with his wife, had gone into an ante-room to look at the Romneys, came hurrying back when he heard Melville's voice. His manner had become authoritative and commanding, and he said to the Chief Whip after he had heard the news,

'I think we'd better encourage everyone to return – we don't want them cluttering up the place. On the whole, though, I think it will be better if dinner is served – everyone's wildly hungry – they can't drive back unfed.'

'Geoffrey thinks –' the Chief Whip began.

'I'm not concerned with Melville at the moment,' said Ormston firmly. 'I think that dinner should be served.'

The Chief Whip had beckoned the steward, and Ormston, looking at the surrounding faces, said,

'The Prime Minister, as you know, has been taken ill, but I'm quite sure he will not want his guests to go hungry.'

'I'm sure he wouldn't,' Mrs Ormston echoed in her clear voice. 'So we will dine as arranged – perhaps we could cut out the first course – and only one wine.'

'Only one wine,' Ormston repeated.

'Very well, sir,' said the steward. Ormston, he knew, often spoke for the Prime Minister. He accepted his orders.

Melville flushed and went outside, followed by Rossiter, Ardrossan, Longmain and Ingleborough to await the arrival of Dr Holmes. After waiting in silence, they returned to find a slow and rather shamefaced straggle of guests into the hall, where dinner was about to be served.

'Why don't you go too?' he asked Elizabeth, who was standing at the foot of the stairs.

'I'm not hungry,' she replied. 'I couldn't possibly eat. But you must. You've hardly eaten anything all day.'

'Not now,' he said. The doctor had climbed out of his car and, accompanied by the secretary, hastened up the stairs. For the past few years he had been visiting the Prime Minister in order to make routine examinations. His name occasionally appeared in bulletins, and his anxiety had grown with his sudden fame at the age of sixty-one. Now his own face was tense and white, as he stopped on the first landing to allow his pounding heart to become calmer.

At first the Prime Minister's empty chair at the head of the table embarrassed the guests and discouraged them from conversation. Ormston sat at the opposite end, his face resolute and preoccupied, answering only an occasional question from those nearest to him. The candles blew in the light breeze from the wide-open window, but now they had acquired a ritual air. After a few murmured remarks about the Prime Minister's relapse, they made no further mention of what was happening upstairs, as if to have done so while they were eating would have been an indelicacy.

Besides, the long drive, the waiting and postponement of dinner had made their hunger obsessive. After the fish, some of the tensions began to disappear. The voices became louder, and Mowbray was heard to say,

'. . . you get to the sea near Luarca. It's exquisite. There's a kind of canyon in the hills, and the river Negro runs right through it. I do recommend it.'

And Ardrossan was saying,

'He played back instead of forward, and that was that. Mind you, he was pretty tired. Moore had made him bowl twenty-two overs the day before, and the poor chap was dehydrated.'

There was a laugh from near by, and gradually the volume of conversation started to rise.

Mrs Ormston was talking to Prebble-Keir about gardening.

'There are lots of border plants,' she said, 'that grow from three to four feet without stakes – wand flowers for example – you know, *Dierama Pulcherrima*.'

With the wine, the dinner party assumed an almost normal mood with the attitudes of sympathy and distress and the moderate voices replaced by the easy clatter of social talk.

'No,' Forbes said, 'I don't see at all how Balthazar can stay three miles. He's big, but he collapsed like a pack of cards just before the hill. Now Pas-de-Deux – that's a different cup of tea.'

'Poor old chap!' said Dawson-Pratt, prodding his *mousse*. 'He was always talking to me about Pas-de-Deux. When I met him at the Gold Cup last year, he bored the pants off me with his training system, and how he'd wished he'd bought Pas-de-Deux.'

Forbes looked thoughtfully around at two Reynolds and the Romney on the walls, at the silver-gilt sconces on each side of the fireplace and the tall eighteenth-century looking-glass and said,

'He could have afforded it.'

'But he was pretty careful, you know. Never knew what he was saving it up for.'

Forbes leaned back to allow his plate to be removed, and then he said, inclining himself towards Dawson-Pratt and lowering his voice,

'The truth is he was getting pretty ga-ga in the last couple of years. I don't like saying this but he should have stepped down at least eighteen months ago. I think the country would have been in rather different shape if Ormston had taken over last year.'

'Well,' said Dawson-Pratt uneasily, 'I wouldn't *quite* say that.'

He owed his appointment as Minister of Aviation directly to the Prime Minister who, despite the resistance of the Air Committee which would have preferred someone with experience of the aircraft industry, had plucked him from the back benches after he had made an effective speech on the Estimates. He hadn't any special liking for the Prime Minister, but, on the other hand, he didn't like Forbes or Ormston particularly. He had been in the Government for at least three months before Ormston had changed his glacial nod into a lukewarm 'good evening'.

'I wouldn't go as far as that,' said Dawson-Pratt. 'After all, he carried us through the Election.'

'That's perfectly true,' said Forbes. 'Although we did lose fifteen seats.'

Dawson-Pratt took up his coffee cup. He had always regarded Forbes as a stuffed prig with a bitchy manner who always seemed to be squabbling with the women in the Government. He could easily do without him, he thought. On the other hand, he had noticed in the House during the past few weeks that he was constantly bouncing behind Ormston through the corridors, letting the heavy brass doors swing into the faces of obscurer Members behind him with the insouciance of a leader of the field in full cry. At this rather tricky stage – Dawson-Pratt sipped his coffee and looked towards the door – he had no wish to antagonize the Ormstonites, least of all a bully like Forbes.

'I imagine,' he murmured, 'that something will have to happen.'

'Oh, of course,' said Forbes, lighting a cigar. 'Quite frankly' – his manner had become magnanimous and expansive – 'quite frankly, David – there'll have to be changes. They're pressing us hard. When a sheep like Newman starts snapping, it shows how the country's feeling. And, I'll tell you another thing. We're going to lose Merchison. I'll give you ten to one we're going to lose Merchison.'

His jaw muscles were bulging, and his cheeks were red from the Beaujolais – an inferior 'year' which the steward had chosen as suitable for the occasion.

'No, David,' he said, putting an arm around the back of the other's chair. 'Whatever happens upstairs, there'll have to be changes.'

'I quite agree,' said Dawson-Pratt. He had reflected and come to the conclusion that it was safe to agree that there would have to be changes.

'What's that?' said Forbes, leaning an ear towards Dawson-Pratt.

'I said I quite agree,' the other replied, raising his voice above the conversation.

'Between ourselves,' said Forbes with an intimate tone which flattered the younger Minister, 'there was a dinner at the New Constitutional last week – Maclennan, Carpenter and Todd –'

'That's a circulation of five million,' said Dawson-Pratt.

'It's a readership of at least fifteen million – plus television.' Dawson-Pratt waited for the conclusion, and Forbes said simply,

'They want Ormston.'

Dawson-Pratt looked around at the shadowed faces beyond the candlelight and said,

'What about Drayford?'

Forbes laughed.

'He isn't a problem. He's very much a business man, you know.'

'And Melville?' Dawson-Pratt asked.

'Melville,' Forbes began. Then he stopped, and puffed at his cigar before he went on,

'The thing about Melville is that he's a natural protégé. He's the sort of man who gets on in the world through – well, not exactly through luck but through choosing a good patron. When he got into the House, first Telfer then the Old Man took a political fancy to him – but, on top of that, he was really good-looking when he was younger.'

'He still is.'

'Ah, yes, but in those days he was outstanding. It was before he began to look like one of those American advertisements for Men of Distinction. At any rate, there was always some woman or other to help him along – but all that seems to be over. You can't be an *ingénu* with white side-pieces.'

He gulped the rest of the wine in his glass.

'What do you conclude from that?' asked Dawson-Pratt.

'I conclude,' said Forbes, 'that the P.M. is the last of the patrons. And that if he goes, Melville's had it. He's the original hollow man.'

'You think so?' said Dawson-Pratt, more comfortable now that he saw Forbes and not himself on the road to indiscretion. 'What did you think of his speech last night?'

'Speech?' said Forbes contemptuously. 'It wasn't a speech; it was a piece of ventriloquism done from the P.M.'s sick-bed. The whole thing was just a bag of tricks.'

'It came off,' said Dawson-Pratt almost to himself.

'Didn't do us any good,' Forbes said flatly. 'It won't go down well in the country. You see, the British like a man they can trust. What do you think they're saying in the clubs and pubs about his climb-down?'

'I don't know,' said Dawson-Pratt.

'Well, I'll tell you,' Forbes went on. 'They're saying that a man who says one thing in private should stick to his guns in public. Take the Ministry of Health. I had a long talk to him before the appointment was made. I told him what I had in mind – the changes I wanted to make – medicine being a family tradition and all the rest of it. Well, I spoke to him rather sharply when I was passed over, and all he could say was, "I detest canvassing".'

'That's a curious thing for a politician to say,' said Dawson-Pratt, following the example of Mrs Ormston, who was rising.

'Dishonest, not curious! The country needs a man it can trust.'

Forbes looked at his watch, and said, 'Something will have to be done.'

Outside the Prime Minister's bedroom, Elizabeth and Melville sat with Palethorpe, waiting for the doctor to reappear.

'How long has he been with him now?' Elizabeth asked.

'Half an hour,' Palethorpe replied.

Someone opened a door in the hall, and the dinner noise rose quickly, then faded as the door was closed again.

Elizabeth stood, and walked across to the landing. When she returned, she said fiercely,

'I do wish they'd shut up downstairs. You'd think it was a celebration.'

The doctor came out of the bedroom, and Melville went to meet him.

'Well?' he asked.

The doctor looked from Melville to Elizabeth, and at the disciplined expression of Palethorpe, who was standing in the background.

'Not very good,' he said, 'not very good! I must wait for Broome's opinion. He ought to be here within the next hour. I've had a message from him. We'll just have to wait – see how things go.'

'Is he speaking?' Melville asked.

'No,' said Holmes. 'He isn't speaking . . . he's in deep unconsciousness.'

He was about to go downstairs when he said, as if in an afterthought,

'Do you want to see him?'

Melville hesitated.

'I don't want to disturb –'

'No – nothing can disturb him,' said Holmes. 'Not even that' – as an outburst of laughter, quickly stifled, came from below.

'I want to see him,' said Elizabeth firmly. 'He sent for me.'

The doctor opened the door of the darkened room, and they went in quietly together. The nurse, sitting in an armchair by the bed-lamp, rose to her feet.

The Prime Minister lay in a halo of light, asleep. His hands were on the counterpane, and as they watched they saw from time to time how his fingers slowly opened and unclenched. His white hair had been neatly combed, and his face, with an earnest and absorbed expression as if wholly intent on matters beyond their concern or understanding, was turned to the wall.

They stood contemplating him, and Melville came closer.

'Andrew!' he said in a whisper. 'Andrew!'

'He can't hear you,' said the nurse in an Irish accent. 'He's far away.'

'Let me stay a few minutes,' said Elizabeth.

She was trembling, Melville saw, but her eyes were dry. She walked to the dark end of the room, and before Melville could help her brought back to the bedside a gilt chair covered with a

195

garment. It was the Prime Minister's old camel-hair dressing-gown, and Elizabeth picked it up and placed it carefully on an armchair.

While they waited, they walked in the gardens, away from the farewell voices, the starting cars and the swirls of light. The moon had begun to rise, and the lawns had turned to a cold steel-blue. From the end of the avenue, Melville looked back at Greystoke in profile against the night sky. Every room seemed to be illuminated, except for the central blackness where the Prime Minister was lying, and Melville said,

'It's like a great cruise-ship.'

'I'm so unhappy,' Elizabeth said.

It was an observation, as she might have spoken of some recent event that they had both experienced and noted.

They walked over the flagstones to the rose-garden, and there they stood by the stone dial, waiting for the other to speak. At last Melville said,

'Tomorrow I'm going to see Frank Dallow. He's a good lawyer.'

'You must do what you think best,' she said with her hand on the damp stone. 'I want you to do what is best for you. Will you bring Sylvia into all this?'

'I don't want to – it needn't be necessary. I hope you will be helpful.'

They were talking without looking at each other, and Elizabeth said,

'He looked so lonely in the huge bed – as if he was already an infinite distance away.'

She stretched out her hand to a bush, and plucked a handful of yellow petals.

'It's late for the roses,' she said. And then, 'How awful to die like that – without any family or anyone else near you!'

'They'll come – they've been sent for.'

He went up to his wife and raised her chin with his hand so that for the first time for many days her eyes were looking directly into his. She tried to turn her face away, but he wouldn't let her.

'Elizabeth,' he said, 'I want to ask you something – I want you now – at this moment – to tell me the truth.'

She stopped turning her head, and said to him,

196

'I will tell you the truth – I'll tell it to you because he's dying, and he asked me here with you –' she stopped, and then said, 'He asked me here with you to face the truth. I'll tell it to you.'

Melville released her chin, and stood away from her. Then he approached and put his arms around her, cupping her head in his hand.

'You must tell me,' he said. 'You must tell me the truth.'

'I will tell you the truth,' she answered in a voice that was like a murmur in sleep.

'Is it true –' he asked, '– is it true about you and Robert?'

She paused for a moment, and frowned. Then she said simply, 'It's true.'

He didn't remove his hand from her head, but began to stroke her hair.

'All the time?' Melville asked, looking over her shoulder at the rose-garden which was filling the air with its heavy scent.

'All the time?' she echoed in a flat voice. 'No – not all the time. That summer – it was a very unhappy summer.'

'Why did it happen?' Melville asked. He held her from him, and examined her pale face as if she were a stranger whom he'd never known.

'He was there,' she said, 'all the time – you left him with me – you condescended to me – I didn't want him but he was there all the time. In our rooms – he was there all the time. Till one afternoon – in the summer – I was resting in bed – he brought me tea – and so it began.'

'You loved him.'

'Oh, no,' Elizabeth said quickly, as if in surprise at the question. 'Not love –'

Her eyes had become frightened.

'Oh, no,' she repeated. 'It wasn't love – nothing like love. I loved you, and nothing changed. It wasn't love it was an afternoon's lust.'

'And in the evening when I came home, you greeted me –?'

'Yes.'

'– and went to bed with me?'

'Yes.'

'Why?'

'Well, I loved you. Don't you understand? I loved you.'

Her voice had become hysterical and insistent.

'And when did it end?'

He lowered his voice, and her panic faded. But his own throat had contracted as if squeezed by a hand.

'It ended,' she said, letting the petals fall to the grass, 'when he killed himself.'

'Killed himself?' Melville asked. And now the horror was swollen.

But she answered calmly,

'Yes – when he killed himself – got killed in his car.'

'And the others?' he went on. 'Broome – Linwood – Holland?' Now there could be no more pain.

She seemed to consider the question, and then she said, 'There were no others – none – not one.'

She began to walk back to the lawns, her head inclined thoughtfully to the path, and Melville followed a few paces behind.

When they reached the house, she stopped and said,

'Forgive me, Geoffrey!'

'No,' Melville said slowly. 'I will never forgive you – neither you nor him. You've taken away all those years. And he was my brother.'

There were still lights downstairs, but most of the guests seemed to have left. Palethorpe came hurrying out to greet Melville, and his lower lip was quivering.

'I'm afraid, sir, he's gone – about four minutes ago,' he said. 'Broome's been here for the last quarter of an hour. But it was quite hopeless.'

Melville ran up the steps into the vestibule. Ormston, surrounded by a group of Ministers, was saying,

'I will, of course, continue as before. I have already informed the Palace, and I will see all the papers. Naturally, I will stay the night.'

The Chief Whip caught sight of Melville, and said,

'It's a great shock but – come on, you look as if you need a drink.'

'No, thank you,' said Melville. 'I'm driving back to London.'

When they left Greystoke, a dozen journalists were already at the gate, waiting to see Ormston.

16

From inside the Abbey, the murmur of the congregation, like the sound of the sea from a cave, reached through the open North Door as far as the crowds which overflowed the pavements in Parliament Square. The August sunshine was already hot as it had been day after day throughout the unusually fine summer, and the watchers, marshalled by the police into queues and enclaves by the railings, consisted as much of tourists who had discovered an accidental diversion as of public mourners who had come to offer their homage.

The sudden grief which had come to the nation after Collard's death in July had now been changed into an acquiescent regret. For a time, it had been difficult to get used to the fact that the well-known face could no longer be associated with the office of Prime Minister. But the shock had been absorbed. Collard, actual and living, potent in making decisions and giving preferment, was now a name belonging to the past, and its very intonation had changed in the mouths of his former colleagues as well as of the general public who had once spoken it with diffidence or ambition or anger or concern. Collard was no longer a subject of argument. The organ fugue running over the assembly as it shuffled into place along the stone floors, was a reminder of transience, the flight of time and the fragility of power.

The policeman at the North Entrance opened the door of Melville's car, and together with Elizabeth he walked towards the arc of photographers who poised their cameras like weapons. Elizabeth half raised her hand to ward off the cameras, and then they were out of the sunlight within the Gothic arch, followed by the murmur of Melville's name, and an usher in morning coat was leading them to their pews. Melville drew aside to let his wife pass, and she half-smiled to him, gratefully. His own face remained impassive and unsmiling as they both knelt for a few seconds, his eyes accustoming themselves to the shadowed stone. When he looked around, the faces displaced from the Parliamentary scene looked unfamiliar. Scott-Bower, Forbes, Ormston, Yates, Ardrossan, Longmain, Newman, Parsons, Greenhill,

Drayford, the notables and ambassadors, peers and commoners – their expressions were composed in a dolorous harmony with the music. Some of them had hated the Prime Minister with a long resentment of his barbs or of his neglect. Today they could join in praise. He was safely dead.

The Order of Service read,

'In memory of Andrew Carlyon Vanbrugh Collard, P.C., C.H., M.P.', and Melville tried to recreate in his memory the rubicund face he had first known, laughing before its jests were ended – Collard, wise, enduring, drinking whiskies and sodas in the Smoking-Room after the House had risen. Instead, he saw the frail dry hand, the eyes searching for reassurance. The remembrance of the thin face and the struggling smile obliterated the Collard who had risen so often, so swiftly at the Despatch Box, his voice emphatic, lucid and challenging. Melville lowered his head.

Elizabeth sat silent now as she often sat with Melville, thankful for the stillness, attentive to his mood and linked with him like a dancing partner who doesn't release her grip. She was wearing a neat black suit which she had specially bought for the occasion, and small black hat with a veil.

Since they had walked in the grounds of Greystoke a month ago, neither had spoken again of their conversation. It was as if they had buried a secret and left it to decompose, unwilling to mention it because of a partnership in guilt and fear. He turned his head to the Ormstons at his side. In the last month they had both developed a stern, proud, expression in public, Ormston himself paler than ever, Mrs Ormston looking at the world through blank eyes, self-contained, aloof and with an air of unshakable indifference. Ormston caught his glance, and they both looked quickly away from each other.

'Are you all right, darling?' Elizabeth asked Melville in the timid voice which she had lately taken to using. He didn't answer, but rose with the others in a great stirring which silenced the mutter of conversation as the Dean and Chapter in their robes were conducted to their places. There was a preliminary rustle, a scrape of feet and a movement of papers before the Dean said in his clear voice, amplified from the tops of the pillars,

'Hear the words of our Lord Jesus Christ.'

The organ played a few bars, and the congregation sang,

200

> 'Guide me, O Thou great Jehovah,
> Pilgrim through this barren land . . .'

Elizabeth's voice was firm and melodious. Her arm pressed against Melville's, and he didn't move his own away. Its warmth touched him like an old companion, a familiar which had been with him almost all his adult life. As he sang, he felt her take breath, observed the trace of sweat on her upper lip and noticed the wisp of hair which had begun to fall over her ear. Melville cleared his throat and, reading the service, prepared to join in the last verse.

> 'When I tread the verge of Jordan,
> Bid my anxious fears subside . . .'

but he gave out no sound, and the hymn swept onwards with the organ in a triumphant conquering peal.

They sat again as the Dean mounted the pulpit.

How many hundreds of times had he sat like this with Elizabeth? How many days had they lived together – and how many nights?

'And though I bestow all my goods to feed the poor,' the Dean intoned, 'and though I give my body to be burned, and have not charity, it profiteth me nothing.'

What merit was there in giving your body to be burned? Melville wondered, when it all came to the same end. He thought of Collard before a Division, counting the heads and noticing the absentees. He was buried, and it made no difference if he had been burned or embalmed in a vault. It was all nothing, and there weren't even tears in all the congregation. Nothing in this remembering but politeness.

But now the choir was singing the psalm, urgently, the music following quietly through the couplets.

> 'For a thousand years in Thy sight,
> Seeing that is past as a watch in the night . . .
> Thou hast set their misdeeds before Thee,
> And our secret sins in the light of Thy
>   countenance.'

He raised the Order of Service to follow the text of the psalm, but the print had suddenly become blurred and his nose congested. He gazed down at the pew so that his wife might not see his face.

The psalm ended.

'As it was in the beginning, is now and ever shall be, world without end. Amen.'

There was a long pause, interrupted only by an occasional cough. Disciplined and attentive, the assembly waited for the Archbishop to climb into the pulpit.

'Give thanks unto Him for a remembrance of His holiness,' he began, and stopped, staring with his light blue eyes at the congregation. Then he went on, 'For His wrath endureth but the twinkling of an eye, and in His pleasure is life. Heaviness' – his voice lamented – 'may endure for a night, but joy cometh in the morning.'

Scott-Bower, who was sitting next to Melville, muttered,

'He won't leave him alone even now – he was always quoting texts at him.'

The Archbishop went on in his rich tones to praise the late Prime Minister's virtues as a batsman at school, a father and a husband, too early separated from a devoted wife, a companion of the great who was at ease with the humble, designer of the New Commonwealth.

'He was a man of deep piety, absorbed by the great mysteries besides which the most opaque problems of State seem translucent. There was nothing in the affairs of men which could surprise him, but in front of the spirit which moves mankind, he stood in silent awe. "Let him that thinketh he standeth,"' the Archbishop's voice resounded, '"take heed lest he fall."'

Melville propped his head on his hand, and remembered Collard walking with his arm around his shoulders down the Library Corridor when he first came into the House.

'There'll be lots for you to do – lots,' he had said. 'Don't hurry your Maiden Speech. Get the feel of the House . . . I enjoyed talking to your wife. She confused me with the Serjeant-at-Arms.'

'Well, they're both bald,' Elizabeth had said later, 'and I did make him laugh. What a darling man he is!'

It was a long time ago. The old Serjeant had died the following year – now Collard. There had been other Memorial Services.

Langham, Callow, Locke, Burton – all had made speeches, asked questions and striven in Party meetings, sought office, talked to Lobby Correspondents, and were gone as all those in the Abbey would one day be gone with their rivalries and ambitions and lusts and appetites, their bravadoes and their regrets.

The Archbishop was ending.

'. . . though men be so strong that they come to four score years, yet is their strength then but labour and sorrow; so soon passeth it away, and we are gone.'

Melville's hand brushed against his wife's, and he withdrew it. The Address was over. The congregation waited. Then the Precentor declared like a testimony,

'Hear also the words of Saint John. If a man say, I love God, and hateth his brother, he is a liar; for he that loveth not his brother whom he hath seen, how can he love God whom he hath not seen?'

And Melville thought that all faith, like all love, is one, and that when one faith is destroyed, no faith survives. *If a man say I love God, and hateth his brother, he is a liar* . . . Could a man love by taking thought? And was not thought the enemy of love?

The Precentor was saying,

'Let silence now be kept for a space while we remember before God Andrew Carlyon Vanbrugh Collard.'

The vast congregation stood, and bowed their heads, and Melville remembered not the Prime Minister but his brother – a child at school when they had run together through the fields beyond the town, how he had fought Griffiths for his brother's sake, and how he had wandered by the sea-shore and wept when they thought he was drowned, only to find that he had gone to the fairground beyond the scrubland. But that was past. There was no more to fear. The far-away death had visited them – Robert and Elizabeth and himself.

They had returned that night from Greystoke, and had sat together by their window till the dawn came like a mourner. Amid the sound of awakening birds, he had shaved and bathed and returned to his study where she was standing, depersonalized as if she had lost an identity which he himself had lent her.

'What are we going to do?' she asked him. 'What am I going to do?'

She came to him, and he took her face in his hands with a sudden compassion.

'Elizabeth!' he said, and looking at her he knew that their happiness would never recur.

But through his recollections, the voice was intoning,

'I have set before you life and death; blessing and cursing; therefore choose life that both thou and thy seed may live.'

The verse lingered in the arcades, then faded away amid the stone flowers of the traceried roof. 'I have set before you life and death . . .' Through the hymn and the Blessing, the words returned to Melville's mind like the ghost of a choice which itself had died. The organist had begun to play Bach's Toccata and Fugue in D Minor. The music rose in triumph and splendour, and the ushers led the family mourners – Collard's two old sisters, his daughters and their husbands – towards the door. They walked with bowed heads, looking neither to left nor right.

'This way, Prime Minister,' said Palethorpe, and the heads of the congregation turned from Collard's relatives to Melville as he took Elizabeth by the elbow, and guided her for a pace or two as they led the rest of the assembly, now impatient to exchange the reminders of death for the daylight streaming through the entrance.

'Pretty good,' said Scott-Bower, close to the Prime Minister's elbow. 'One o'clock exactly. They said it would take half an hour.'

Melville had been preparing to go for a walk in the Park on the day after Collard's death when a special messenger arrived at his house requesting him to be at Buckingham Palace at 9.30. He had gone into Elizabeth's bedroom where she was sitting at her dressing-table making up her face. She had looked at him uncertainly, and then she had read in his expression something which he had hoped not to feel.

'What is it, darling?' she asked.

She rose and went towards him, and he said, as if he were at the top of a high mountain,

'I've been sent for – to Buckingham Palace. They've sent for me.'

With her eyes swimming with joy, she approached him carefully, afraid that he might reject her, and said,

'It's wonderful – wonderful, Geoffrey.'

'No,' he said, turning away. 'It's not wonderful – it's not wonderful.'

In the evening, Ormston, congratulating him, said that he would not be able to serve in the new administration.

Outside, there were greetings between friends, restrained salutes as if they were unsure as to the propriety of a smile. The sun dazzled the eyes of the congregants as they emerged and brightened the clothes of the onlookers who with their holiday air seemed to be wearing a different national dress.

'How well you look, Elizabeth, I really don't know how you do it. Aren't you madly busy moving in?' said Mrs Drayford, intercepting them.

Elizabeth looked at Melville as if for guidance, and said in a restrained voice,

'Not really. Somehow everything has happened all at once, but it all seems to be happening *to* me.'

'Ah, well,' said Mrs Drayford gaily, 'whoever would have thought *I'd* be setting off to Africa next week? How is that charming daughter of yours – Sybil?'

'Sylvia,' said Elizabeth. 'We had a letter from her only yesterday from Philadelphia. She's very happy there.'

Drayford, who had joined them, raised his silk hat courteously to Melville, and they walked off to their car.

'Very touching!' said Lord Gradwell, supported under his left arm by a pretty secretary. 'My best friend! Ah, well, Prime Minister – that's how life is. We start to die the minute we're born.'

His faded old eyes looked into the distance, and he mumbled as if to himself.

'Glad we backed you against that scoundrel Yates!'

Yates had appeared with a group of his friends, and bare-headed, talking in a resonant voice, was making his way through the crowd in the direction of the House of Commons. He appeared to be approaching Mrs Drayford, face to face, but she called 'Godfrey!' over his shoulder and addressed herself with delight to one of Melville's new junior Ministers.

'*Lady* Drayford!' said Scott-Bower to the Prime Minister, savouring the title. They both smiled, and Melville said,

'Next week! She'll enjoy it.'

Close by, a young Member of Parliament had pressed his way to Ormston, and said,

'Congratulations, sir. I was delighted to read about your . . .' he groped for the word.

Ormston smiled his melancholy smile.

'I always wanted to be an M.P. without constituents. I'll enjoy the other place. But I'll miss the House. You know my wife, of course.'

'My name is Farleigh,' said the young Member, 'I'm one of the new boys – I came in with the Merchison by-election. I hope you both enjoy –'

Mrs Ormston began to smile to him, but changed her mind and held her husband's arm more closely. Farleigh said,

'I'd better hurry on.'

The police held the crowds back as Melville and Elizabeth, accompanied by their detectives, made their way to the car. A woman said loudly, 'She's nice – isn't she?' But before there could be more than a surge of curiosity and a patter of handclapping, the chauffeur had already begun to move away.

'Could we possibly just drive around the Park?' said Elizabeth. 'I'd rather like a little air before we return.'

'Of course,' said Melville. 'We'll be back long before they arrive. I imagine they'll walk.'

He gave the order to the driver, and they swung around Parliament Square where a dark line of M.P.s and their wives were crossing Old Palace Yard. Then they drove slowly down Birdcage Walk.

Although there were picnickers on the warm, dry grass, a few leaves had already fallen from the chestnut trees and a breeze, ruffling the lake, had driven the ducks to the shelter of the islands. Elizabeth turned her face towards her husband, who sat with a preoccupied, unsmiling expression.

'Geoffrey,' she said hesitantly, 'I want to ask you . . . Can we start again?'

She looked timidly at his face, and went on,

'For so many years – can't we remember all that was good and hopeful in our lives?'

'No,' said Melville.

She put her hand on his, and he let it rest there.

206

'It will be different,' said Elizabeth. 'Perhaps better.'
Her face was reflective.

'Not better,' said Melville, 'but different!'

The promenade was over. The car turned off Whitehall into Downing Street where a considerable crowd had gathered to greet the Prime Minister. Now the applause was loud as they got out of the car, and stood on the pavement. There was a holiday mood in the air. 'Good old Geoff!' someone shouted. And the cry was taken up. 'Good old Geoff!' From now on it would be, 'Good old Geoff!' Avoiding the police a woman tried to give Melville a sprig of heather, and Elizabeth took it from her hand. The crowd roared with delight. 'Good old Geoff! Good luck, Prime Minister!' Other cars bringing their Cabinet guests to the luncheon edged into the narrow street. With a quick wave, Melville made for the open door, but one of the photographers whose cameras had been clicking called, 'Could we have just one more, sir? You and Mrs Melville – by the door. A happy, smiling one.'

Elizabeth stood at the door, diffident next to her husband, and clasped his arm.

'Smile!' said the photographer.

They both smiled to the cameras.